£ 2.99

HE WH

C000077716

Born in 1906, John Dickson Carr was an American author of Golden Age 'British-style' detective stories. He published his first novel, *It Walks by Night*, in 1930 while studying in Paris to become a barrister. Shortly thereafter he settled in his wife's native England where he wrote prolifically, averaging four novels per year until the end of WWII. Well known as a master of the locked-room mystery, Carr created eccentric sleuths to solve apparently impossible crimes. His two most popular series detectives were Dr. Fell, who debuted in *Hag's Nook* in 1933, and barrister Sir Henry Merrivale (published under the pseudonym of Carter Dickson), who first appeared in *The Plague Court Murders* (1934). Eventually, Carr left England and moved to South Carolina where he continued to write, publishing several more novels and contributing a regular column to *Ellery Queen's Mystery Magazine*. In his lifetime, Carr received the Mystery Writers of America's highest honor, the Grand Master Award, and was one of only two Americans ever admitted into the prestigious – but almost exclusively British – Detection Club. He died in 1977.

HE WHO WHISPERS

JOHN DICKSON CARR

THE LANGTAIL PRESS
LONDON

This edition published 2010 by
The Langtail Press

www.langtailpress.com

ISBN 978-1-78002-002-0

CONTENTS

CHAPTER 1

'A DINNER *of the Murder Club — our first meeting in more than five years — will be held at Beltring's Restaurant on Friday, June 1st, at 8.30 p.m. The speaker will be Professor Rigaud. Guests have not hitherto been permitted; but if you, my dear Hammond, would care to come along as my guest …?'*

That, he thought, was a sign of the times.

A fine rain was falling, less a rain than a sort of greasy mist, when Miles Hammond turned off Shaftesbury Avenue into Dean Street. Though you could tell little from the darkened sky, it must be close on half-past nine o'clock. To be invited to a dinner of the Murder Club, and then to get there nearly an hour late, was more than mere discourtesy; it was infernal, unpardonable cheek even though you had a good reason.

And yet, as he reached the first turning where Romilly Street trails along the outskirts of Soho, Miles Hammond stopped.

A sign of the times, that letter in his pocket. A sign, in this year nineteen-forty-five, that peace had crept back unwillingly to Europe. And he couldn't get used to it.

Miles looked round him.

On his left, as he stood at the corner of Romilly Street, was the east wall of St Anne's Church. The grey wall, with its big round-arched window, stood up almost intact. But there was no glass in the window, and nothing beyond except a grey-white tower seen through it. Where high explosive had ripped along Dean Street, making chaos of matchboard houses and spilling strings of garlic into the road along with broken glass and mortar-dust, they had now built a neat static-water tank — with barbed wire so that children shouldn't fall in and get drowned. But the scars remained, under whispering rain. On the east wall of St Anne's, just under that gaping window, was an old plaque commemorating the sacrifice of those who died in the last war.

Unreal!

No, Miles Hammond said to himself, it was no good calling this feeling morbid or fanciful or a product of war-nerves. His whole life now, good fortune as well as bad, *was* unreal.

Long ago you enter the Army, with a notion that solid walls are crumbling and that something must be done about it somehow. You get, unheroically, that form of Diesel-oil-poisoning which in the Tank Corps is nevertheless as deadly as anything Jerry throws at you. For eighteen months you lie in a hospital bed, between white galling sheets, with a passage of time so slow that time itself grows meaningless. And then, when the trees are coming into leaf for the second time, they write and tell you that Uncle Charles has died – cosily as always, in a safe hotel in Devon – and that you and your sister have inherited everything.

Have you always been naggingly short of money? Here's all you want.

Have you always been fond of that house in the New Forest, with Uncle Charles's library attached? Enter!

Have you – far more than either of these things – longed for freedom from the stifle of crowding, the sheer pressure of humanity like the physical pressure of travellers packed into a bus? Freedom from regimentation, with space to move and breathe again? Freedom to read and dream, without a sense of duty towards anybody and everybody? All this should be possible too, if the war is ever finished.

Then, gasping out to the end like a *gauleiter* swallowing poison, the war is over. You come out of hospital – a little shakily, your discharge-papers in your pocket – into a London still pinched by shortages; a London of long queues, erratic buses, dry pubs; a London where they turn on the street-lights, and immediately turn them off again to save fuel; but a place free at last from the intolerable weight of threats.

People didn't celebrate that victory hysterically, as for some reason or other the newspapers liked to make out. What the news-reels showed was only a bubble on the huge surface of the town. Like himself, Miles Hammond thought, most people were a little apathetic because they could not yet think of it as real.

But something awoke, deep down inside human beings' hearts, when the cricket results crept back into the papers and the bunks began to disappear from the Underground. Even peace-time institutions like the Murder Club ...

2

'This won't do!' said Miles Hammond. He pulled his dripping hat further over his eyes, and turned to the right down Romilly Street towards Beltring's Restaurant.

There was Beltring's on the left, four floors once painted white and still faintly whitish in the dusk. Distantly a late bus rumbled in Cambridge Circus, making the street vibrate. Lighted windows gathered strength against the mist of rain, which seemed to splash more loudly here. There, just as of old, was the uniformed commissionaire at the entrance to Beltring's.

But, if you were to attend a dinner of the Murder Club, you did not go in by the front door. Instead you went round the corner, to the side entrance in Greek Street. Beyond a low door, and up a thick-carpeted flight of stairs – according to popular legend, this was once royalty's discreet way of entering – you emerged into an upstairs passage with the doors of private rooms along one side.

Half-way up the stairs, faintly hearing that rich subdued murmur which is the background of a rich subdued restaurant, Miles Hammond knew a moment of sheer panic.

He was the guest to-night of Dr Gideon Fell. But, even as a guest, he was none the less an outsider.

This Murder Club had become as famous in legend as the exploits of that scion of royalty whose private stair he was now ascending. The Murder Club's membership was restricted to thirteen: nine men and four women. The names of its members were celebrated, some all the more celebrated for being unobtrusively so, in law, in literature, in science, in art. Mr Justice Coleman was a member. So was Dr Banford, the toxicologist, and Merridew, the novelist, and Dame Ellen Nye, the actress.

Before the war they were accustomed to meet four times a year, in two private rooms at Beltring's always assigned to them by Frédéric, the head-waiter. There was an outer room with an improvised bar, and an inner room for the dinner. In the inner room – where Frédéric, for the occasion, always hung the engraving of the skull on the wall – these men and women, as solemn as children, sat far into the night discussing murder cases which had come to be known as classics.

Yet here was he, Miles Hammond ...

Steady!

Here was he – an outsider, almost an impostor – dripping in his sodden hat and raincoat up the stairs of a restaurant where in the old days he could seldom afford to eat. Scandalously late, feeling shabby in his very bones, nerving himself to face craned necks and inquiring eyebrows as he walked in ...

Steady, curse you!

He had to remind himself that once upon a time, in the far-off hazy days before the war, there had been a scholar named Miles Hammond: last of a long line of academic for-bears of whom his uncle, Sir Charles Hammond, had only recently died. A scholar named Miles Hammond had won the Nobel Prize for History in nineteen-thirty-eight. And that person, amazingly enough, was himself. He mustn't let illness gnaw away his nerves. He had every right to be here! But the world is always changing, always altering its shape; and people forget very easily.

In such a mood of cynicism Miles reached the upstairs hall, where discreet lights behind frosted glass shone on polished mahogany doors. It was deserted and quiet, except for a distant murmur of conversation. It might have been Beltring's before the war. Over one door was an illuminated sign that said, 'Gentlemen's Cloakroom', and he hung his hat and overcoat inside. Across the hall from it he saw a mahogany door bearing the placard, 'Murder Club'.

Miles opened the door, and stopped short.

'Who —' A woman's voice struck across at him, suddenly. It went up with something like a note of alarm, before it regained its soft and casual level. 'Excuse me,' the voice added uncertainly, 'but who are you?'

'I'm looking for the Murder Club,' said Miles.

'Yes, of course. Only ...'

There was something wrong here. Something very wrong.

A girl in a white evening-gown was standing in the middle of the outer room, her gown vivid against thick dark carpet. The room was rather dimly lighted, behind buff shades. Its heavy curtains, obscurely patterned in gold, had been drawn across the two windows facing Romilly Street. A long white-covered table had been pushed in front of these windows to serve as a bar; a bottle of sherry, a bottle of gin and another of bitters, stood beside a dozen polished unused glasses. Except for the girl, there was nobody else in this room.

In the right-hand wall Miles could see double-doors, partly open, leading into the inner room. He could see a big circular table set for dinner, with chairs set stiffly round it; the gleaming silver was ranged just as stiffly; the table decorations, roses, made a scarlet pattern against green ferns on the white cloth; the four tall candles remained unlighted. Over the mantelpiece beyond, grotesquely, hung the framed engraving of the skull as a sign that the Murder Club was in session.

But the Murder Club was not in session. There was nobody there, either.

Then Miles became conscious that the girl had moved forward.

'I'm awfully sorry,' she said. The low, hesitant voice, infinitely delightful after the professionally pleasant tones of nurses, warmed his heart. 'It was very rude of me to shout out like that.'

'Not at all! Not at all!'

'I – I suppose we'd better introduce ourselves.' She raised her eyes. 'I'm Barbara Morell.'

Barbara Morell? Barbara Morell? Which one of the celebrities could this be?

For she was young, and she had grey eyes. Most of all you were conscious of her extraordinary vitality, her aliveness, in a world grown half bloodless from war. It showed in the sparkle of the grey eyes, the turn of the head and mobility of the lips, the faint pink flush of the skin in face and neck and shoulders above the white gown. How long was it, he wondered, since he had last seen a girl in evening-dress?

And, in the face of that – what a scarecrow *he* must look!

In the wall between the two curtained windows facing Romilly Street there was a long mirror. Miles could see duskily reflected the back of Barbara Morell's gown, cut off at the waist by the bar-table, and the sleek knot into which she had done her sleek ash-blonde hair. Over her shoulder was reflected his own countenance: gaunt, wry, and humorous, with the high cheek-bones under long red-brown eyes, and the thread of grey in his hair making him seem forty-odd instead of thirty-five; rather like an intellectual Charles the Second, and (God's fish!) just as unprepossessing.

'I'm Miles Hammond,' he told her, and looked about desperately for someone to whom he could apologize for his lateness.

'Hammond?' There was a slight pause. Her grey eyes were fixed on him, wide open. 'You aren't a member of the club, then?'

'No. I'm a guest of Dr Gideon Fell.'

5

'Of Dr Fell? So am I! I'm not a member, either. But that's just the trouble.' Miss Barbara Morell spread out her hands. 'Not a single member has turned up to-night. The whole club has just ... disappeared.'

'*Disappeared?*'

'Yes.'

Miles stared round the room.

'There's nobody here,' the girl explained, 'except you and me and Professor Rigaud. Frédéric the head-waiter is nearly frantic, and as for Professor Rigaud ... well!' She broke off. 'Why are you laughing?'

Miles had not meant to laugh. In any case, he told himself, you could hardly call it laughing.

'I beg your pardon,' he hastened to say. 'I was only thinking –'

'Thinking what?'

'Well! For years this club has been meeting, each time with a different speaker to give them the inside story of some celebrated horror. They've discussed crime; they've revelled in crime; they've even hung the picture of a skull on the wall as their symbol.'

'Yes?'

He was watching the line of her hair, hair of such pale ash-blonde that it seemed almost white, parted in the middle after what seemed to him an old-fashioned manner. He met the upturned grey eyes, with their dark lashes and dead-black points of iris. Barbara Morell pressed her hands together. She had an eager way of giving you her whole attention, of seeming to hang on every word you uttered, very flattering to the scarred nerves of a man in convalescence.

He grinned at her.

'I was only thinking,' he answered, 'that it would be a triumph of sensationalism if on the night of this meeting each member of the club mysteriously disappeared from his home. Or if each were found, as the clock struck, sitting quietly at home with a knife in his back.'

The attempt at a joke fell flat. Barbara Morell changed colour slightly.

'What a horrible idea!'

'Is it? I'm sorry. I only meant ...'

'Do you by any chance write detective stories?'

'No. But I read a lot of them. That is – oh, well!'

'This is *serious*,' she assured him, with a small-girl naïveté and still a heightened colour in her face. 'After all, Professor Rigaud has come a very

6

long distance to tell them about this case, this murder on the tower; and then they treat him like this! Why?'

Suppose something *had* happened? It was incredible, it was fantastic, yet anything seemed possible when the whole evening was unreal. Miles pulled his wits together.

'Can't we do something about finding out what's wrong?' he demanded. 'Can't we telephone?'

'They have telephoned!'

'To whom?'

'To Dr Fell; he's the Honorary Secretary. But there wasn't any reply. Now Professor Rigaud is trying to get in touch with the President, this judge, Mr Justice Coleman ...'

It became clear, however, that he had not been able to get in touch with the President of the Murder Club. The door to the hall opened, with a sort of silent explosion, and Professor Rigaud came in.

Georges Antoine Rigaud, Professor of French Literature at the University of Edinburgh, had a savage catlike roll in his gait. He was short and stout; he was bustling; he was a little untidy, from bow tie and shiny dark suit to square-toed shoes. His hair showed very black above the ears, in contrast to a large bald head and a faintly purplish complexion. In general, Professor Rigaud varied between a portentous intensity of manner and a sudden expansive chuckle which showed the gleam of a gold tooth.

But no expansiveness was in evidence now. His thin shells of eyeglasses, even his patch of black moustache, seemed to tremble with rigid indignation. His voice was gruff and husky, his English almost without accent. He held up a hand, palm outwards.

'Do not speak to me, please,' he said.

On the seat of a pink-brocaded chair against the wall lay a soft dark hat with a flopping brim, and a thick cane with a curved handle. Professor Rigaud bustled over and pounced on them.

His manner was now one of high tragedy.

'For years,' he said, before straightening up, 'they have asked me to come to this club. I say to them: No, no, no! – because I do not like journalists. "There will be no journalists," they tell me, "to quote what you say." "You promise that?" I ask. "Yes!" they say. Now I have come all the way from Edinburgh. And I could not get a sleeper on the train,

7

either, because of "priority".' He straightened up and shook a bulky arm in the air. 'This word priority is a word which stinks in the nostrils of honest men!'

'Hear, hear, *hear*,' said Miles Hammond with fervour.

Professor Rigaud woke up from his indignant dream, fixing Miles with a hard little glittering eye from behind the thin shells of glasses.

'You agree, my friend?'

'Yes!'

'That is good of you. You are —?'

'No,' Miles answered his unspoken question, 'I'm not a missing member of the club. I'm a guest too. My name is Hammond.'

'Hammond?' repeated the other. Interest and suspicion quickened in his eye. 'You are not Sir Charles Hammond?'

'No. Sir Charles Hammond was my uncle. He …'

'Ah, but of course!' Professor Rigaud snapped his fingers. 'Sir Charles Hammond is dead. Yes, yes, yes! I read of this in the newspapers. You have a sister. You and your sister have inherited the library.'

Barbara Morell, Miles noticed, was looking more than a little perplexed.

'My uncle,' he said to her, 'was a historian. He lived for years in a little house in the New Forest, accumulating thousands of books piled up in the wildest and craziest disorder. As a matter of fact, my main reason for coming to London was to see whether I couldn't get a trained librarian to put the books in order. But Dr Fell invited me to the Murder Club …'

'The library!' breathed Professor Rigaud. 'The library!'

A strong inner excitement seemed to kindle and expand inside him like steam, making his chest swell and his complexion a trifle more purplish.

'That man Hammond,' he declared with enthusiasm, 'was a great man! He was curious! He was alert! He' – Professor Rigaud twisted his wrist, as one who turns a key – 'pried into things! To examine his library I would give much. To examine his library I would give … But I forgot. I am furious.' He clapped on his hat. 'I will go now.'

'Professor Rigaud,' the girl called softly.

Miles Hammond, always sensitive to atmospheres, was conscious of a slight shock. For some reason there had been a subtle change in the attitude of both his companions, or so it seemed to him, ever since he had mentioned his uncle's house in the New Forest. He could not analyse this; perhaps he had imagined it.

But when Barbara Morell suddenly clenched her hands and called out, there could be no doubt about the desperate urgency in her tone.

'Professor Rigaud! Please! Couldn't we – couldn't we hold the meeting of the Murder Club after all?'

Rigaud swung round.

'Mademoiselle?'

'They've treated you badly. I know that.' She hurried forward. The half-smile on her lips contrasted with the appeal in the eyes. 'But I've looked forward *so* much to coming here! This case he was going to talk about' – briefly, she appealed to Miles – 'was rather special and sensational. It happened in France just before the war, and Professor Rigaud is one of the few remaining people who know anything about it. It's all about ...'

'It is about,' said Professor Rigaud, 'the influence of a certain woman on human lives.'

'Mr Hammond and I would make an awfully good audience. And we wouldn't breathe a word to the press, either of us! And after all, you know, we've got to dine somewhere; and I doubt whether we could get anything at all to eat if we left here. Couldn't we, Professor Rigaud? Couldn't we? Couldn't we?'

Frédéric the head-waiter, dispirited and angry and sorry, slipped unobtrusively through the half-opened door to the hall, making a flicking motion of the fingers to someone who hovered outside.

'Dinner is served,' he said.

9

CHAPTER 2

THE story told to them by Georges Antoine Rigaud – over the coffee, following an indifferent dinner – Miles Hammond was at first inclined to dismiss as a fable, a dream, an elaborate leg-pull. This was partly because of Professor Rigaud's expression: one of portentous French solemnity, shooting little glances from one of his companions to the other, yet with a huge sardonic amusement behind everything he said.

Afterwards, of course, Miles discovered that every word was true. But by that time ...

It was muffled and quiet in the little dining-room, with the four tall candles burning on the table as its only light. They had drawn back the curtains and opened the windows, to let in a little air on that stuffy night. Outside the rain still splashed, against a purplish dusk spotted with one or two lighted windows in the red-painted restaurant across the street.

It formed a fitting background for what they were about to hear.

'Crime and the occult!' Professor Rigaud had declared, flourishing his knife and fork. 'These are the only hobbies for a man of taste!' He looked very hard at Barbara Morell. 'You collect, mademoiselle?'

An eddying breeze, moist-scented, curled in through the open windows and made the candle-flames undulate. Moveing shadows were thrown across the girl's face.

'Collect?' she repeated.

'Criminal relics?'

'Good heavens, no!'

'There is a man in Edinburgh,' said Professor Rigaud rather wistfully, 'who has a pen-wiper made of human skin, from the body of Burke, the body-snatcher. Do I shock you? But as God is my judge' – suddenly he chuckled, showing his gold tooth, and then became very serious again – 'I could name you a lady, a very charming lady like yourself, who stole the headstone from the grave of Dougal, the Moat Farm murderer, at Chelmsford Prison; and has the headstone set up in her garden now.'

'Excuse me,' said Miles. 'But do all students of crime ... well, carry on like that?'

Professor Rigaud considered this.

'It is a blague, yes,' he conceded. 'But all the same it is amusing. As for myself, I will show you presently.'

He said no more until the table was cleared and the coffee poured. Then, lighting a cigar with concentration, he hitched his chair forward and put his thick elbows on the table. His cane, of polished yellow wood which shone under the candle-light, was propped against his leg.

'Outside the little city of Chartres, which is some sixty-odd kilometres south of Paris, there lived in the year nineteen-thirty-nine a certain English family. You are perhaps familiar with Chartres?

'One thinks of the place as medieval, as all black stone and a dream of the past, and in a sense that is true. You see it in the distance, on a hill, amid miles of yellow grain-fields, with the unequal towers of the Cathedral rising up. You enter through the round-towers of the Porte Guillaume, where geese and chickens fly in front of your motor-car, and go up steep little cobbled streets to the Hotel of the Grand Monarch.

'At the foot of the hill winds the River Eure, with the old walls of the fortifications overhanging it, and willows drooping into the water. You see people walking on these walls, in the cool of the evening, where the peach-trees grow.

'On market-days − ouf! The noise of cattle is like the devil blowing horns. There are absurdities to buy, at lines of stalls where the vendors sound as loud as the cattle. There are' − Professor Rigaud hesitated slightly − 'superstitions here, as much a part of the soil as moss on rock. You eat the best bread in France, you drink good wine. And you say to yourself, "Ah! This is the place to settle down and write a book."

'But there are industries here: milling, and iron-founding, and stained-glass, and leather manufacture, and others I do not investigate because they bore me. I mention them because the largest of the leather manufactories, Pelletier et Cie., was owned by an Englishman. Mr Howard Brooke.

'Mr Brooke is fifty years old, and his happy wife is perhaps five years younger. They have one son, Harry, in his middle twenties. All are dead now, so I may speak of them freely.'

A slight chill – Miles Hammond could not have said why – passed through the little dining-room.

Barbara Morell, who was smoking a cigarette and watching Rigaud in a curious way from behind it, stirred in her chair.

'Dead?' she repeated. 'Then no more harm can be done by ...'

Professor Rigaud ignored this.

'They live, I repeat, a little way outside Chartres. They live in a villa – grandiosely called a château, though it is not – on the very bank of the river. Here the Eure is narrow, and still, and dark green with the reflexion of its banks. Let us see, now!'

Bustling with concentration, he pushed forward his coffee-cup.

'This,' he announced, 'is the villa, built of grey stone round three sides of a courtyard. This' – dipping his finger into the dregs of a glass of claret, Professor Rigaud drew a curved line on the tablecloth – 'this is the river, winding past in front of it.

'Up here, some two hundred yards northwards from the house, is an arched stone bridge over the river. It is a private bridge; Mr Brooke owns the land on either side of the Eure. And still farther along from there, but on the opposite bank of the river from the house, stands an old ruined tower.

'This tower is locally known as la Tour d'Henri Quatre, the tower of Henry the Fourth, for absolutely no reason relating to that king. It was once a part of a château, burnt down by the Huguenots when they attacked Chartres towards the end of the sixteenth century. Only the tower remains: round, stone-built, its wooden floors burnt out, so that inside it is only a shell with a stone staircase climbing spirally up the wall to a flat stone roof with a parapet.

'The tower – observe! – cannot be seen from this villa where the Brooke family live. But the prospect is pretty, pretty, pretty!

'You walk northwards, through thick grass, past the willows, along the river-bank where it curves *here*. First there is the stone bridge, mirrored in a glitter of water. Farther on is the tower, overhanging the moss-green bank, round and grey-black with vertical window-slits, perhaps forty feet high, and framed against a distant line of poplars. It is used by the Brooke family as a kind of bathing-hut, to change clothes when they go for a swim.

'So this English family – Mr Howard the father, Mrs Georgina the mother, Mr Harry the son – live in their comfortable villa, happily and perhaps a little stodgily. Until ...'

'Until?' prompted Miles, as Professor Rigaud paused.

'Until a certain woman arrives.'

Professor Rigaud was silent for a moment.

Then, exhaling his breath, he shrugged the thick shoulders as though disclaiming any responsibility.

'Myself,' he went on, 'I arrive in Chartres in May of thirty-nine. I have just finished my *Life of Cagliostro*, and I wish for peace and quiet. My good friend Coco Legrand, the photographer, introduces me to Mr Howard Brooke one day on the steps of the *hôtel de ville*. We are different types, but we like each other. He smiles at my Frenchness, I smile at his Englishness; and so everybody is happy.

'Mr Brooke is grey-haired, upright, reserved but friendly, a hardworking executive at his leather business. He wears plus-fours, which seem as strange in Chartres as a curé's skirts in Newcastle. He is hospitable, he has a twinkle in the eye, but he is so conventional you can bet your shilling on exactly what he will do or say at any time. His wife, a plump, pretty, red-faced woman, is much the same.

'But the son Harry ...

'Ah! There is a different person!

'This Harry interested me. He has sensitiveness, he has imagination. In height and weight and way of carrying himself he is much like his father. But under that correct outside of his, he is all wires and all nerves.

'He is a good-looking young fellow, too: square jaw, straight nose, good wide-spaced brown eyes, and fair hair that (I think to myself) will be grey like his father's if he does not control his nerves. Harry is the idol of both his parents. I tell you I have seen doting fathers and mothers, but never any like those two!

'Because Harry can swipe a golf-ball two hundred yards, or two hundred miles, or whatever is the asinine distance, Mr Brooke is purple with pride. Because Harry plays tennis like a maniac in the hot sun, and has a row of silver cups, his father is in the seventh heaven. He does not mention this to Harry. He only says, "Not bad, not bad." But he brags about it interminably to anybody who will listen.

'Harry is being trained in the leather business. He will inherit the factory one day; he will be a very rich man like his father. He is sensible; he knows his duty. And yet this boy wants to go to Paris and study painting.

'My God, how he wants it! He wants it so much he is inarticulate. Mr Brooke is gently firm with this nonsense about becoming a painter. He is broad-minded, he says; painting is all very well as a hobby; but as a serious occupation – really, now! As for Mrs Brooke, she is almost hysterical on the subject, since the impression in her mind is that Harry will live in an attic among beautiful girls without any clothes on.

' "My boy," says the father, "I understand exactly how you feel. I went through a similar phase at your age. But in ten years' time you will laugh at this."

' "After all," says the mother, "couldn't you always stay at home and paint animals?"

'After which Harry goes out blindly and hits a tennis-ball so hard he blows his opponent off the court, or sits on the lawn with a white-faced, brooding, swearing look. These people are all so honest, so well-meaning, so thoroughly sincere!

'I never learned, I tell you now, whether Harry was serious about his life's work. I never had the opportunity to learn. For, in late May of that year, Mr Brooke's personal secretary – a hard-faced, middle-aged woman named Mrs McShane – grows alarmed at the international situation and returns to England.

'Now that was serious. Mr Brooke's private correspondence – his personal secretary has no connexion with the work at the office – is enormous. Ouf! Often it made my head swim, how that man wrote letters! His investments, his charities, his friends, his letters to the newspapers in England: he would pace up and down as he dictated, his hands behind his back, grey-haired and bony-faced, with a look of stern moral indignation about his mouth.

'As a personal secretary he must have the very best. He wrote to England for the best. And there arrived at Beauregard – that is what the Brookes called their house – there arrived at Beauregard, Miss Fay Seton.

'Miss Fay Seton ...

'It was on the afternoon of the thirtieth of May, I remember. I was taking tea with the Brookes. Here was Beauregard, a grey stone house of the early eighteenth century, with stone faces carved on the walls and white-painted window-frames, built round three sides of a front courtyard. We were sitting in the court, which is paved with smooth grass, having tea in the shadow of the house.

'In front of us was the fourth wall, pierced by big iron-grilled gates that stood open. Beyond these gates lay the road that ran past, and beyond this a long grassy bank sloping down to the river fringed with willows.

'Papa Brooke sits in a wicker chair, his shell-rimmed spectacles on his nose, grinning as he holds out a piece of biscuit for the dog. In English households there is always a dog. To the English it is a source of perpetual astonishment and delight that a dog has sense enough to sit up and ask for food.

'However!

'There is Papa Brooke, and the dog is a dark-grey Scotch terrier like an animated wire brush. On the other side of the tea-table sits Mama Brooke – with brown bobbed hair, pleasant and ruddy of face, not very smartly dressed – pouring out a fifth cup of tea. At one side stands Harry, in a sports-coat and flannels, practising golf-strokes with a driver against an imaginary ball.

'The tops of the trees faintly moving – a French summer! – and the noise of the leaves rippling and rustling, and the sun that winks on them, and fragrance of grass and flowers, and all the drowsy peacefulness – it makes you close your eyes even to think of ...

'That was when a Citroën taxi rolled up outside the front gates.

'A young woman got out of the taxi, and paid the driver so generously that he followed her in with her luggage. She walked up the path towards us, diffidently. She said her name was Miss Fay Seton, and that she was the new secretary.

'Attractive? *Grand ciel!*

'Please to remember – you will excuse my admonitory fore-finger – please to remember, however, that I was not conscious of this full attractiveness at first, or all at once. No. For she had the quality, then and always, of being unobtrusive.

'I remember her standing in the path on that first day, while Papa Brooke punctiliously introduced her to everybody including the dog, and Mama Brooke asked her whether she wanted to go upstairs and wash. She was rather tall, and soft and slender, wearing some tailored costume that was unobtrusive too. Her neck was slender; she had heavy, smooth, dark-red hair; her eyes were long and blue and dreaming, with a smile in them, though they seldom seemed to look at you directly.

15

'Harry Brooke did not say anything. But he took another swing at an imaginary golf-ball, so that there was a swish and a *whick* as the clubhead flicked cropped grass.

'So I smoked my cigar – being always, always, always violently curious about human behaviour – and I said to myself, "Aha!"

'For this young woman grew on you. It was odd and perhaps a bit weird. Her spiritual good looks, her soft movements, above all her extraordinary aloofness …

'Fay Seton was, in every sense of your term, a lady: though she seemed rather to conceal this and be frightened of it. She came of a very good family, old impoverished stock in Scotland, and Mr Brooke discovered this and it impressed him powerfully. She had not been trained as a secretary; no, she had been trained as something else.' Professor Rigaud chuckled and eyed his auditors keenly. 'But she was quick and efficient, and deft and cool-looking. If they wanted a fourth at bridge, or someone to sing and play at the piano when the lamps were lighted in the evening, Fay Seton would oblige. In her way she was friendly, though shy and somewhat prudish, and she would often sit looking into the distance, far away. And you thought to yourself, in exasperation: what *is* this girl thinking about?

'That blazing hot summer …!

'When the very water of the river seemed thick and turgid under the sun, and there was a wiry hum of crickets after nightfall: I am never likely to forget it, now.

'Like a sensible person Fay Seton did not indulge much in athletics, but this was really because she had a weak heart. I told you of the stone bridge, and of the ruined tower they used as a bathing-hut when they went for a swim. Once or twice only she went for a swim – tall and slender, her red hair done up under a rubber cap; exquisite! – with Harry Brooke encouraging her. He rowed her on the river, he took her to the cinema to hear MM. Laurel and Hardy speaking perfect French, he walked with her in those dangerous romantic groves of Eure-et-Loir.

'It was obvious to me that Harry would fall in love with her. It was not, you understand, quite so quick as in the delicious description of Anatole France's story: "I love you! What is your name?" But it was quick enough.

'One night in June Harry came to me in my room at the Hotel of the Grand Monarch. He would never speak to his parents. But he poured out

16

confessions to me: perhaps because, as I smoke my cigar and say little, I am sympathetic. I had been teaching him to read our great romantic writers, moulding his mind towards sophistication, and it may be in a sense playing the devil's advocate. His parents would not have been pleased.

'On this night, at first, he would only stand by the window and fiddle with an ink-bottle until he upset it. But at last he blurted out what he had come to say.

' "I'm mad about her," he said. "I've asked her to marry me."

' "Well?" said I.

' "She won't have me," cried Harry – and for a second I thought, quite seriously, he was going to dive out of the open window.

'Now this astonished me: the statement, I mean, and not any suggestion of love-sick despair. For I could have sworn that Fay Seton was moved and drawn towards this young man. That is, I could have sworn it as far as one could read that enigmatic expression of hers: the long-lidded blue eyes that would not look directly at you, the elusive and spiritual quality of remoteness.

' "Your technique, perhaps it is clumsy."

' "I don't know anything about that," said Harry, hitting his fist on the table where he had upset the ink-bottle. "But last night I went walking with her, on the river bank. It was moonlight ..."

' "I know."

' "And I told Fay I loved her. I kissed her mouth and her throat" – hah! that is significant – "until I nearly went out of my mind. Then I asked her to marry me. She went as white as a ghost in the moonlight, and said, 'No, no, no!' as though I'd said something that horrified her. A second later she ran away from me, over into the shadow of that broken tower.

' "All the time I'd been kissing her, Professor Rigaud, Fay had stood there as rigid as a statue. It made me feel pretty sick, I can tell you. Even though I knew I wasn't worthy of her. So I followed her over to the tower, through the weeds, and asked whether she was in love with anybody else. She gave a kind of gasp and said no, of course not. I asked her whether she didn't like me, and she admitted she did. So I said I wouldn't give up hoping. And I *won't* give up hoping."

'*Enfin!*

17

'That was what Harry Brooke told me, standing by the window of my hotel room. It puzzled me still more, since this young woman Fay Seton was obviously a woman in every sense of the word. I spoke consolingly to Harry. I said to him that he must have courage; and that doubtless, if he used tact, he could get round her.

'He did get round her. It was not three weeks later when Harry triumphantly announced – to me, and to his parents – that he was engaged to be married to Fay Seton.

'Privately, I do not think Papa Brooke and Mama Brooke were too well pleased.

'Mark you, it was not that a word could be said against this girl. Or against her family, or her antecedents, or her reputation. No! To any eye she was suitable. She might be three or four years older than Harry; but what of that? Papa Brooke might feel, in a vague British way, that it was somehow undignified for his son to marry a girl who had first come there in their employ. And this marriage was sudden. It took them aback. But they would not really have been satisfied unless Harry had married a millionairess with a title, and even then only if he had waited until he was thirty-five or forty before leaving home.

'So what could they say except, "God bless you"?

'Mama Brooke kept a stiff upper lip, with the tears running down her face. Towards his son Papa Brooke became very bluff and hearty and man-to-man, as though Harry had suddenly grown up overnight. At intervals papa and mama would murmur to each other in hushed tones, "I'm sure it'll be all right!" – as one might speculate, at a funeral, about the destination of the deceased's soul.

'But please to note: both parents were now enjoying themselves very much. Once used to the idea, they began to take pleasure in it. That is the way of families everywhere, and the Brookes were nothing if not conventional. Papa Brooke was looking forward to his son working harder in the leather business, building up an even sounder name for Pelletier et Cie. After all, the newly wedded pair would live at home or at least reasonably close to home. It was ideal. It was lyrical. It was Arcadian.

'And then ... tragedy.

'Black tragedy, I tell you, as unforeseen and as unnerving as a bolt of magic.'

Professor Rigaud paused.

18

He had been sitting forward with his thick elbows on the table, arms upraised, the forefinger of his right hand tapping impressively against the forefinger of his left hand each time he made a point, his head a little on one side. He was like a lecturer. His shining eyes, his bald head, even his rather comical patch of moustache, had a fervour of intensity.

'Hah!' he said.

Exhaling his breath noisily through the nostrils, he sat upright. The thick cane, propped against his leg, fell to the floor with a clatter. He picked it up and set it carefully against the table. Reaching into his inside pocket, he produced a folded sheaf of manuscript and a photograph about half cabinet size.

'This,' he announced, 'is a photograph of Miss Fay Seton. It was done in colour, not crudely either, by my friend Coco Legrand. The manuscript is an account of this case, which I have specially written for the archives of the Murder Club. But look, please, at the photograph!'

He pushed it across the tablecloth, brushing away crumbs as he did so.

A soft face, a disturbingly haunting face, looked out past the shoulder of the beholder. The eyes were wide-spaced, the brows thin; the nose was short; the lips were full and rather sensual, though this was contradicted by the grace and fastidiousness about the carriage of the head. Those lips just avoided the twitch of a smile at their outer corners. The weight of dark red hair, smooth as fleece, seemed almost too heavy for the slender neck.

It was not beautiful. Yet it troubled the mind. Something about the eyes – was it irony, was it bitterness under the far-away expression? – at once challenged you and fled from you.

'Now tell me!' said Professor Rigaud, with the proud satisfaction of one who believes himself to be on sure ground. 'Can you see anything wrong in that face?'

CHAPTER 3

'WRONG?' echoed Barbara Morell.

Georges Antoine Rigaud seemed convulsed by some vast inner amusement.

'Exactly, exactly, exactly! Why do I designate her as so very dangerous a woman?'

Miss Morell had been following this narrative with the utmost absorption, and a faintly contemptuous expression. Once or twice she had glanced at Miles, as though about to speak. She watched Professor Rigaud as he picked up his dead cigar from the edge of a saucer, took a triumphant puff at it, and put it down again.

'I'm afraid,' – suddenly her voice went high, as though she were somehow personally concerned in this – 'I'm afraid we must get back to a matter of definition. How do you mean, dangerous? So attractive that she … well, turned the head of every man she met?'

'No!' said Professor Rigaud with emphasis.

Again he chuckled.

'I admit, mark you,' he hastened to add, 'that with many men this might well be the case. Look at the photograph there! But it was not what I meant.'

'Then in what way dangerous?' persisted Barbara Morell, a lustre of intentness, even slight anger, coming into her grey eyes. She shot out the next question as something like a challenge. 'You mean – a criminal?'

'My dear young lady! No, no, no!'

'An adventuress, then?'

Barbara struck her hand against the edge of the table.

'A trouble-maker of some kind, is that it?' she cried. 'Malicious? Or spiteful? Or tale-bearing?'

'I say to you,' declared Professor Rigaud, 'that Fay Seton was none of those things. Forgive me if I, the old cynic, insist that in her puritanical way she was altogether gentle and good-hearted.'

'Then what's left?'

'What is left, mademoiselle, is the real answer to the mystery. The mystery of the unpleasant rumours that began to creep through Chartres and the surrounding country. The mystery of why our sober, conservative Mr Howard Brooke, her prospective father-in-law, cursed her aloud in a public place like the Crédit Lyonnais Bank ...'

Under her breath Barbara uttered a curious sound which was either incredulity or contempt, either disbelieving this or dismissing it as of no importance whatever. Professor Rigaud blinked at her.

'You doubt me, mademoiselle?'

'No! Of course not!' Her colour went up. 'What do *I* know about it?'

'And you, Mr Hammond: *you* say little?'

'Yes,' Miles replied absently. 'I was –'

'Looking at the photograph?'

'Yes. Looking at the photograph.'

Professor Rigaud opened his eyes delightedly.

'You are impressed, eh?'

'There's a kind of spell about it,' said Miles, brushing his hand across his forehead. 'The eyes there in the picture! And the way she's got her head turned. Confound the photograph!'

He, Miles Hammond, was a tired man only recently recovered from a very long illness. He wanted peace. He wanted to live in seclusion in the New Forest, among old books, with his sister to keep house for him until her marriage. He didn't want to have his imagination stirred. Yet he sat staring at the photograph, staring at it under the candle-light until its subtle colours grew blurred, while Professor Rigaud went on.

'These rumours about Fay Seton ...'

'What rumours?' Barbara asked sharply.

Blandly, Professor Rigaud ignored this.

'For myself, blind bat and owl that I am, I had heard nothing of them. Harry Brooke and Fay Seton became engaged to be married in the middle of July. Now I must tell you about the twelfth of August.

'On that day, which seemed to me like any other day, I am writing a critical article for the *Revue des Deux Mondes*. All morning I write in my pleasant hotel room, as I have been doing for nearly a week. But after lunch I step across the Place des Epars to get my hair cut. And while I am there, I think to myself, I will just go into the Crédit Lyonnais and cash a cheque before the bank closes.

'It was very warm. All morning the sky had been heavy and dark, with fits of vague prowling thunder and sometimes spatters of rain. But nothing more than a drizzle; no cloud-burst; nothing to let the heat out and give us peace. So I went into the Crédit Lyonnais. And the first person I saw, coming out of the manager's office, was Mr Howard Brooke.

'Odd?

'Rather odd, yes! For I had imagined he would be at his office, like the conscientious fellow he was.

'Mr Brooke regarded me very strangely. He wore a raincoat and a tweed cap. Over his left arm was hung the crook of a cane, and in his right hand he carried an old black-leather brief-case. It seemed to me even then that his light-blue eyes looked strangely watery; nor had I ever noticed before, in a man so fit, that there was sagging flesh under his chin.

' "My dear Brooke!" I said to him, and shook hands with him in spite of himself. His hand felt very limp. "My dear Brooke," I said, "this is an unexpected pleasure! How is everyone at home? How is your good wife, and Harry, and Fay Seton?"

' "Fay Seton?" he said to me. "Damn Fay Seton."

'Ouf!

'He had spoken in English, but so loudly that one or two persons in the bank glanced round. He flushed with embarrassment, this good man, but he was so troubled that he did not really seem to care. He marched me to the front of the bank, beyond hearing of anyone else. Then he opened the brief-case, and showed me.

'Inside, in solitary state, were four slender packets of English banknotes. Each packet contained twenty-five twenty-pound notes: two thousand pounds.

' "I had to send to Paris for these," he told me, and his hands were trembling. "I thought, you know, that English notes would be more tempting. If Harry won't give the woman up, I must simply buy her off. Now you must excuse me."

'And he straightened his shoulders, shut up the brief-case, and walked out of the bank without another word.

'My friends, have you ever been hit very hard in the stomach? So that your eyesight swims, and your stomach rises up, and you feel suddenly like

22

a rubber toy squeezed together? That was how I felt then. I forgot to write a cheque. I forgot everything. I walked back to my hotel, through a drizzling rain that was turning black and greasy the cobble-stones of the Place des Epars.

'But it was impossible to write, as I discovered. About half an hour later, at a quarter past three, the telephone rang. I think I guessed what it might be about, though I did not guess what it was. It was Mama Brooke, Mrs Georgina Brooke, and she said:

' "*For God's sake, Professor Rigaud, come out here immediately.*"

'This time, my friends, I am more than disturbed.

'This time I am thoroughly well frightened, and I confess it!

'I got out my Ford; I drove out to their house as fast as I could, and with an even more execrable style of driving than usual. Still it would not rain properly, would not burst a hole in this hollow of thundery heat that enclosed us. When I reached Beauregard, it was like a deserted house. I called aloud in the downstairs hall, but nobody answered. Then I went into the drawing-room, where I found Mama Brooke sitting bolt upright on a sofa, making heroic efforts to keep her face from working, but with a damp handkerchief clutched in her hand.

' "Madame," I said to her, "what is happening? What is wrong between your good husband and Miss Seton?"

'And she cried out to me, having nobody else to whom she could appeal.

' "I don't know!" she said; it was plain she meant it. "Howard won't tell me. Harry says it's all nonsense, whatever it is, but he won't tell me anything either. Nothing is real any longer. Only two days ago ..."

'Only two days before, it appeared, there had been a shocking and unexplained incident.

'Near Beauregard, on the main road to Le Mans, lived a market-gardener named Jules Fresnac, who supplied them with eggs and fresh vegetables. Jules Fresnac had two children – a daughter of seventeen, a son of sixteen – to whom Fay Seton had been very kind, so that the whole Fresnac family was very fond of her. But two days ago Fay Seton had met Jules Fresnac driving his cart in the road, in the white road with the tall poplars and grain-fields on either side. Jules Fresnac got down from his cart, his fate bluish and swollen with fury, and shouted and screamed at her until she put up a hand to cover her eyes.

23

'All this was witnessed by Mama Brooke's maid, Alice. Alice was too far away to catch what was being said; the man's voice, in any case, was so hoarse with rage as to be almost unrecognizable. But, as Fay Seton turned round to hurry away, Jules Fresnac picked up a stone and flung it at her.

'A pretty story, eh?

'This was what Mama Brooke told me, with helpless gestures of her hands, while she sat on the sofa in that drawing-room.

' "And now," she said, "Howard has gone out to that tower, to Henry the Fourth's tower, to meet poor Fay. Professor Rigaud, you have got to help us. You have got to do something."

' "But, madame! What can I do?"

' "I can't tell you," she answered me; she might once have been pretty. "But something dreadful is going to happen! I know it!"

'Mr Brooke, it developed, had returned from the bank at three o'clock with his brief-case full of money. He told his wife that he meant to have what he called a show-down with Fay Seton, and that he had arranged to meet her at the tower at four o'clock.

'He then asked Mama Brooke where Harry was, because he said he wanted Harry to be present at the show-down. She replied that Harry was upstairs in his room, writing a letter, so the father went upstairs to get him. He didn't find Harry – who, actually, was tinkering with a motor in the garage – and presently he came downstairs again. "So *pitiful* he looked," said Mama Brooke, "and so aged, and walking slowly as though he were ill." That was how Papa Brooke went out of the house towards the tower.

'Not five minutes later, Harry himself turned up from the garage and asked where his father was. Mama Brooke told him, rather hysterically. Harry stood for a moment thinking to himself, muttering, and then *he* went out of the house towards Henri Quatre's tower. During this time there was no sign of Fay Seton.

' "Professor Rigaud," the mother cried to me, "you've got to follow them and do something. You're the only friend we have here, and you've got to follow them!"

'A job, eh, for old Uncle Rigaud?

'My word!

'And yet I followed them.

'There was a crack of thunder as I left the house, but still it would not rain in earnest. I walked northwards along the east bank of the river, until I came to the stone bridge. There I crossed the bridge to the west bank. The tower stood on that side, overhanging the bank a little farther up.

'It looks desolate enough, I tell you, when you stumble across the few old bits of blackened stone – fire-razed, over-grown in the earth with weeds – which are all that remain of the original building. The entrance to the tower is only a rounded arch cut in the wall. This doorway faces west, away from the river, towards open grass and a wood of chestnut trees beyond. I approached there with the sky darkening, and the wind blowing still harder.

'In the doorway, looking at me, stood Fay Seton.

'Fay Seton, in a thin flowered-silk frock, stockingless, with white openwork leather sandals. She carried over her arm a bathing-dress, a towel, and a bathing-cap; but she had not been in to swim, since not even the edges of the shining dark-red hair were damp or tumbled. She breathed slowly and heavily.

' "Mademoiselle," I said to her, not at all certain what I was supposed to do, "I am looking for Harry Brooke and his father."

'For some five seconds, which can seem a very long time, she did not answer.

' "They're here," she told me. "Upstairs. On the roof of the tower." All of a sudden her eyes (I swear it!) were the eyes of one who remembers a horrible experience of some kind. "They seem to be having an argument. I don't think I shall intrude just now. Excuse me."

' "But, mademoiselle – !"

' "Please excuse me!"

'Then she was gone, keeping her face turned away from me. One or two raindrops stung the wind-blown grass, followed by others.

'I put my head inside the doorway. As I told you, that tower was no more than a stone shell, up whose wall a spiralling stone staircase climbed to a square opening giving on the flat roof. It smelt inside of age and the river. It was empty, as bare as your hand, except for a couple of wooden benches and a broken chair. Long narrow windows along the staircase lighted it fairly well, though there was a wild enough stormlight flying over the sky now.

'Angry voices were speaking up there. I could hear them faintly. I gave them a shout, my voice making a hollow echo in that stone jug, and the voices stopped instantly.

25

'So I plodded up the corkscrew stair – a dizzy business, also very bad for one scant of breath – and emerged through the square opening on to the roof.

'Harry Brooke and his father stood facing each other on a circular stone platform, with a high parapet, well above the trees. The father, in his raincoat and tweed cap, had his mouth set implacably. The son pleaded with him; Harry was hatless and coatless, in a corduroy suit whose wind-blown tie emphasized his state of mind. Both of them were pale and worked up, but both seemed rather relieved it was I who had interrupted them.

' "I tell you, sir – !" Harry was beginning.

' "For the last time," said Mr Brooke in a cold buttoned-up voice, "will you allow me to deal with this matter my own way?" He turned to me and added: "Professor Rigaud!"

' "Yes, my dear fellow?"

' "Will you take my son away from here until I have adjusted certain matters to my own satisfaction?"

' "Take him where, my dear fellow?"

"Take him anywhere," replied Mr Brooke, and turned his back on us.

'It was now, as I saw by a surreptitious glance at my watch, ten minutes to four o'clock. Mr Brooke was due to meet Fay Seton there at four o'clock, and he meant to wait. Harry was beaten and deflated; that leapt to the eyes. I said nothing about having met Miss Fay a moment before, since I wanted to pour ointment on the situation instead of inflaming it. Harry allowed me to lead him away.

'Now I wish to impress on you – very clearly! – the last thing we saw as we went downstairs.

'Mr Brooke was standing by the parapet, his back uncompromisingly turned. On one side of him his cane, of light yellowish-coloured wood, was propped upright against the parapet. On the other side of him, also resting against the parapet, was the bulging brief-case. Round the tower-top this battlemented parapet ran breast-high: its stone broken, crumbling, and scored with whitish hieroglyphics where people had cut their initials.

'That is clear? Good!

'I took Harry downstairs. I led him across the open space of grass, into the shelter of the big wood of chestnut trees stretching westwards and northwards. For the rain was beginning to sprinkle pretty heavily now, and we had no cover. Under the hissing and pattering leaves, where it was almost dark, my curiosity reached a point of mania. I begged Harry, as his friend and in a sense his tutor, to tell me the meaning of these suggestions against Fay Seton.

'At first he would hardly listen to me. He kept opening and shutting his hands, this handsome mentally unformed young man, and replied that it was all too ridiculous to be talked about.

' "Harry," said Uncle Rigaud, lifting an impressive fore-finger like this. "Harry, I have spoken to you much of French literature. I have spoken to you of crime and the occult. I have covered a broad field of human experience. And I tell you that the things which cause the most trouble in this world are the things which are too ridiculous to be talked about."

'He regarded me quickly, with a strange, sullen, shining eye.

' "Have you," he asked, "have you heard about Jules Fresnac, the market gardener?"

' "Your mother mentioned him," I said, "but I have yet to hear what is wrong with Jules Fresnac."

' "Jules Fresnac," said Harry, "has a son of sixteen."

' "Well?"

'That was the point where – in the twilight woods, out of sight of the tower – we heard a child screaming.

'Yes: a *child* screaming.

'I tell you, it scared me until I felt my scalp crawl. A drop of rain filtered through the thick leaves overhead, and landed on my bald head, and I jumped throughout every muscle in my body. For I had been congratulating myself that trouble was averted: that Howard Brooke and Harry Brooke and Fay Seton were for the moment separated, and that these three elements were not dangerous unless they came together all at once. And now …

'The screaming came from the direction of the tower. Harry and I ran out of the woods, and emerged into the open grassy space with the tower and the curve of the river-bank in front of us. That whole open space now seemed to be full of people.

'What had happened we learned soon enough.

'Inside the fringe of the wood there had been, for some half an hour, a picnic-party composed of a Monsieur and Madame Lambert, their niece, their daughter-in-law, and four younger children aged from nine to fourteen.

'Like true French picnickers, they had refused to let the weather put them off an appointed day. The land was private, of course. But private property means less in France than it does in England. Knowing that Mr Brooke was supposed to be crotchety about trespassers, they had hung back until they had seen the departure first of Fay Seton and then of Harry and myself. They would assume the coast was clear. The children erupted into the open space, while Monsieur and Madame Lambert sat them down against a chestnut-tree to open the picnic-basket.

'It was the two youngest children who went to explore the tower. As Harry and I rushed out of the wood, I can see yet that little girl standing in the doorway of the tower, pointing upwards. I hear her voice, shrill and raw.

' "*Papa! Papa! Papa! There's a man up there all covered with blood!*"

'That was what she said.

'Myself, I cannot say what the others said or did at that moment. Yet I remember the children turning faces of consternation towards their parents, and a blue-and-white rubber ball rolling across the grass to splash into the river. I walked towards that tower, not quite running. I climbed the spiral stair. A strange, wild, fanciful thought occurred to me as I went: that it was very inconsiderate to ask Miss Fay Seton, with her weak heart, to climb up all these steps.

'Then I got out on to the roof, where the wind blew freshly.

'Mr Howard Brooke – still alive, still twitching – lay flat on his face in the middle. The back of his raincoat was soaked and sodden with blood, showing a half-inch rent where he had been stabbed through the back just under the left shoulder-blade.

'I have not yet mentioned that his own cane, the cane he always carried, was really a sword-stick. It now lay in two halves on either side of him. The handle-part, with its long thin pointed blade stained with blood, was lying near his right foot. The wooden sheath had rolled away to rest against the inside of the parapet opposite. But the brief-case containing two thousand pounds had disappeared.

'All this I saw in a kind of daze, while the family of Lambert screamed below. The time was exactly six minutes past four o'clock: I noted this not from any police sense, but because I wondered whether Fay Seton had kept her appointment.

'I ran over to Mr Brooke, and raised him up to a sitting position. He smiled at me and tried to speak, but all he could get out was, "Bad show."

Harry joined me among the smears of blood, though Harry was not much help. He said, "Dad, who did this?" but the old man was past articulation. He died in his son's arms a few minutes later, clinging to Harry as though he himself were the child.'

Here Professor Rigaud paused his narrative.

Looking rather guilty, he lowered his head and glowered down at the dinner-table, his thick hands spread out on either side of it. There was a long silence until he shook himself, impatiently.

With extraordinary intensity he added:

'Remark well, please, what I tell you now!

'We *know* that Mr Howard Brooke was unhurt, in the best of health, when I left him alone on top of the tower at ten minutes to four o'clock.

'Following that, the person who murdered him must have visited him on top of the tower. This person, when his back was turned, must have drawn the sword-cane from its sheath and run him through the body. Indeed, the police discovered that several fragments of crumbling rock had been detached from one of the broken battlements on the river-side, as though someone's fingers had torn them loose in climbing up there. And this must have occurred between ten minutes to four and five minutes past four, when the two children discovered him in a dying condition.

'Good! Excellent! Established!'

Professor Rigaud hitched his chair forward.

'Yet the evidence shows conclusively,' he said, 'that during this time not a living soul came near him.'

CHAPTER 4

'YOU hear what I say?' insisted Rigaud, snapping his fingers rapidly in the air to attract attention.

Whereupon Miles Hammond woke up.

To any person of imagination, he thought, this narrative of the stout little professor – its sounds and scents and rounded visual detail – had the reality of the living present. Momentarily Miles forgot that he was sitting in an upper room at Beltring's Restaurant, beside candles burning low and windows opening on Romilly Street. Momentarily he *lived* amid the sounds and scents and visual outlines in that story, so that the whisper of the rain in Romilly Street became the rain over Henri Quatre's tower.

He found himself emotionally stirred up, worrying and fretting and taking sides. He liked this Mr Howard Brooke, liked him and respected and sympathized with him, as though the man had been a personal friend. Whoever *had* killed the old boy ...

And all this time, even more disturbingly, the enigmatic eyes of Fay Seton were looking back at him from the tinted photograph now lying on the table.

'I beg your pardon,' said Miles, rousing himself with a start at the snapping of Professor Rigaud's fingers. 'Er – would you mind repeating that last sentence?'

Professor Rigaud uttered his sardonic chuckle.

'With pleasure,' he replied politely. 'I said that the evidence showed not a living soul had come near Mr Brooke during those fatal fifteen minutes.'

'Had come near him?'

'Or could have come near him. He was utterly alone on top of the tower.'

Miles sat up straight.

'Let's get this clear!' he said. 'The man *was* stabbed?'

'He was stabbed,' assented Professor Rigaud. 'I am in the proud position of being able to show you, now, the weapon with which the crime was committed.'

With modest deprecation he reached out to touch the thick cane of light yellowish wood, which throughout the dinner had never left his side and which was now propped against the edge of the table.

'That,' cried Barbara Morell, 'is –?'

'Yes. This belonged to Mr Brooke. I think I intimated to mademoiselle that I am a collector of such relics. It is a beauty, eh?'

With a dramatic gesture, picking up the cane in both hands, Professor Rigaud unscrewed the curved handle. He drew out the long, thin, pointed steel blade, wickedly caught by candle-light, and he laid it with some reverence on the table. Yet the blade had little life or gleam; it had not been cleaned or polished in some years; and Miles could see, as it lay there across the edge of Fay Seton's photograph, the darkish rust-coloured stains that had dried along it.

'A beauty, eh?' Professor Rigaud repeated. 'There are also blood-stains inside the scabbard, if you care to hold it up to the eye.'

Abruptly Barbara Morell pushed back her chair, got to her feet, and backed away.

'Why on earth,' she cried, 'must you bring such things here? And positively gloat over them?'

The good professor's eyebrows went up in astonishment.

'Mademoiselle does not like it?'

'No. Please put it away. It's – it's ghoulish!'

'But mademoiselle must like such things, surely? Or else she would not be a guest of the Murder Club?'

'Yes. Yes, of course!' she corrected herself hastily. 'Only …'

'Only what?' prompted Professor Rigaud in a soft, interested voice.

Miles, himself wondering not a little, watched her as she stood grasping the back of the chair.

Once or twice he had been conscious of her eyes fixed on him across the table. But for the most part she had looked steadily at Professor Rigaud. She must have been smoking cigarettes furiously throughout the narrative: for the first time Miles noticed at least half a dozen stubs in the saucer of her coffee-cup. At one point, during the description of Jules

31

Fresnac's tirade against Fay Seton, she had bent down as though to pick up something from under the table.

A vital, not-very-tall figure – it may have been the white gown which gave her such a small-girl appearance – Barbara stood moving and twisting her fingers on the back of the chair.

'Yes, yes, yes?' went on the probing voice of Professor Rigaud. 'You are very much interested in such things. Only …?'

Barbara forced out a laugh.

'Well!' she said. 'It doesn't do to make crimes *too* real. Any fiction-writer can tell you that.'

'Are you a writer of fiction, mademoiselle?'

'Not – exactly.' She laughed again, trying to dismiss the subject with a turn of her wrist. 'Anyway,' she hurried on, 'you tell us *somebody* murdered this Mr Brooke. Who murdered him? Was it – Fay Seton?'

There was a pause, a pause of slightly tense nerves, before Professor Rigaud eyed her as though trying to make up his mind. Then he chuckled.

'What assurance will you have, mademoiselle? Have I not told you that this lady was not, in the accepted sense, a criminal of any kind?'

'Oh!' said Barbara Morell. 'Then *that's* all right.'

And she drew back her chair and sat down again, while Miles stared at her.

'If you think it's all right, Miss Morell, I can't say I agree. According to Professor Rigaud here, nobody went near the victim at any time –'

'Exactly! And I repeat the statement!'

'How can you be sure of it?'

'Among other things, witnesses.'

'Such as?'

With a quick glance at Barbara, Professor Rigaud tenderly picked up the blade-part of the sword-stick. He replaced it in the cane-scabbard, screwed its threads tight again, and once more propped it up with nicety against the side of the table.

'You will perhaps agree, my friend, that I am an observant man?'

Miles grinned. 'I agree without a struggle.'

'Good! Then I will show you.'

Professor Rigaud illustrated the next part of his argument by again sticking his elbows on the table, lifting his arms, tapping the forefinger of his right hand against the forefinger of his left, and at the same time bringing his intent, gleaming eyes so close to the fingers that he almost grew cross-eyed.

'First of all, I myself can testify that there was no person in or on the tower – hiding there – when we left Mr Brooke alone. Such an idea is absurd! The place was as bare as a jug! I saw for myself! And the same truth applies to my return at five minutes past four, when I can take my oath that no murderer was lurking inside to make subsequent escape.

'Next, what happens as soon as Harry and I go away? The open grass space, surrounding the tower on every side except for the narrow segment where it overhangs the river, is instantly invaded by a family of eight persons: Monsieur and Madame Lambert, their niece, their daughter-in-law, and four children.

'I am a bachelor, thank God.

'These people take possession of the open space. By sheer numbers they fill it. Papa and Mama are in sight of the doorway. Niece and eldest child keep walking round the tower and looking at it. The two youngest are actually *inside*. And all agree that no person either entered or left the tower during that time.'

Miles opened his mouth to make a protest, but Professor Rigaud intervened before he could speak.

'It is true,' the professor conceded, 'that these people could not speak as to the side of the round-tower facing the river.'

'Ah!' said Miles. 'There were no witnesses on that side?'

'Alas, none.'

'Then it's fairly obvious, isn't it? You told us a while ago that one of the battlements round the parapet, on the side facing the river, had crumbling pieces of rock broken off as though someone's fingers had clawed at them in climbing up. The murderer must have come from the river-side.'

'Consider,' said Professor Rigaud in a persuasive voice, 'the difficulties of such a theory.'

'What difficulties?'

The other checked them off on his forefinger, tapping again.

'No boat approached the tower, or it would have been seen. The stone of that tower, forty feet high, was as smooth as a wet fish. The lowest window (as measured by the police) was fully twenty-five feet above the surface of the water. How does your murderer scale the wall, kill Mr Brooke, and get down again?'

33

There was a long silence.

'But, hang it all, the thing *was* done!' protested Miles. 'You're not going to tell me this crime was committed by a ...'

'By a what?'

The question was fired back so quickly, while Professor Rigaud lowered his lands and leaned forward, that Miles felt an eerie and disturbing twinge of nerves. It seemed to him that Professor Rigaud was trying to tell him something, trying to lead him, trying to draw him on, with that sardonic amusement behind it.

'I was going to say,' Miles answered, 'by some sort of supernatural being that could float in the air.'

'How curious for you to use those words! How very interesting!'

'Would you mind if I interrupted for a moment?' asked Barbara, fiddling with the tablecloth. 'The main thing, after all, is about – is about Fay Seton. I think you said she had an appointment with Mr Brooke for four o'clock. Did she keep that appointment at all?'

'She was, at least, not seen.'

'*Did* she keep that appointment, Professor Rigaud?'

'She arrived there afterwards, mademoiselle. When it was all over.'

'Then what was she doing during that time?'

'Ah!' said Professor Rigaud, with such relish that both his auditors half dreaded what he might say. 'Now we come to it!'

'Come to what?'

'The most fascinating part of the mystery. This puzzle of a man alone when he is stabbed' – Professor Rigaud puffed out his cheeks – 'it is interesting, yes. But to me the great interest of a case is not in material clues, like a bright little puzzle-box with all the pieces numbered and of a different colour. No! To me it lies in the human mind, the human behaviour: if you like, the human soul.' His voice sharpened. 'Fay Seton, for example. Describe for me, if you can, *her* mind and soul.'

'It might help us,' Miles pointed out, 'if we learned what she had been doing which upset people so much, and changed everybody's feelings towards her. Forgive me, but – you do know what it was?'

'Yes.' The word was clipped off. 'I know.'

'And where she was at the time of the murder,' continued Miles, with questions boiling inside him. 'And what the police thought about her position in the affair. And what happened to her romance with Harry Brooke. And, in short, the whole end of the story!'

Professor Rigaud nodded.

'I will tell you,' he promised. 'But first' – like a good connoisseur, tantalizingly, he beamed as he held them in suspense – 'we must have a glass of something to drink. My throat is as dry as sand. And you must drink too.' He raised his voice. 'Waiter!'

After a pause he shouted again. The sound filled the room; it seemed to draw vibrations from the engraving of the skull hung over the mantelpiece, it made the candle-flames curl slowly; but there was no reply. Outside the windows the night was now pitch-black, gurgling as though from a water-spout.

'Ah, zut!' fussed Professor Rigaud, and began to look about for a bell.

'To tell you the truth,' ventured Barbara, 'I'm rather surprised we haven't been turned out of here long ago. The Murder Club seem to be very favoured people. It must be nearly eleven o'clock.'

'It *is* nearly eleven o'clock,' fumed Professor Rigaud, consulting his watch. Then he bounced to his feet. 'I beg of you, mademoiselle, that you will not disturb yourself! Or you, either, my friend: *I* will get the waiter.'

The double-doors to the outer room closed behind him, again whisking the candle-flames. As Miles got up automatically to anticipate him, Barbara stretched out her hand and touched his arm. Her eyes, those friendly sympathetic grey eyes under the smooth forehead and the wings of ash-blonde hair, said silently but very clearly that she wanted to ask him a question in private.

Miles sat down again.

'Yes, Miss Morell?'

She withdrew her hand quickly. 'I ... I don't know how to begin, really.'

'Then suppose I begin?' said Miles, with that tolerant and crooked smile which so much inspired confidence.

'How do you mean?'

'I don't want to pry into anything, Miss Morell. This is entirely between ourselves. But it has struck me, once or twice to-night, that you're far more interested in the specific case of Fay Seton than you are in the Murder Club.'

'What makes you think that?'

35

'Isn't it true? Professor Rigaud's noticed it too.'

'Yes. It's true.' She spoke after a hesitation, nodding vigorously and then turning her head away. 'That's why I owe you an explanation. And I want to give you an explanation. But before I do' – she turned back to face him – 'may I ask you a horribly impertinent question? *I* don't want to pry either; really I don't; but may I ask it?'

'Of course. What do you want to know?'

Barbara tapped the photograph of Fay Seton, lying between them beside the folded sheaf of manuscript.

'You're fascinated by that, aren't you?' she asked.

'Well – yes. I suppose I am.'

'You wonder,' said Barbara, 'what it would be like to be in love with her.'

If her first remark had been a trifle disconcerting, the second took him completely aback.

'Are you setting up as a mind-reader, Miss Morell?'

'I'm sorry! But isn't it true?'

'No! Wait! Hold on! That's going a bit too far!'

The photograph *had* been having a hypnotic effect; he could not in honesty deny it. But that was curiosity, the lure of a puzzle. Miles had always been rather amused by those stories, usually romantic stories with a tragic ending, in which some poor devil falls in love with a woman's picture. Such things had actually happened in real life, of course; but it failed to lessen his disbelief. And, in any case, the question didn't arise here.

He could have laughed at Barbara for her seriousness.

'Anyway,' he countered, 'why do you ask that?'

'Because of something you said earlier this evening. Please don't try to remember what it was!' Humour, a wryness about the mouth to contradict the smile in her eyes, showed in Barbara's face. 'I'm probably only tired, and imagining things. Forget I said it! Only ...'

'You see, Miss Morell, I'm a historian.'

'Oh?' Her manner was quickly sympathetic.

Miles felt rather sheepish. 'That's a highfalutin' way of putting it, I'm afraid. But it does happen to be true, in however small a way. My work, the world I live in, is made up of people I never knew. Trying to visualize, trying to understand, a lot of men and women who were only heaps of dust before I was born. As for this Fay Seton ...'

'She *is* wonderfully attractive, isn't she?' Barbara indicated the photograph.

'Is she?' Miles said coolly. 'It's not a bad piece of work, certainly. Coloured photographs are usually an abomination. Anyway,' fiercely he groped back to the subject, 'this woman is no more real than Agnes Sorel or – or Pamela Hoyt. We don't know anything about her.' He paused, startled. 'Come to think of it, we haven't even heard whether she's still alive.'

'No,' the girl agreed slowly. 'No, we haven't even heard that.'

Barbara got up slowly, brushing her knuckles across the table as though throwing something away. She drew a deep breath.

'I can only ask you again,' she said, 'please to forget everything I've just said. It was only a silly idea of mine; it couldn't possibly come to anything. What, a queer evening this has been! Professor Rigaud does rather cast a spell, doesn't he? And, as far as that's concerned' – she spoke suddenly, twitching her head round – 'isn't Professor Rigaud being a long time in finding a waiter?'

'Professor Rigaud!' called Miles. He lifted up his voice powerfully. '*Professor Rigaud!*'

Again, as when the absent one had himself called for a waiter, only the rain gurgled and splashed in the darkness. There was no reply.

CHAPTER 5

MILES rose to his feet and went over to the double-doors. He threw them open, and looked into an outer room sombre and deserted. Bottles and glasses had been removed from the improvised bar; only one electric light was burning.

'A queer evening,' Miles declared, 'is absolutely right. First the whole Murder Club disappears. Professor Rigaud tells us an incredible story,' Miles shook his head as though to clear it, 'which grows even more incredible when you have time to think. Then *he* disappears. Common sense suggests he's only gone to – never mind. But at the same time …'

The mahogany door to the hall opened. Frédéric, the head-waiter, his round-jowled face aloof with reproach, slipped in.

'Professor Rigaud, sir,' he announced, 'is downstairs. At the telephone.'

Barbara, who had stopped only long enough, apparently, to pick up her handbag and blow out one candle which was fluttering and flaring in a harsh gush of wax-smoke, had followed Miles into the outer room. Again she stopped short.

'At the telephone?' Barbara repeated.

'Yes, miss.'

'But' – the words sounded almost comic as she flung them out – 'he was looking for someone to serve us drinks!'

'Yes, miss. The call came through while he was downstairs.'

'From whom?'

'I believe, miss, from Dr Gideon Fell.' Slight pause. 'The Honorary Secretary of the Murder Club.' Slight pause. 'Dr Fell learned Professor Rigaud had been ringing up from here earlier in the evening; so Dr Fell rang back.' Was there a dangerous quality, now, about Frédéric's eye? 'Professor Rigaud seems very angry, miss.'

'Oh, good Lord!' breathed Barbara in a voice of honest consternation.

Over the back of one of the pink-brocaded chairs, chairs ranged as stiffly round the room as in an undertaker's parlour, hung the girl's fur wrap and an umbrella. Assuming an air of elaborate unconcern which would have deceived nobody, Barbara picked them up and twisted the wrap round her shoulders.

'I'm awfully sorry,' she said to Miles. 'I shall have to go now.'

He stared at her.

'But, look here! You can't go now! Won't the old boy be annoyed if he comes back and finds you're not here?'

'Not half as annoyed,' Barbara said with conviction, 'as if he comes back and finds I *am* here.' She fumbled at her handbag. '– I want to pay for my share of the dinner. It's been very nice. I –' Confusion, utter and complete, overcame her down to the finger-tips. Her handbag overflowed, spilling coins and keys and a compact on the floor.

Miles restrained an impulse to laugh, though certainly not at her. A great dazzle of illumination came into his mind. He bent down, picked up the fallen articles, dropped them into her handbag, and closed it with a snap.

'You arranged all this, didn't you?' he asked her.

'Arranged? I ...'

'*You* dished the meeting of the Murder Club, by God! In some way you put off Dr Fell and Mr Justice Coleman and Dame Ellen Nye and Uncle Tom Cobleigh and all! All except Professor Rigaud, because you wanted to hear his first-hand account about Fay Seton! But you knew the Murder Club had never entertained any guests except the speaker, so you hadn't bargained on *my* turning up ...'

Her dead-serious voice recalled him.

'Please! Don't make a fool of me!'

Wrenching loose from the hand he had put on her arm, Barbara ran for the door. Frédéric, a stony eye on one corner of the ceiling, slowly moved aside for her as one who calls attention to the fact that he could have sent for the police. Miles hurried after her.

'Here! Wait! I wasn't blaming you! I ...'

But she was already flying down the soft-carpeted hall, in the direction of the private stair to Greek Street.

Miles glanced round desperately. Opposite him was the illuminated sign of the gentleman's cloakroom. He snatched up his raincoat, crammed his hat on his head, and returned to face the speaking eye of Frédéric.

'Are the dinners of the Murder Club paid for by somebody in a lump sum? Or does each person pay for his own?'

'It is the rule for each person to pay for his own, sir. But to-night –'

'I know, I know!' Miles thrust banknotes into the man's hand, with pleasurable exhilaration at the thought that he could nowadays afford to do so. 'This is to cover everything. Present my distinguished compliments to Professor Rigaud, and say I'll ring him in the morning to apologize. I don't know where he's staying in London,' this was an impasse he swept aside, 'but I can find out. Er – have I given you enough money?'

'More than enough *money*, sir. At the same time ...'

'Sorry. My fault. Good night!'

He dared not run too hard, since his old illness was apt to claw at him and make his head swim. But his pace was tolerably fast all the same. As he got downstairs and outside, he could just see the glimmer of Barbara's white dress, under the short fur wrap, moving in the direction of Frith Street. Then he really did run.

A taxi rolled down Frith Street in the direction of Shaftesbury Avenue, its motor whirring with great distinctness in the hollow-punctuated silence of London at night. Miles shouted at it without much hope, but to his surprise it hesitatingly swerved in towards the kerb. With his left hand Miles caught at Barbara Morell's arm; with his right he twisted open the handle of the cab door before someone else should appear, ghostly out of the rain-pattering gloom, to lay claim to it.

'Honestly,' he said to Barbara, with such a warmth of sincerity that her arm relaxed, 'there was no reason to run away like that. You can at least let me drop you off at home. Where do you live?'

'St John's Wood. But ...'

'Can't do it, governor,' said the taxi-driver in a fierce voice of defiance mingled with martyrdom. 'I'm going Victoria way, and I've only just got enough petrol to get home.'

'All right. Drop us at Piccadilly Circus tube-station.'

The car door slammed. There was a slur of tyres on wet asphalt. Barbara, in the far corner of the seat, spoke in a small voice.

'You'd like to kill me, wouldn't you?' she asked.

'For the last time, my dear girl: no! On the contrary. Life has been made so uncomfortable for us that every little bit helps.'

'What on earth do you mean?'

'A high-court judge, a barrister-politician, and a number of other important people have been carefully flummoxed at something they'd arranged. Wouldn't it delight your heart if you heard – as you never will – of an Important Person who couldn't make a reservation or got thrown back to the tail-end of a queue?'

The girl looked at him.

'You *are* nice,' she said seriously.

This threw Miles a little off balance.

'It isn't a question of what you call niceness,' he retorted with some violence. 'It's a question of the Old Adam.'

'But poor Professor Rigaud –! '

'Yes, it's a bit rough on Rigaud. We must find a way to make amends. All the same! – I don't know why you did it, Miss Morell, but I'm very glad you did it. Except for two reasons.'

'What reasons?'

'In the first place, I think you should have confided in Dr Fell. He's a grand old boy; he'd have sympathized with anything you told him. And how he would have enjoyed that case of the man murdered while alone on a tower! That is,' Miles added, with the perplexity and strangeness of the night wrapping him round, 'if it *was* a real case and not a dream or a leg-pull. If you'd told Dr Fell ...'

'But I don't even know Dr Fell! I lied about that too.'

'It doesn't matter!'

'It does matter,' said Barbara, and pressed her hands hard over her eyes. 'I'd never met any of the members. But I was in a position, you see, to learn all their names and addresses, and that Professor Rigaud was speaking on the Brooke case. I phoned everybody except Dr Fell as Dr Fell's private secretary, and said the dinner had been postponed. Then I got in touch with Dr Fell as representing the President. And hoped to heaven those two would be away from home to-night if someone *did* ring up for confirmation.'

She paused, staring straight ahead at the glass partition behind the driver's seat, and added slowly:

'I didn't do it for a joke.'

'No. I guessed that.'

'Did you?' cried Barbara. 'Did you?'

The cab jolted. Motor-car lamps, odd in newness, once or twice swept the back of the cab with their brief unaccustomed glare through dingy rain-misted windows.

Barbara turned towards him. She put out a hand to steady herself against the glass partition in front. Anxiety, apology, a curious embarrassment, and – yes! her obvious liking for him – shone in her expression as palpably as her wish to tell him something else. But she did not speak that something else. She only said:

'What was the other reason?'

'Other reason?'

'You told me there were two reasons why you regretted this – this foolishness of mine to-night. What's the other one?'

'Well!' He tried to sound light and casual. 'Hang it all, I *was* a good deal interested in that case of the murder on the tower. Since Professor Rigaud probably isn't on speaking terms with either of us –'

'You may never hear the end of the story. Is that it?'

'Yes, that's it.'

'I see.' She was silent for a moment, tapping her fingers on her handbag, her mouth moving in an odd way and her eyes shining almost as though there were tears in them. 'Where are you staying in town?'

'At the Berkeley. But I'm going back to the New Forest to-morrow. My sister and her fiancé are coming up for the day, and we're all travelling back together.' Miles broke off. 'Why do you ask?'

'Maybe I can help you.' Opening her handbag, she drew out a folded sheaf of manuscript and handed it to him. 'This is Professor Rigaud's own account of the Brooke case, specially written for the archives of the Murder Club. I – I stole it from the table at Beltring's when you went to look for him. I was going to post it on to you when I'd finished reading, but I've already learned the only thing I really wanted to know.'

Insistently she thrust the manuscript back into his hands.

'I don't see how I can be of any use now,' she cried. 'I don't *see* how I can be of any use now!'

With a grind of gears into neutral, with the whush of tyres erratically scraping a kerb, the taxi drew up. Ahead loomed the cavern of Piccadilly Circus from the mouth of Shaftesbury Avenue, murmurous and shuffling with a late crowd. Instantly Barbara was across the cab and outside on the pavement.

42

'Don't get out!' she insisted, backing away. 'I can go straight home in the Underground from here. And the taxi's going your way in any case. – Berkeley Hotel!' she called to the driver.

The door slammed just before eight American G.I.'s, in three different parties, bore down simultaneously on the cab. Against the gleam of a lighted window Miles caught a glimpse of Barbara's face, smiling brightly and tensely and unconvincingly in the crowd as the taxi moved away.

Miles sat back, holding Professor Rigaud's manuscript and feeling it figuratively burn his hand.

Old Rigaud would be furious. He would demand to know, in a frenzy of Gallic logic, why this trick had been played on him. And that was not funny; that was only just and reasonable; for Miles himself had still no notion why. All of which he could be certain was that Barbara Morell's motive had been a strong one, passionately sincere.

As for Barbara's remark about Fay Seton ...

'You wonder what it would be like to be in love with her.'

What infernal nonsense!

Had the mystery of Howard Brooke's death ever been solved, by the police or by Rigaud or by anyone else? Had they learned who committed the murder, and how it was done? Evidently not, from the tenor of the professor's remarks. He had said he knew what was 'wrong' with Fay Seton. But he had also said – though in queer, elusive terms – that he did not believe she was guilty. Every statement concerning the murder, through all that tortuous story, rang the clear indication that there had been no solution.

Therefore all this manuscript could tell him ... Miles glanced at it in the semi-darkness ... would be the routine facts of the police investigation. It might tell him some sordid facts about the character of a pleasant-faced woman with red hair and blue eyes. But no more.

In an utter revulsion of feeling Miles hated the whole thing. He wanted peace and quiet. He wanted to be free from these clinging strands. With a sudden impulse, before he should think better of it, he leaned forward and tapped the glass panel.

'Driver! Have you got enough petrol to take me back to Beltring's Restaurant, and then on to the Berkeley? – Double fare if you do!'

The silhouette of the driver's back contorted with angry indecision; but the cab slowed down, slurred, and circled Eros's island back into Shaftesbury Avenue.

43

Miles was inspired by his new resolution. After all, he had been gone from Beltring's only a comparatively few minutes. What he proposed doing now was the only sensible thing to do. His resolution blazed brightly inside him when he jumped out of the taxi in Romilly Street, hurried round the corner to the side entrance, and up the stairs.

In the upstairs hall he found a dispirited-looking waiter occupied with the business of closing up.

'Is Professor Rigaud still here? A short stoutish French gentleman with a patch of moustache something like Hitler's carrying a yellow cane?'

The waiter looked at him curiously.

'He is downstairs in the bar, monsieur. He ...'

'Give him this, will you?' requested Miles, and put the still-folded manuscript into the waiter's hand. 'Tell him it was taken by mistake. Thank you.'

And he strode out again.

On the way home, lighting his pipe and inhaling the soothing smoke, Miles was conscious of a sensation of exhilaration and buoyancy. To-morrow afternoon, when he had attended to the real business which brought him to London, he would meet Marion and Steve at the station. He would return to the country, to the secluded house in the New Forest where they had been established for only a fortnight, as a man plunges into cool water on a hot day.

That was disposed of, cut off at the root, before it could really trouble his mind. Whatever secret appertained to a phantom image called Fay Seton, it was no concern of his.

To claim his attention there would be his uncle's library, that alluring place hardly as yet explored during the confusion of moving in and settling down. By this time to-morrow night he would be at Greywood, among the ancient oaks and beeches of the New Forest, beside the little stream where rainbow trout rose at dusk when you flicked bits of bread on the water. Miles felt, in some extraordinary way, that he had got out of a snare.

His taxi dropped him at the Piccadilly entrance to the Berkeley: he paid the driver in an expansive mood. Seeing that the lounge inside was still pretty well filled at its little round tables, Miles, with his passionate hatred of crowds, deliberately walked round to the Berkeley Street entrance so that he might breathe solitude a little longer. The rain was clearing away. A freshness tinged the air. Miles pushed through the revolving doors into the little foyer, with the reception desk on his right.

He got his key at the desk, and stood debating the advisability of a final pipe and whisky-and-soda before turning in, when the night reception clerk hurried out of the cubicle with a slip of paper in his hand.

'Mr Hammond!'

'Yes?'

The clerk scrutinized the slip of paper, trying to read his own handwriting.

'There's a message for you, sir. I think you applied to the – to this employment agency for a librarian to do cataloguing work?'

'I did,' said Miles. 'And they promised to send an applicant round this evening. The applicant didn't turn up, which made me very late for a dinner I was attending.'

'The applicant *did* turn up, sir, eventually. The lady says she's very sorry, but it was unavoidable. She says could you please see her to-morrow morning? She says things are very difficult, since she's only just been repatriated from France …'

'Repatriated from France?'

'Yes, sir.'

The hands of a gilt clock on the grey-green wall pointed to twenty-five minutes past eleven. Miles Hammond stood very still, and stopped twirling the key in his hand.

'Did the lady leave her name?'

'Yes, sir. Miss Fay Seton.'

CHAPTER 6

ON the following afternoon, Saturday, the second of June, Miles reached Waterloo Station at four o'clock.

Waterloo, its curving acre of iron-girdered roof still darkened over except where a few patches of glass remained after the shake of bombs, had got over most of the Saturday rush to Bournemouth. But it still rang with a woman's spirited voice over a loud-speaker, telling people what queues to join. (If this voice ever begins to say something you want to hear, it is instantly drowned out by a hiss of steam or the thudding chest-notes of an engine.) Streams of travellers, mainly in khaki against civilian drabness, wound back among the benches behind the bookstall and, to the ladylike annoyance of the loud-speaker, got mixed up in each other's queues.

Miles Hammond was not amused. As he put down his suitcase and waited under the clock, he was almost blind to everything about him.

What the devil, he said to himself, *had* he done?

What would Marion say? What would Steve say?

Yet if anybody on this earth represented sanity, it was his sister and her fiancé. He was heartened to see them a few minutes later, Marion laden with parcels and Steve with a pipe in his mouth.

Marion Hammond, six or seven years younger than Miles, was a sturdy, nice-looking girl with black hair like her brother but a practicality that he perhaps lacked. She was very fond of Miles and tirelessly humoured him; because she really did believe, though she never said so, that he was not mentally grown up. She was proud, of course, of a brother who could write such learned books, though Marion confessed she didn't understand such things herself: the point was that books had no relation to serious affairs in life.

And, as Miles sometimes had to admit to himself, perhaps she was right.

So she came hurrying along under the echoing roof of Waterloo, well dressed even in this year because of new tricks with old clothes, her hazel eyes at ease with life under their dark straight brows, and intrigued – even pleased – by a new vagary of Miles's nature.

'Honestly, Miles!' said his sister. 'Look at the clock! It's only a few minutes past four!'

'I know that.'

'But the train doesn't go until half-past *five*, dear. Even if we've got to be here early to have a prayer of getting a seat, why must you make us get here as early as this?' Then her sisterly eye caught the expression on his face, and she broke off. 'Miles! What's wrong? Are you ill?'

'No, no, no!'

'Then what is it?'

'I want to talk to both of you,' said Miles. 'Come with me.'

Stephen Curtis took the pipe out of his mouth. 'Ho?' he observed.

Stephen's age might have been in the late thirties. He was almost completely bald – a sore subject with him – though personable-enough looking and with much stolid charm. His fair moustache gave him a vaguely R.A.F. appearance, though in fact he worked at the Ministry of Information and Strongly resented jokes about this institution. He had met Marion there two years ago after being invalided out very early in the war. He and Marion, in fact, were themselves an institution already.

So he stood looking at Miles with interest from under the brim of a soft hat.

'Well?' prompted Stephen.

Opposite platform number eleven at Waterloo there is a restaurant, up two steep flights of stairs. Miles picked up his suitcase and led the way there. When they had installed themselves at a window table overlooking the station platform, in a big imitation-oak-panelled room only sparsely filled, Miles first ordered tea with care.

'There's a woman named Fay Seton,' he said. 'Six years ago, in France, she was mixed up in a murder case. People accused her of some kind of unnamed bad conduct which set the whole district by the ears.' He paused. 'I've engaged her to come to Greywood and catalogue the books.'

There was a long silence while Marion and Stephen looked at him. Again Stephen took the pipe out of his mouth.

'Why?' he asked.

'I don't know!' Miles answered honestly. 'I'd made up my mind to have absolutely nothing to do with it. I was going to tell her firmly that the post had been filled. I couldn't sleep all last night for thinking about her face.'

'Last night, eh? When did you meet her?'

'This morning.'

With great carefulness Stephen put down the pipe on the table between them. He pushed the bowl a fraction of an inch to the left, and then a fraction of an inch to the right, delicately.

'Look here, old man –' he began.

'Oh, Miles,' cried his sister, what *is* all this?'

'I'm trying to tell you!' Miles brooded. 'Fay Seton was trained as a librarian. That's why both Barbara Morell and old What's-his-name, at the Murder Club, both looked so strange when I mentioned the library and said I was looking for a librarian. But Barbara was even quicker-minded than the old professor. *She* guessed. What with the present terrific labour shortage, if I went to the agencies for a librarian and Fay Seton was in the market for a job, it was twenty to one Fay would be sent to me. Yes. Barbara guessed in advance.'

And he drummed his fingers on the table.

Stephen removed his soft hat, showing the pinkish bald head above an intent, worried-looking face set in an expression of affection and expostulation.

'Let's get this straight,' he suggested. 'Yesterday morning, Friday morning, you came to London in search of a librarian –'

'Actually, Steve,' Marion cut in, 'he'd been invited to a dinner of something called the Murder Club.'

'That,' said Miles, 'was where I first heard about Fay Seton. I'm not crazy and this isn't at all mysterious. Afterwards I met her ...'

Marion smiled.

'And she told you some heart-rending story?' said Marion. 'And your sympathies were roused as usual?'

'On the contrary, she doesn't even know I've heard a word about her. We simply sat in the lounge at the Berkeley and talked.'

'I see, Miles. Is she young?'

'Fairly young, yes.'

'Good-looking?'

'In a certain way, yes. But that wasn't what influenced me. It was —'

'Yes, Miles?'

'Just something about her!' Miles gestured. 'There isn't time to tell you the whole story. The point is that I *have* engaged her and she's travelling down with us by this afternoon's train. I thought I'd better tell you.'

Conscious of a certain relief, Miles sat back as the waitress came and clanked down tea-things on the table with a wrist-motion suggestive of someone throwing quoits. Outside, under the dusty windows beside which they sat, moved the endless sluggish knots of travellers in front of black white-numbered gates leading to the platforms.

And it suddenly occurred to Miles, as he watched his two companions, that history was repeating itself. There could be no persons more conventional, better representing the traditions of home life, than Marion Hammond and Stephen Curtis. Exactly as Fay Seton had been introduced into the Brooke family six years ago, she would now enter another such household.

History repeating itself. Yes.

Marion and Stephen exchanged a glance. Marion laughed.

'Well, I don't know,' she observed, in the musing tone of a woman not altogether displeased. 'It might be rather fun, in a way.'

'*Fun?*' exclaimed Stephen.

'Did you tell her, Miles, to be sure to bring her ration-book?'

'No,' His tone was bitter. 'I'm afraid that detail escaped me.'

'Never mind, dear. We can always …' Abruptly Marion sat up, a flash of consternation in her hazel eyes under the sensible straight brows. 'Miles! Wait! This woman didn't *poison* anybody?'

'My dear Marion,' said Stephen, 'will you please tell me what difference it makes whether she poisoned anybody or shot anybody or beat in some old man's head with a poker? The point is —'

'Just a minute,' interposed Miles quietly. He tried to be very quiet, very measured, and to control the thumping of his pulses. 'I didn't say this girl was a murderess. On the contrary, if I have any judgement of human character, she certainly isn't anything of the kind.'

'Yes, dear,' Marion said indulgently, and leaned across the tea-service to pat his hand. 'I'm sure you're *quite* convinced of that.'

'God damn it, Marion, will you stop misjudging my motives in this thing?'

49

'Miles! Please!' Marion clucked her tongue, more from force of habit than anything else. 'We're in a public place.'

'Yes,' agreed Stephen. 'Better lower your voice, old boy.'

'All right, all right! Only ...'

'Here!' soothed Marion, and poured tea with deftness. 'Take this, and try one of the cakes. There! Isn't that better? This interesting lady of yours, Miles: how old did you say she was?'

'In her early thirties, I should think.'

'And going out as a librarian? How is it the Labour Exchange hasn't got her?'

'She's only just been repatriated from France.'

'From France? Really? I wonder if she's brought over any French perfume with her?'

'Come to think of it,' said Miles, who in fact could remember it quite well, 'she *was* wearing some kind of perfume this morning. I happened to notice.'

'We want to hear all about her past history, Miles. There's plenty of time, and we can save an extra cup of tea for her in case she turns up soon. It *wasn't* poison? You're sure of that? Steve, darling! – you're not having any tea!'

'*Listen!*' said Stephen, at last in the authoritative voice of one who calls for the floor.

Picking up his pipe from the table, he twisted at it and thrust it bowl-upwards into his breast-pocket.

'What I can't understand,' he complained, 'is how all this came about. Do they keep murderers at the Murder Club, or what? All right, Miles! Don't get on your high horse! I like to get my facts in order, that's all. How long will it take Miss What-is-it to put the books in order? A week or so?'

Miles grinned at him.

'Properly to catalogue that library, Steve, with all the cross-referencing of the old books, will take between two and three months.'

Even Marion looked startled.

'Well,' murmured Stephen, after a pause, 'Miles will always do exactly what he wants to do. So that's all right. But I can't go back to Greywood with you this evening ...'

'You can't go back this evening?' cried Marion.

'My darling,' said Steve, 'I kept trying to tell you in the taxi – only you haven't the gift of worshipful silence – that there's a crisis on again at the office. It's only until to-morrow morning.' He hesitated. 'I suppose it's all right to send you two down there alone with this interesting female?'

There was a brief silence.

Then Marion chortled with mirth.

'Steve! You *are* an idiot!'

'Am I? Yes. I suppose I am.'

'What can Fay Seton do to us?'

'Not being acquainted with the lady, I can't say. Nothing, actually.' Stephen smoothed at his cropped moustache. 'It's only –'

'Drink up your tea, Steve, and don't be so old-fashioned. *I* shall be glad of her help about the house. When Miles said he was going to employ a librarian I rather imagined an old man with a long white beard. What's more, I shall put her in my room, and that will give me an excuse to move into that glorious ground-floor room even if it does still smell of paint. It's tiresome about the Ministry of Information; but I don't think the woman will frighten us to death in one night even if you're not there. What train are you taking to-morrow morning?'

'Nine-thirty. And mind you don't mess about with that kitchen boiler unless I'm there to help. Let it *alone*, do you hear?'

'I'm a dutiful bride-to-be, Steve.'

'Dutiful my foot,' said Stephen, without stress or resentment; he simply stated a fact. At the same time, obviously soothed and shaken back to normal by this talk, he dismissed the subject of Fay Seton. 'By George, Miles, you must take *me* to a meeting of this Murder Club one day! What do they do there?'

'It's a dinner club.'

'You mean you pretend the salt is poison? That sort of thing? And score a point if you can shove it into somebody's coffee without being detected? All right, old man: don't be offended! I must be pushing off now.'

'Steve!' Marion spoke in a voice whose inflexion her brother knew only too well. 'I forgot something. May I have a word with you? You *will* excuse us for a moment, Miles!'

Talking about him, eh?

Miles glowered at the table, trying to pretend he was unconscious of this, as Marion moved with Stephen towards the door. Marion was speaking

51

in an animated undertone, Stephen shrugging his shoulders and smiling as he put on his hat. Miles took a drink of tea that had begun to grow cold.

He had an uncomfortable suspicion that he was somehow making a fool of himself, certainly that he was losing his sense of humour. But why? The true answer to that occurred to him a moment later. It was because he wondered whether he might not be loosing in his own household certain forces over which he had no control.

A cash-register rang: outside the windows rose the chug of a train; the burring voice of the loud-speaker recalled him to Waterloo Station. Miles told himself that this fleeting idea – the momentary intense chill which touched his heart – was all nonsense. He repeated it, summoning up a laugh, and felt his spirits improved when Marion returned.

'Sorry if I sounded bad-tempered, Marion.'

'My dear boy!' She dismissed this with a gesture. Then she eyed him persuasively. 'But now that we're all alone, Miles, tell your little sister all about it.'

'There isn't anything to tell! I met this girl, I liked her manners, I was convinced she'd been slandered ...'

'But you didn't tell her you knew anything about her?'

'Not a word. She didn't mention it, either.'

'She gave you references, of course?'

'I didn't ask for them. Why should you be so interested?'

'Miles, Miles!' Marion, shook her head. 'Practically every woman falls for that sauntering Charles-the-Second air of yours, the more so as you're so superbly unconscious of it yourself. Now don't draw yourself up and look stuffy! You hate it when I take *any* interest in your welfare!'

'I only meant that these constant sisterly character analyses –!'

'And when I hear of a woman who seems to have impressed you so much, naturally I'm interested!' Marion's eyes remained steady. 'What was the trouble she was mixed up in?'

Miles' gaze wandered out of the window.

'Six years ago she went over to Chartres as private secretary to a wealthy leather manufacturer named Brooke. She became engaged to be married to the son of the house ...'

'Oh.'

' ... a young neurotic named Harry Brooke. Afterwards there was a row of some kind.' Inwardly Miles choked over the words. He couldn't

52

physically couldn't, tell Marion about Howard Brooke's determination to buy off this girl.

'What kind of a row, Miles?'

'Nobody knows; or at least *I* don't. One afternoon the father climbed up to the top of a tower that's a landmark in the district, and ...' Miles broke off. 'By the way, you won't mention any of this to Miss Seton? You won't give her any intimation you know?'

'Do you think I could be so tactless, Miles?'

'It was a wild, rainy, thundery day over the tower, like a scene in a German ghost-story. Mr Brooke was found stabbed through the back with his own sword-stick. But that's the amazing part of the whole business, Marion. The evidence showed he must have been alone when he died. Nobody came near him or could have come near him. It almost seemed that the murder, if it was a murder, must have been committed by someone who could rise up unsupported in the air ...'

Again he paused. For Marion was contemplating him in a strange, wide-eyed, searching way, bursting and balanced on the edge of laughter.

'Miles Hammond!' she cried. 'Who's been stuffing you full of this awful rubbish?'

'I am simply,' he said through his teeth, 'stating the facts of the official police investigation.'

'All right, dear. But who told you?'

'Professor Rigaud of Edinburgh University. A distinguished man in the academic world. You must have come across his *Life Cagliostro*?'

'No. Who's Cagliostro?'

(Why is it – Miles had often pondered the question – that in debates with your own family you are inclined to lose your temper over questions which from an outsider would be greeted with mildness, even amusement?)

'Count Cagliostro, Marion, was a famous wizard and charlatan of the eighteenth century. Professor Rigaud takes the line that Cagliostro, though he was a thundering fraud in most respects, really did possess certain psychic powers which ...'

For the third time he checked himself. Marion was whooping. And, hearing what his own voice must sound like, Miles had enough sense of proportion left to agree that possibly he might have made a better choice of words.

'Yes,' he admitted. 'It does sound a bit funny, doesn't it?'

'It certainly does, Miles. I'll believe that sort of thing when *I* see it. But never mind Count Cagliostro. Stop pulling my leg and tell me about this *girl*! Who is she? What's she like? What sort of influence does she have?'

'You can find out for yourself, Marion.'

'Still gazing down out of the window, Miles rose to his feet. He was looking at one of the green-painted signs opposite the platform gates, the sign where travellers already drifted by ones and twos in readiness for the five-thirty train to Winchester, Southampton Central, and Bournemouth. And with great deliberation Miles nodded towards it.

'There she is now.'

CHAPTER 7

GREY twilight hung over Greywood in the New Forest, that evening which afterwards was to be so well remembered.

Off the main motor-road from Southampton branches another motor-road. Follow this into tall green depths where forest ponies browse at the edges. Presently turn left at a broad wooden gate, down the curve of a gravel path dusky even at noonday, cross a rustic bridge over the stream which winds through the estate, and just ahead is Greywood – set against a green lawn, encircled by the might of beeches and oaks.

Long and narrow-built, not large, its narrow side faces you as you cross the rustic bridge. You must climb up a few stone-flagged steps, and go round a flagged terrace to what seems the side of the house, in order to reach the front door. Built of wood and of brick plastered over, it stands out brown and white against the sun-dusted forest. It has friendliness and it is touched with magic.

One or two lights gleamed in the windows to-night. They were paraffin lamps, since the electric power-plant of Sir Charles Hammond's day had not yet been put in order.

Their light grew stronger, yellow, and tremulous, as the cool dusk deepened. Perceptible now, almost unnoticed by day, was the silky splash of water over the miniature dam. Dusk blurred the outlines of the bright-canopied garden swing, with wicker chairs and a table for serving tea, which stood on the open lawn westwards towards the curve of the stream.

And in a long room at the rear of the house – a room after his own heart – stood Miles Hammond, holding a lamp above his head.

'It's all right,' he was saying to himself. 'I didn't make a mistake in bringing her here. It's all right.'

But he knew in his heart that it wasn't all right.

The flame of the little lamp, in its tiny cylindrical glass shade, partly drew the shadows from a mummified world of books. It was wrong, of course, to call this place a library. It was a stack-room, a repository, an immensely long dust-heap for the two or three thousand volumes accumulated like dust by his late uncle. Books old and broken, books newish and shiny, books in quarto and octavo and folio, books in fine bindings and books withered black: breathing their exhilarating mustiness, a treasure-house hardly yet touched.

Their shelves reached to the ceiling, built even round the door to the dining-room and enclosing the row of little-paned windows that faced east. Books piled the floor in ranks, mounds, and top-heavy towers of unequal height, a maze of which the lanes between were so narrow that you could hardly move without knocking books over in a fluttering puff of dust.

Standing in the middle of this, Miles held the lamp high and slowly looked round him.

'It's all *right*!' he fiercely said aloud.

And the door opened, and Fay Seton came in.

'Did you call me, Mr Hammond?'

'Call you, Miss Seton? No.'

'I beg your pardon. I thought I heard you call.'

'I must have been talking to myself. But it might interest you to have a look at this confusion.'

Fay Seton stood there framed in the doorway, with the many-hued books on either side of her. Rather tall and soft and slender, her head a little on one side. She herself was carrying a paraffin lamp; and, as she lifted the lamp so that it illuminated her face, Miles was conscious of a sense of shock.

In daylight, at the Berkeley and later on the train journey, she had seemed ... not older, though in fact she was older; not less attractive ... but subtly and disquietingly different from the image in his mind.

Now, by artificial light, under the softened radiance of the lamp, it was as though for the first time the photographic image of last night had sprung to life. It was only a brief glimpse, of eye and cheek and mouth, as she raised the lamp to glance round her. But the very *passiveness* of those aloof features, with their polite smile, flowed out and troubled the judgement.

Miles held up his own lamp, so that the light of the two clashed in an unsteady shadow-play, slow and yet wild, across the walls of books.

56

'The place *is* a mess, isn't it?'

'It's not nearly as bad as I'd expected,' answered Fay. She spoke in a low voice and seldom raised her eyes.

'I'm afraid I haven't dusted or cleaned up for you.'

'That doesn't matter, Mr Hammond.'

'My uncle, if I remember correctly, bought a card-index cabinet and an incredible number of reference cards. But he never did any cataloguing. The things are somewhere in this jumble.'

'I can find them, Mr Hammond.'

'Is my sister – er – making you comfortable?'

'Oh, yes!' She gave him a quick smile. 'Miss Hammond wanted to move out of her bedroom up there' – she nodded towards the ceiling of the library – 'and move me in there. But I couldn't have her do that. Anyway, there are reasons why I much, much prefer to be on the ground floor. You don't mind?'

'Mind? Of course not! Won't you come in?'

'Thank you.'

The piles of books on the floor ranged from breast-high to waist-high. Obediently Fay moved forward, with that extraordinary and unconscious grace of hers, edging sideways among the lanes so that her rather shabby dove-grey dress hardly brushed them. She set down the little lamp on a heap of folios, raising a breath of dust, and looked round again.

'It looks interesting,' she said. 'What were your uncle's interests?'

'Almost anything. He specialized in medieval history. But he was also keen on archaeology and sport and gardening and chess. Even crime and –' Miles checked himself abruptly. You're *sure* you're quite comfortable here?'

'Oh, yes! Miss Hammond – she asked me to call her Marion – has been very kind.'

Well, yes: yes, Miles supposed, she *had* been kind. During the train journey, and afterwards while she and Fay prepared a scratch meal in the big kitchen, Marion had talked away twenty to the dozen. Marion had almost gushed over their guest. Yet Miles, who knew his sister, was uneasy in his mind.

'I'm sorry about the servant situation,' he told her. 'They can't be obtained in this part of the world for love or money. At least, by newcomers. I didn't want you to have to … to …'

Her tone was deprecating.

'But I like it. It's cosy. We three are all alone here. And this is the New Forest!'

'Yes.'

Hesitantly, with that same sinuous grace, Fay edged through the lanes over to the row of small-paned windows – themselves framed all round with books – in the east wall. The stationary lamp threw an elongated shadow of her. Two of the window-lights stood open, propped open on catches like little doors. Fay Seton leaned her hands on the window-sill and looked out. Miles, holding his own lamp high, blundered over to join her.

Outside it was not quite dark.

A grass terrace sloped up a few feet to another open space of grass bounded by a straggling iron fence. Beyond that – remote, mysterious, ash-grey turning to black in that unreal light – the tall forest pressed in on them.

'How large is the forest, Mr Hammond?'

'About a hundred thousand acres.'

'As large as that? I hadn't realized …'

'Very few people do. But you can walk into the forest, over there, and get lost and wander about for hours, so that they have to send out a search-party for you. It sounds absurd in a small country like England, but my uncle used to tell me it happened time after time. As a newcomer, I haven't liked to venture too far myself.'

'No, of course not. It looks … I don't know! …'

'Magical?'

'Something like that.' Fay moved her shoulders.

'You see where I'm pointing, Miss Seton?'

'Yes?'

'Not a very great walk from here is the spot where William Rufus, the Red King, was killed with an arrow while he was out hunting. There's an iron monstrosity to mark it now. And – you know *The White Company*?'

She nodded quickly.

'The moon rises very late to-night,' said Miles. But one night soon you and I – and Marion too, of course – must take a walk by full moonlight in the New Forest.'

'That would be awfully nice.'

She was still leaning forward, the palms of her hands flat on the window-sill; she nodded as though she had hardly heard him. Miles was

58

standing close to her. He could look down on the soft line of her shoulders, the whiteness of her neck, the heavy dark-red hair glistening under lamplight. The perfume she used was faint but distinctive. Miles became aware of the disturbing nearness of her physical presence.

Perhaps she realized this; for abruptly, but in her unobtrusive way, she moved away from him and threaded a path back through the books to where she had left the lamp. Miles also turned abruptly and stared out of the window.

He could see her reflexion, ghostly in the window-glass. Picking up an old newspaper, she shook it out for dust, opened it, and put it down on a pile of books. Then she sat down, beside the little lamp.

'Careful!' he warned without turning round. 'You'll get yourself dirty.'

'That doesn't matter.' She kept her eyes lowered. 'It's lovely here, Mr Hammond. I imagine the air is very good?'

'Excellent. You'll sleep like the dead to-night.'

'Do *you* have difficulty in going to sleep?'

'Sometimes, yes.'

'Your sister said you'd been very ill.'

'I'm all right now.'

'War?'

'Yes. The peculiar and painful and unheroic form of poisoning you get in the Tank Corps.'

'Harry Brooke was killed in the retreat to Dunkirk in nineteen-forty,' remarked Fay, with absolutely no change of tone. 'He joined the French Army as liaison-officer with the British – being bi-lingual, you see – and he was killed in the retreat to Dunkirk.'

During a thunderclap of silence, while Miles's ears seemed to ring and Fay Seton's voice remained exactly the same, he stood staring at her reflexion in the window-glass. Then she added:

'You know all about me, don't you?'

Miles put down the lamp on the window-sill, because his hand was shaking and he felt a constriction across his chest. He swung round to face her.

'*Who told you* ...?'

'Your sister intimated it. She said you were moody and had imaginative fits.'

(Marion, eh?)

59

'I think it was awfully decent of you, Mr Hammond, to give me this position – and I *am* rather badly off! – without asking me anything about it. They very nearly sent me to the guillotine, you know, for the murder of Harry's father. But don't you think you ought to hear *my* side of it?'

Long pause.

A cool breeze, infinitely healing, crept in through the window-lights and mingled with the fustiness of old books. From the corner of his eye Miles noticed a black strand of cobweb swaying from the ceiling. He cleared his throat.

'It's none of my business, Miss Seton. And I don't want to upset you.'

'It doesn't upset me. Really it doesn't.'

'But don't you feel …?'

'No. Not now.' She spoke in a very odd tone. The blue eyes, their whites very luminous in lamplight, turned sideways. She put one hand against her breast, a hand very white in contrast to the grey silk dress, and pressed hard there. 'Self-sacrifice!' she said.

'I beg your pardon?'

'What we won't do,' murmured Fay Seton, 'if we get a chance to sacrifice ourselves!' She was silent for a long time, the wide-spaced blue eyes expressionless and lowered. 'Forgive me, Mr Hammond. It doesn't really matter, but I wonder who told you about this.'

'Professor Rigaud.'

'Oh, Georges Rigaud.' She nodded. 'I heard he'd escaped from France during the German occupation, and taken a university post in England. I only asked that, you see, because your sister wasn't sure. For some reason she seemed to think the source of your information was Count Cagliostro.'

They both laughed. Miles was glad of an excuse to laugh, glad to relieve his feelings by shouting at the top of his lungs; but the noise of that laughter went up with inexplicable eeriness under the towering walls of books.

'I – I didn't kill Mr Brooke,' said Fay. 'Do you believe that?'

'Yes.'

'Thank you, Mr Hammond. I …'

(God knows, Miles thought to himself, I, *do* want to hear your story! Go on! Go on! Go on!)

'I went out to France,' she told him in her low voice, 'to be Mr Brooke's personal secretary. I wasn't what you might call,' she looked away from him, 'experienced.'

Miles nodded without speaking, since she had paused.

'It was awfully pleasant there. The Brookes were pleasant, or so I thought. I ... well, you've probably heard that I fell in love with Harry Brooke. I really did fall in love with him, Mr Hammond, from the very start.'

Miles's question, a question he had not meant to ask, was wrung out of him. 'But you refused Harry the first time he proposed marriage?'

'Did I? Who told you that?'

'Professor Rigaud.'

'Oh, I see.' (What was that strange, secret, inner amusement about her eyes? Or did he imagine it?) 'In any case, Mr Hammond, we did become engaged. I think I was very happy, because I've always been domestic-minded. We were making plans for the future, when someone began circulating reports about me.'

Miles's throat felt dry.

'What sort of reports?'

'Oh, of gross immorality.' Faint colour stained the smooth white cheeks; still she kept her eyelids lowered. 'And something else which is really,' Fay half laughed, 'too stupid to bother you with. *I* never heard any of this, of course. But Mr Brooke must have been hearing for some weeks, though he never said anything. First of all I think he had been getting anonymous letters.'

'Anonymous letters?' exclaimed Miles.

'Yes.'

'Professor Rigaud didn't say anything about *that!*'

'Perhaps not. It's – it's only what I think, of course. Matters were awfully strained at the house: in the study when Mr Brooke was dictating, and at meals, and in the evening. Even Mrs Brooke seemed to guess something had gone wrong. Then we came to that awful day of the twelfth of August, when Mr Brooke died.'

Backing away, never taking his eyes from her, Miles Hammond hauled himself up to sit on the wide ledge of the windows.

The tiny lamp-flames burned clearly; the shadows were steady. But in Miles's imagination this long library might have been swept away. He was again outside Chartres beside the Eure, with its backgrounds as the villa called Beauregard and the stone tower looming above the river. The old scenes took form again.

'What a hot day it was!' Fay said dreamily, and moved her shoulders. 'Damp and thundery, but so *hot!* Mr Brooke asked me after breakfast, privately, whether I would meet him at Henri Quatre's tower about four o'clock. Of course I never dreamed he was going in to the Crédit Lyonnais in Chartres to get the famous two thousand pounds.

'*I* left the house at shortly before three o'clock, just before Mr Brooke returned from the bank with that money in his brief-case. You see, I can tell you ... oh, I told the police so often afterwards! ... all the times. I meant to go for a dip in the river, so I took along a bathing-suit. But instead I simply wandered along the river-bank.'

Fay paused.

'When I left that house, Mr Hammond,' – she uttered a strange, far-off kind of laugh – 'it was outwardly a very peaceful house. Georgina Brooke, that's Harry's mother, was in the kitchen speaking to the cook. Harry was upstairs in his room writing a letter. Harry – poor fellow! – wrote once a week to an old friend of his in England, named Jim Morell.'

Miles sat up.

'Just a minute, Miss Seton!'

'Yes?'

And now she did lift her eyes, with a quick blue glance, startled, as though she were suddenly wondering.

'Was this Jim Morell,' asked Miles, 'any relation to a girl named Barbara Morell?'

'Barbara Morell. Barbara Morell.' She repeated it, and the momentary interest died out of her face. 'No, I can't say I have any knowledge of the girl. Why do you ask?'

'Because ... nothing at all! It doesn't matter.'

Fay Seton smoothed at her skirt, as though earnestly occupied in choosing just what words to say. She seemed to find it a delicate business.

'I don't know anything about the murder!' she exclaimed, with delicate insistence. 'Over and over I told the police so afterwards! At just before three o'clock I went for a stroll along the river-bank, northwards, and far beyond the tower.

'You've undoubtedly heard what was happening in the meantime. Mr Brooke returned from the bank and looked for Harry. Since Harry was by that time in the garage instead of his room, Mr Brooke walked slowly out of the house to keep his appointment with me – miles ahead of time, really! – at the tower. Shortly afterwards Harry learned where he had gone, and snatched up his raincoat and followed Mr Brooke. Mrs Brooke phoned to Georges Rigaud, who drove out there in his car.

'At half-past three ... I knew that by my wrist-watch ... I thought it was time for me to stroll back towards the tower, and I went inside. I heard voices talking from the direction of the roof. As I started up the stairs I recognized the voices of Harry and his father.'

Fay moistened her lips.

To Miles it seemed, by the subtle alteration in her tone, that she used by force of habit – sincerely, yet glibly – a series of words made familiar to her by repetition.

'No, I did not hear what they were talking about. It is simply that I dislike unpleasantness, and I would not remain. In going out of the tower I met Monsieur Rigaud, who was going in. Afterwards ... well! I went for my dip after all.'

Miles stared at her.

'For a swim in the river?'

'I felt hot and tired. I believed it would cool me. I undressed in the woods by the river, as many persons do. This was not near the tower; it was well away from the tower, northwards, on the west bank. I swam and floated and dreamed in the cool water. I did not know anything was wrong until I was walking back home at a quarter to five. There was a great clamour of people round the tower, with policemen among them. And Harry walked up to me, putting out his hands, and said, "My God, Fay, somebody's killed Dad."'

Her voice trailed away.

Putting up a hand to shade her eyes, Fay shielded her face well. When she looked at Miles again, it was with a wistful and apologetic smile.

'Please do forgive me!' she said, giving her head that little sideways toss which made the dim yellow light ripple across her hair. 'I *lived* it again, you see. It's a habit lonely people have.'

'Yes. I know.'

'And that's the limit of my knowledge, really. Is there anything you want to ask me?'

Acutely uncomfortable, Miles spread out his hands. 'My dear Miss Seton! I'm not here to question you like a public prosecutor!'

'Perhaps not. But I'd rather you did, if you have any doubts.'

Miles hesitated.

'The only thing the police really could urge against me,' she said, 'was that most unfortunate swim of mine. I had been in the river. And there were no witnesses who could testify about the part of the tower facing the river: who went near it, or who didn't. Of course it was perfectly absurd that someone – in a bathing-dress: really! – could get up a smooth wall forty feet high. They were compelled to see that, eventually. But in the meantime …!'

Smiling as though the matter were of no importance now, yet shivering a little nevertheless, Fay rose to her feet. She edged forward among the waist-high piles of books, as though impulsively, before changing her mind. Her head was still a little on one side. About her eyes and her mouth there was a passive gentleness, a sweetness, which went straight to Miles's heart. He jumped down from the edge of the window-sill.

'You do believe me?' cried Fay. 'Say you believe me!'

CHAPTER 8

MILES smiled at her.

'Of course I' believe you!'

'Thank you, Mr Hammond. Only I thought you looked a little doubtful, a little – what shall I call it?'

'It isn't that. It's only that Professor Rigaud's account was more or less cut off in the middle, and there were certain things that kept tormenting me. What was the official police view of the whole matter?'

'They finally decided it was suicide.'

'*Suicide?*'

'Yes.'

'But why?'

'I suppose, really,' and Fay lifted her thin-arched eyebrows in a timidly whimsical way, 'it was because they couldn't find any other explanation. That verdict saved their faces.' She hesitated. 'And it's true that Mr Brooke's fingerprints, and only Mr Brooke's fingerprints, were on the handle of the sword-stick. You heard it was a sword-stick?'

'Oh, yes. I even saw the infernal thing.'

'The police surgeon, a nice funny little man named Doctor Pommard, almost had a fit whenever he thought of the verdict. He gave some technicalities, which I'm afraid I don't understand, to show that the angle of the wound was very nearly impossible for a suicide: certainly impossible unless Mr Brooke had held the weapon by the blade instead of by the handle. All the same ...' She lifted her shoulders.

'But wait a minute!' protested Miles. 'As I understand it, the brief-case with the money was missing?'

'Yes. That's true.'

'If nobody got up on top of the tower to stab Mr Brooke, what did they think had happened to the brief-case?'

Fay looked away from him.

'They thought,' she replied, 'that in Mr Brooke's dying convulsion he – he had somehow knocked it off the parapet into the river.'

'Did they drag the river?'

'Yes. Immediately.'

'And they didn't find it?'

'Not then ... or ever.'

Fay's head was bent forward, her eyes on the floor.

'And it wasn't for want of trying!' she cried out softly. The tips of her fingers brushed across books and left streaks in the dust. 'That affair was the sensation of France during the first winter of the war. Poor Mrs Brooke died during that winter; they say she died of grief. Harry, as I told you, was killed in the retreat to Dunkirk.

'Then the Germans came. They were always glad of any excuse to give publicity to a sensational murder case, especially one that had – that had a woman's immorality concerned in it, because they believed it kept the French public amused and out of mischief. Oh, *they* saw to it that popular curiosity didn't lapse!'

'I gather,' said Miles, 'that you were caught in the invasion? You didn't come back to England before then?'

'No,' answered Fay. 'I was ashamed'

Miles turned away from her, turned his back to her, and fiercely struck his fist on the window-sill.

'We've talked about this long enough,' he declared.

'Please! It's perfectly all right.'

'It's *not* all right!' Miles stared grimly out of the window. 'I hereby give you my solemn promise that this subject is finished; that I will never refer to it again; that I will never ask you another ques –' He stopped. 'You didn't marry Harry Brooke, then?'

Reflected in the little panes of the windows, black illuminated glass, he saw her begin to laugh before he heard a sound. He saw Fay throw back her head and shoulders, he saw the white throat working, the closed eyes and the tensely out-thrown arms, before her almost hysterical laughter choked and sobbed and rang in the quiet library, dazing him with its violence from so passive a girl.

Miles swung round. Over him, penetrating to his inner heart, flowed such a wave of sympathy and protectiveness – dangerously near love – that it unstrung his nerves. He blundered towards her, putting out his hand. He knocked over a toppling heap of books, with a crash and drift of dust which floated up against the dim light, just as Marion Hammond opened the door and came in.

'Do you two,' inquired Marion's common-sense voice, cutting off emotion as a string is snapped, 'do you two have any idea what time it is?'

Miles stood still, breathing rapidly. Fay Seton also stood still, as placid-faced now as she had ever been. That outburst might have been an illusion seen in glass or heard in a dream.

Yet there was a sense of strain even about the bright-eyed, brisk-looking Marion.

'It's nearly half-past eleven,' she went on. 'Even if Miles wants to stay up for most of the night, as he generally does, I've got to see to it that all of us don't lose our sleep.'

'Marion, for the love of ...!'

Marion cooed at him.

'Now don't be so snappish, Miles. Can you imagine,' she appealed to Fay, 'can you imagine how he can be almost *too* sympathetic towards everyone else in the world, and yet an absolute beast to me?'

'I expect most brothers are like that, really.'

'Yes. Maybe you're right.' Wearing a house-apron, trim and sturdy and black-haired, Marion wormed with dislike and distrust through the morass of books. With a firm managing gesture she picked up Fay's lamp and pressed it into her guest's hand.

'I like my lovely present so much,' she told Fay cryptically, 'that I'm going to give you something in return. Yes, I am! A *box* of something! It's upstairs in my room now. You run along up and see it, and I'll join you in just one moment; and afterwards I'm going to send you straight downstairs to bed. You – you know your way?'

Holding up the lamp, Fay smiled back at her.

'Oh, yes! I think I could find my way anywhere in the house. It's awfully kind of you to ... to ...'

'Not at all, my dear! Run along!'

'Good night, Mr Hammond.'

Giving Miles a backward glance, Fay closed the door as she went out. With only one lamp left, it was a little difficult to see Marion's face as she stood over there in the gloom. Yet even an outsider would have realized that a state of emotion, a dangerous state of emotion, was already gathering in this house. Marion spoke gently.

'Miles, old boy!'

'Yes?'

'It was frightfully overdone, you know.'

'What was?'

'*You* know what I mean.'

'On the contrary, my dear Marion, I haven't the remotest idea what you're talking about,' said Miles. He roared this out in what he recognized to be a pompous and stuffed-shirt manner; he knew this, he knew that Marion knew it, and it was beginning to make him angry. 'Unless it by any chance means you've been listening at the door?'

'Miles, don't be so *childish!*'

'Would you mind explaining that rather offensive remark?' He strode towards her, sending books flying. 'What it actually means, I suppose, is that you don't like Fay Seton?'

'That's where you're wrong. I *do* like her! Only …'

'Go on, please.'

Marion looked rather helpless, lifting her hands and then dropping them against the house-apron.

'You get angry with me, Miles, because I'm practical and you're not. I can't *help* being practical. That's how I'm made.'

'I don't criticize you. Why should you criticize me?'

'It's for your own good, Miles! Steve – and heaven knows, Miles, I love Steve a very great deal –!'

'Steve ought to be practical enough for you.'

'Under that moustache and that slowness, Miles, he's nervy and romantic and a bit like you. Maybe all men are; I don't know. But Steve rather likes being bossed, whereas you won't be bossed in any circumstances …'

'No, by God, I won't!'

'… or even take a word of advice, which you must admit is silly of you. Anyway, let's not quarrel. I'm sorry I brought the subject up.'

'Listen, Marion.' He had himself under control. He spoke slowly, and thoroughly believed every word he was saying. 'I've got no deep personal interest in Fay Seton, if that's what you think. I'm academically interested in a murder case. A man was killed on top of a tower where nobody, NOBODY, could possibly have come near him –'

'All right, Miles. Don't forget to lock up before you go to bed, dear. Good night.'

There was a strained silence between them as Marion moved towards the door. It irked Miles; it chafed his conscience.

'Marion!'

'Yes, my dear?'

'No offence, old girl?'

Her eye twinkled. 'Of course not, stupid! And I *do* like your Fay Seton, in a way. Only, Miles: as for your floating murderers and things that can walk on air – I only wish I could meet one of them, that's all!'

'As a matter of scientific interest, Marion, what would you do if that did happen?'

'Oh, I don't know. Shoot at it with a revolver, I suppose. Be *sure* to lock up, Miles, and don't go wandering away into the forest with all the doors wide open. Good night!'

And the door closed after her.

For a little while after she had gone, turning over unruly thoughts, Miles stood motionless. In a mechanical way he picked up and replaced the books he had knocked over.

What had these women got against Fay Seton, anyway? Last night, for instance, Barbara Morell had practically warned him against Fay – or had she? There was a good deal in Barbara's behaviour he could not fit into any pattern. He could only be sure that she was emotionally upset. Fay, on the other hand, had denied knowing Barbara Morell; though Fay had mentioned, with a sharp hinting insistence, some man of the same surname ...

'Jim Morell.' That was it.

Damn it all!

Miles Hammond swung himself up again to sit on the window-ledge. Glancing behind at the darkling shape of the New Forest pressing up to within twenty yards of the house, he saw its darkness and breathed its fragrance as a balm for fever. And so, pushing one of the swinging lights wider open, he slid through and jumped down outside.

To breathe this dew-scented dimness was like a weight off the lungs. He climbed up the little grass slope of the terrace to the open space between here and the line of the forest. A few feet below him now lay the long narrow side of the house; he could see into the library, into the dark dining-room, into the sitting-room with its low-glimmering lamp, then the dark reception hall. Most of the other rooms at Greywood were bedrooms, chiefly unused and in a bad state of repair.

He glanced upwards and to his left. Marion's bedroom was at the rear of the house, over the library. The bedroom windows on the side facing him – eastwards – were covered with curtains. But its rear windows, looking south towards another loom of the encircling woods, threw out dim yellow light the edge of whose reflexion he could see as it touched the trees. Though Miles was out of sight of these rear windows, that yellow light lay plain enough at the corner of his eye. And, as he watched, a woman's shadow slowly passed across it.

Marion herself? Or Fay Seton talking to her before she retired?

It was all *right!*

Muttering to himself, Miles swung round and walked northwards towards the front of the house. It was a bit chilly; he might at least have brought a raincoat. But the singing silence, the hint of moonrise beginning to make a white dawn behind the trees, at once soothed and exalted him.

He walked down to the open space in front of Greywood. Just before him lay the stream spanned by the rustic bridge. Miles went out on the bridge, leaned against its railing, and stood listening to the little whispering noises of the water at night. He might have stood there for twenty minutes, lost in thoughts where a certain face kept obtruding, when the jarring bump of a motor-car roused him.

The car, approaching unseen through the trees in the direction of the main road, jolted to a stop on gravel. Two men got out of it, one of them carrying an electric torch. As they toiled up on foot towards the rustic bridge, Miles could see in outline that one of them was short and stoutish, bouncing along with quick little inward-turning steps. The other was immensely tall and immensely fat, his long dark cape making him appear even more vast; he strode along with a rolling motion like an emperor, and the sound of his throat-clearing preceded him like a war-cry.

The smaller man, Miles saw, was Professor Georges Antoine Rigaud. And the immense man was Miles's friend, Dr Gideon Fell.

He called out their names in astonishment, and both of them stopped.

Dr Fell, absent-mindedly turning the light of the torch on his own fare as he whirled it round to seek the source of the voice, stood briefly revealed as being even more ruddy of face and vacant of eye than Miles remembered him. His several chins were drawn in as though for argument. His, eye-glasses on the broad black ribbon were stuck wildly askew on his nose. His big mop of grey-streaked hair seemed to quiver with argument like the bandit's moustache. So he stood peering round, huge and hatless, in every direction except the right one.

'I'm here, Dr Fell! On the bridge! Walk forward.'

'Oh, ah!' breathed Dr Fell.

He came rolling forward majestically, swinging a cane, and towered over Miles as his footsteps thundered and shook on the planks of the bridge.

'Sir,' intoned Dr Fell, adjusting his eyeglasses as he peered down like a very large djinn taking form, 'good evening. You may safely trust two men of – harrumph – mature years and academic pursuits to do something utterly harebrained. I refer, of course ...'

Again the planks of the bridge quivered.

Rigaud, like a barking little terrier, achieved the feat of worming past Dr Fell's bulk. He stood gripping the railing of the bridge, staring at Miles with that same inextinguishable curiosity in his face.

'Professor Rigaud,' said Miles, 'I owe you an apology. I meant to ring you up this morning; I honestly meant it. But I didn't know where you were staying in London, and ...'

The other breathed quickly.

'Young man,' he replied, 'you owe me no apology. No, no, no! It is I who owe you one.'

'What's that?'

'*Justement!*' said Professor Rigaud, nodding very rapidly. 'Last night I had my merry joke. I teased and tantalized the minds of you and Mees Morell until the very last. Is it not so?'

'Yes, I suppose it is. But –'

'Even when you mentioned casually that you sought after a librarian, young man, it struck me as no more than an amusing coincidence. I never guessed, not I, that this woman was within five hundred miles of here! I never knew – never! – that the lady was in England!'

'You mean Fay Seton?'

'I do.'

Miles moistened his lips.

71

'But this morning,' pursued Professor Rigaud, 'comes Mees Morell, who *does* ring up on the telephone with confused and incoherent explanations about last night. Mees Morell further tells me that she too knows Fay Seton is in England, knows her address, and believes the lady may be sent to you for employment. A call to the Berkeley Hotel, tactfully made, confirms this.' He nodded over his shoulder. 'You see that motor-car?'

'What about it?'

'I have borrowed it from a friend of mine, a Whitehall official, who has the petrol. I have broken the law to come and tell you. You must find some polite excuse to get this lady away from your house at once.'

White glimmered Professor Rigaud's face under the rising moon, his patch of moustache no longer comical and a desperate seriousness in his manner. Under his left arm he gripped the thick yellow sword-stick with which Howard Brooke had been stabbed. Long afterwards Miles Hammond remembered the tinkling stream, the loom of Dr Fell's huge outline, the stout little Frenchman with his right hand holding tightly to the railing of the bridge. Now Miles took a step backwards.

'*Not you too!*'

Professor Rigaud's eyebrows went up.

'I do not understand.'

'Candidly, Professor Rigaud, every single person has been warning me against Fay Seton. And I'm getting damned sick and tired of it!'

'It *is* true, of course? You did engage the lady?'

'Yes! Why not?'

Professor Rigaud's quick eyes moved over Miles's shoulder towards the house in the background.

'Who else is here to-night besides yourself?'

'Only my sister Marion.'

'No servants? No other person?'

'Not for to-night, no. But what difference does that make? What *is* all this? Why shouldn't I ask Miss Seton to come here and stay as long as she likes?'

'Because you will die,' answered the other simply. 'You and your sister will both die.'

CHAPTER 9

EVEN more white, very white, glimmered Rigaud's face under the rising moon, whose light now touched the water beneath them.

'Will you come with me, please?' Miles said curtly.

And he turned round and led the way back towards the house.

Towards the western side of Greywood lay the broad flat stretch of lawn, as close-clipped as a bowling green, where you could dimly make out the wicker chairs, the little table, and the bright-canopied garden swing. Miles glanced towards that side of the house as he walked. No lights showed there, though Fay Seton had been given a bedroom on the ground floor. Fay must have turned in.

Miles led the way round to the east side, through the reception-hall which housed his uncle's little collection of medieval arms, and into the long sitting-room. This sitting-room was a pleasant place of tapestry chairs, low, white-painted bookshelves, and a small Leonardo in oils above the mantelpiece. Only one lamp burned there as a night-light, with a very tiny flame which made immense shadows; but Miles had no wish to make it brighter.

In the hush of the New Forest at past midnight, he swung round.

'I think I ought to tell you,' he said in a louder voice than was necessary, 'that I've already had a long talk with Miss Seton ...'

Professor Rigaud stopped short. 'She told you!'

(Steady, now! No reason at all to have a lump in your throat or a furiously hammering heart!)

'She told me about the facts of Mr Brooke's death, yes. The police eventually decided it was suicide, because only Mr Brooke's fingerprints were on the handle of the swords-tick. Is that true?'

'It is.'

'And, at the time of – at the time it happened, Fay Seton had gone for a swim in the river some distance away from the tower. Is *that* true?'

'As far as it goes,' Professor Rigaud nodded, 'yes. But did she tell you about the young man Pierre Fresnac? The son of Jules Fresnac?'

'Need we,' Miles almost shouted, 'need we be so infernally censorious nowadays? After all! If there did happen to be anything between this young man Fresnac and Fay Seton ...'

'The English!' breathed Professor Rigaud in a tone of awe. And then, after a pause: 'My God, the English!'

He stood staring back in a light so dim as to take away expression, with Dr Fell's big shape behind him. He propped the yellow sword-cane against the arm of a tapestry chair, and removed his hat. There was something in the tone of his voice, not a loud voice, which twitched along Miles's nerves.

'You are like Howard Brooke,' breathed Professor Rigaud. 'I say one thing, and you think I mean only ...'

Again he paused.

'Do you think it likely, young man,' he went on with a sort of pounce, 'that a peasant farmer of Eure-et-Loir would care two sous, would care *that*,' he snapped his fingers, 'about a little affair of the passions between his son and a lady of the district? It would only amuse him, if in fact he noticed it at all. It would not, I assure you, start the thunder-storm which swept with terror every peasant in that district. It would not make Jules Fresnac throw a stone at the woman in a public road.'

'What *was* it, then?'

'Can you cast your mind back to the days just before Howard Brooke's death?'

'I can.'

'This young man, Pierre Fresnac, lived with his parents in a stone farm-house off the road between Chartres and Le Mans.

It is necessary to emphasize that his bedroom was in an attic up three flights of stairs.'

'Well?'

'For some days Pierre Fresnac had been ill, had been weak, had been dazed. Partly because he dared not speak, partly because he did not understand and thought it was all a night-mare, he said nothing to anyone. Like all young people, he was frightened of being thrashed for something that was not his fault. So he bound a scarf round his neck and said not a word.

'He thought it was a dream when he saw, night after night, the white face floating outside the upstairs window. He thought it was a dream when he saw the body taking form in the air metres above ground, and felt the anaesthesia that dims the mind and muscles as that lamp is dimmed when you turn down the wick. It was his father, presently, who tore away the bandage from the throat. And they found the sharp teeth-marks in the neck where the life-blood had been drained away.'

In the pause that followed, with a sort of wild patience, Miles Hammond waited for someone to laugh.

He waited for this emptiness to be broken. He waited for Rigaud to throw back his head and utter that chuckle which showed a gold tooth. He waited for the Gargantuan chuckle of Dr Fell. And nothing happened. No one as much as smiled, or asked him how he liked the joke. What struck his wits numb, what held him in a kind of paralysis, was the uttering of those solid flat police-court-like words, 'the sharp teeth-marks in the neck where the life-blood had been drained away.'

As though from a distance Miles heard his own voice.

'Are you crazy?'

'No.'

'You mean —?'

'Yes,' said Professor Rigaud. 'I mean the vampire. I mean the un-dead. I mean the drainer of bodies and killer of souls.'

The white face floating in the air outside the upstairs window.

The white face floating in the air outside the upstairs window ...

In spite of himself Miles couldn't laugh. He tried to do so, but the sound stuck in his throat.

'The good simple-minded Mr Howard Brooke,' said Professor Rigaud, 'understood nothing of this. *He* saw in it only a vulgar intrigue between a peasant lad and a woman older than the boy. He was shocked to the very depths of his British soul. He had the simple conviction that any immoral woman can be bought off with money. And so ...'

'And so?'

'He died. That is all.'

Professor Rigaud shook his bald head, in a very fever and passion of earnestness. He picked up the sword-cane, clutching it under his arm.

'I tried last night ... alas for my idiotic sense of humour! ... to tease you with a puzzle. I stated facts quite fairly, if obliquely. I told you that this woman was not, in the accepted sense, a criminal of any kind. I told you truly that in the workaday world she is gentle and even prudish.

'But this does not apply to the soul inside, which she can no more help than I can help greed or inquisitiveness. It does not apply to the soul which can leave the body in trance or sleep, and take form visible to the eye. That soul, like the white face at the upstairs window, feeds on and draws life from the blood of the living.

'If Howard Brooke had told me any of this beforehand, I could have helped him. But no, no, no! This woman is immoral; this must be kept quiet. Perhaps I should have guessed for myself, from the outward signs and from the story I gave you. The physical characteristics, the red hair and the slender figure and the blue eyes, are always in folklore associated with the vampire because in folklore they are signs of eroticism. But as usual I do not recognize what is under my nose. I am left to learn it after Howard Brooke's death, from a mob of peasants who wish to lynch her.'

Miles passed a hand across his forehead and pressed hard.

'But you can't seriously mean this! You can't mean it was this ... this ...'

'This thing,' supplied Professor Rigaud.

'This person, let's say. You tell me that Fay Seton killed Howard Brooke?'

'The vampire did. Because the vampire hated him.'

'It was plain murder with a sharp sword-blade! No supernatural agency is involved!'

'How then,' asked Professor Rigaud coolly, 'did the murderer approach and leave his victim?'

Again there was a long silence.

'Listen, my good friend!' cried Miles. 'I tell you again, you can't seriously mean this! You, a practical man, can't put forward as an explanation this superstitious ...'

'No, no, no!' said Professor Rigaud with three separate words like hammer-blows, and suddenly snapped his fingers in the air.

'How do you mean, no?'

'I mean,' returned Professor Rigaud, 'it is an argument I often have with my academic colleagues about the word "superstitious". Can you dispute the facts I present?'

'Apparently not.'

'*Justement!* And supposing – I say supposing! – any such creature as a vampire to exist, do you agree that it may explain Fay Seton's every action while she lived with the Brooke family?'

'But look here – !'

'I say to you,' Professor Rigaud's little eye gleamed in a sort of logical frenzy, 'I say to you: "Here are certain facts; please to explain them." Facts, facts, facts! You reply to me that you cannot explain them, but that I must not – must not, must not! – talk such superstitious nonsense, because the thing I suggest upsets your universe and makes you afraid. You may be right in saying so. You may be wrong in saying so. But it is I who am practical and you who are superstitious.'

He peered round at Dr Fell.

'*You* agree, dear doctor?'

Dr Fell had been standing over against the low line of the white-painted bookshelves, his arms folded under his long box-pleated cape, and his eyes fixed with absent-minded absorption on the dim flame of the lamp. Miles was assured of his presence by a gentle wheezing of breath, with occasional snorts and stoppages as though the doctor had suddenly waked out of a half-dream, and by the flutter of the broad black eyeglass-ribbon when his chest rose and fell.

His face, as ruddy as a furnace, radiated that sort of geniality which as a ride made him tower in heartening comfort like Old King Cole. Gideon Fell, Miles knew, was an utterly kind-hearted, utterly honest, completely absent-minded and scatterbrained man whose best hits occurred half through absent-mindedness. His face at the moment, with the under-lip drawn up and the bandit's moustache drawn down, appeared something of a study in ferocity.

'*You* agree, dear doctor?' persisted Rigaud.

'Sir – ' began Dr Fell, rearing up with a powerful oratorical flourish like Dr Johnson. Then he seemed to change his mind; he subsided and scratched his nose.

'Monsieur?' prompted Rigaud with the same formality.

'I do not deny,' said Dr Fell, sweeping out one arm in a gesture which gravely endangered a bronze statuette on the bookshelves, 'I do not deny that supernatural forces may exist in this world. In fact, I firmly believe they do exist.'

'Vampires!' said Miles Hammond.

'Yes,' agreed Dr Fell, with a seriousness which made Miles's heart sink. 'Perhaps even vampires.'

Dr Fell's own crutch-handled stick was propped against the book-shelves. But he was now looking, with even more witless vacancy, at the thick yellow sword-cane still clutched under Professor Rigaud's arm.

Wheezing as he lumbered forward, Dr Fell took the cane from Rigaud. He turned it over in his fingers. Holding it in the same absent-minded fashion, he wandered over and sat down – very untidily – in a big tapestry chair by the empty fireplace. The whole room shook as he sat down, though this was a solidly constructed house.

'But I believe,' he pursued, 'like any honest psychical researcher, in first of all examining the facts.'

'Monsieur,' cried Professor Rigaud, 'I *give* you facts!'

'Sir,' replied Dr Fell, 'no doubt.'

Scowling, he blinked at the sword-cane. He slowly unscrewed the blade-handle, removed it from the scabbard, and studied it. He held the threads of the handle close to his lopsided eyeglasses, and tried to peer into the scabbard. When the learned doctor spoke again, rousing himself, it was in a voice like a schoolboy.

'I say! Has anybody got a magnifying-glass?'

'There's one here in the house,' answered Miles, who was trying to adjust his mind to this. 'But I can't seem to remember where I saw it last. Would you like me to …?'

'Candidly speaking,' said Dr Fell, with an air of guilty frankness, 'I'm not sure it would be much good to me. But it makes an impressive picture, and gives the user a magnificent sense of self-importance. Harrumph.' His voice changed. 'I think someone said there were bloodstains *inside* this scabbard?'

Professor Rigaud was almost at the point of jumping up and down on the floor.

'There *are* bloodstains inside it! I said so last night to Miss Morell and Mr Hammond. I said so again to you this morning.' His voice grew challenging: 'And then?'

'Yes,' said Dr Fell, nodding in a slow and lion-like way, 'that is still another point.'

Fumbling into his inside coat pocket under the big cape, Dr Fell drew out a folded sheaf of manuscript. Miles had no difficulty in recognizing it.

It was Professor Rigaud's account of the Brooke case, written for the archives of the Murder Club and restored by Miles himself after it had been taken away by Barbara Morell. Dr Fell weighed it in his hand.

'When Rigaud brought me this manuscript to-day,' he said in a tone of real reverence, 'I read it with a pop-eyed fascination beyond words. O Lord! O Bacchus! This *is* one for the club! But it does rather prompt a strong question.' His eyes fixed on Miles. 'Who is Barbara Morell, and why does she up-set the dinner of the Murder Club?'

'Ah!' breathed Professor Rigaud, nodding very rapidly and rubbing his hands together, 'that also interests me very much! Who *is* Barbara Morell?'

Miles stared back at them.

'Hang it, don't look at me! *I* don't know!'

Professor Rigaud's eyebrows went up. 'Yet one remembers that you accompanied her home?'

'Only as far as the Underground station, that's all.'

'You did not, perhaps, discuss this matter?'

'No. That is – no.'

The stout little Frenchman had a very disconcerting eye.

'Last night,' Professor Rigaud said to Dr Fell, after a long scrutiny of Miles, 'this little Mees Morell is several times very much upset. Yes! The one obvious thing is that she is much concerned about Fay Seton, and undoubtedly knows her very well.'

'On the contrary,' said Miles. 'Miss Seton denies ever having met Barbara Morell, or knowing anything about her.'

It was as though you had struck a gong for silence. Professor Rigaud's expression was almost ghoulish.

'She told you this?'

'Yes.'

'When?'

'To-night, in the library, when I – asked her about things.'

'So!' breathed Professor Rigaud, with an air of refreshed interest. 'You, among her victims' – the word struck Miles like a blow in the face – 'you, among her victims, at least have courage! You introduced the subject and questioned her about it?'

'I didn't exactly introduce the subject, no.'

'*She* volunteered the information?'

'Yes, I suppose you could call it that.'

'Sir,' said Dr Fell, sitting back in the chair with the manuscript and sword-cane across his knees and a very curious expression on his face, 'it would help me enormously – by thunder, how it would help me! – if you told me everything the lady said to you. If you told me here, at this moment (forgive me) without prejudice and without editing.'

It must, Miles thought, be growing very late. Such an intensity of stillness held the house that he imagined he could hear a clock strike far back in the kitchen. Marion would be fast asleep, up there over the library; Fay Seton would be fast asleep downstairs. Through the windows moonlight strengthened with deathly pallor, dimming the mere spark of the lamp and rearing on the opposite wall shadow-images of the little oblong panes.

Miles began to speak out of a dry throat, slowly and carefully. Only once did Dr Fell interrupt with questions.

"'Jim Morell!'" the doctor repeated, so sharply that Professor Rigaud jumped. 'A great friend of Harry Brooke, to whom Harry regularly wrote once a week.' He turned his big head towards Rigaud. 'Were you acquainted with any James Morell?'

Rigaud, perched on the edge of a side-table, bending forward eagerly with his hand cupped behind his ear, returned a violent negative.

'To the best of my knowledge, dear doctor, this name is completely new to me.'

'Harry Brooke never even mentioned him to you?'

'Never.'

'Nor' – Dr Fell tapped the manuscript – 'is he mentioned in this admirably clear narrative of yours. Even the attached affidavits, of other witnesses concerned, make no reference to him. Yet Harry Brooke was writing to him on the very day –' Dr Fell was silent for a moment. Was it an effect of the light, that momentary expression about his eyes? 'Never mind!' he said. 'Go on!'

Yet Miles saw the same expression there again, briefly, before he finished his story. Dr Fell's look had been that of a man dazed, startled, half blinking at the sight of truth, and yet in it there were elements of sheer horror. That was what was so unnerving. All the time that Miles went on speaking, mechanically, frantic thoughts ran across the inner screen of his mind.

Dr Fell couldn't believe, of course, in this nonsense about vampires. Professor Rigaud might sincerely credit the reality of evil spirits inhabiting flesh, evil spirits that could leave the body and materialize high in the air, with their white faces outside windows.

But not Dr Fell. That could be taken for granted! All Miles wanted was to hear him say so.

All Miles wanted was a word, a gesture, a twinkle in the eye, which should blow away this poisonous mist which Georges Antoine Rigaud would call the mist of the vampire. 'Come, now! Come now! Archons of Athens!' – in uproarious delight. A twitch of the several chins, a shaking of the huge waistcoat, the old-time familiar amusement as Gideon Fell rolled back in the chair, hammering the ferrule of a stick against the floor.

And Miles was not getting that word.

Instead, as Miles finished speaking, Dr Fell sat back with a hand shading his eyes, and the bloodstained sword-stick across his lap.

'That is all?' he inquired.

'Yes. That's all.'

'Oh, ah. And to you, my friend' – Dr Fell had to clear his throat powerfully before he addressed Rigaud – 'I should like to put a vitally important question.' He held up the manuscript. 'When you wrote this, of course, you chose your words with care?'

Professor Rigaud drew himself up stiffly.

'Is it necessary to say that I did?'

'You wouldn't wish to change any of it?'

'No, I assure you! Why should I?'

'Let me read you,' said Dr Fell persuasively, 'two or three lines from your account of the last time you saw Mr Howard Brooke, on top of the tower, before he was attacked.'

'Well?'

Dr Fell moistened his thumb, adjusted his eyeglasses on the black ribbon, and leafed back through the manuscript.

' "Mr Brooke," ' he read aloud, ' "was standing by the parapet, his back uncompromisingly turned. On one side of him –" '

'Excuse me for interrupting,' said Miles, 'but those sound like exactly the same words Professor Rigaud used last night when he was telling it instead of writing it.'

'They *are* the same words,' smiled Professor Rigaud. 'It flowed trippingly, yes? It was memorized. Anything I spoke to you, young man, will also be found in that manuscript. Continue, continue, continue!'

Dr Fell eyed him curiously.

' "On one side of him" – you are still describing Mr Brooke – "on one side of him his cane, of light yellowish-coloured wood, was propped upright against the parapet. On the other side of him, also resting against the parapet, was the bulging brief-case. Round the tower-top this battlemented parapet ran breast-high, its stone broken, crumbling, and scored with whitish hieroglyphics where people had cut their initials." '

Dr Fell closed up the manuscript and tapped it again.

'That,' he demanded, 'is all accurate?'

'But perfectly accurate!'

'Only one other small thing,' begged Dr Fell. 'It's about this sword-stick. You say in your lucid account that the police, after the murder, took away the two halves of the sword-stick for expert examination. I presume the police didn't fit them together before removing them? They were taken away just as found?'

'But naturally!'

Miles couldn't stand it any longer.

'For God's sake, sir, let's get things straight! Let's know at least what we think and where we are!' His voice went up. '*You don't believe all this, do you?*'

Dr Fell blinked at him. 'Believe what?'

'Vampires!'

'No,' Dr Fell said gently. 'I don't believe it.'

(Miles had known it all along, of course. He told himself this, with a small inner laugh, while he settled his mental shoulders and prepared to laugh aloud. But the breath rushed out of his lungs, and he felt a hot wave of relief over his whole body, at the realization that there could be no terrors now.)

'It is only fair to say that,' Dr Fell went on gravely, 'before we leave. This wild night ride to the New Forest, on a – harrumph! – a sudden romantic impulse of Rigaud's, who also wanted to see your uncle's library, is one that two elderly gentlemen will regret when they arrive back in London. But before we do go …'

'By the powers of all evil,' said Miles with some vehemence, 'you're not going back to-night!'

'Not going back to-night?'

'I'm going to put you up here,' said Miles, 'in spite of the shortage of habitable bedrooms. I want to see you both in daylight and feel sane again. And my sister Marion! When she hears the rest of the story ...?'

'Your sister already knows something about it?'

'A little, yes. Come to think of it, I asked her to-night what she would do if *she* met a ... well, a supernatural horror that could walk on air. And that was even before I'd heard this vampire story.'

'Indeed!' murmured Dr Fell. 'And what did she say she would do?'

Miles laughed.

'She said she'd probably fire a revolver at it. The only sensible thing is to be just as amused as Marion was.' He bowed to Professor Rigaud. 'I thank you deeply, sir, for coming all this distance to put me on my guard against a vampire with white face and blood-bedabbled mouth. But it seems to me that Fay Seton has had a hard enough time already. And I scarcely think ...'

He broke off.

The sound they all heard then came from upstairs and a little distance away. But it was magnified by the night stillness. It was shattering and unmistakable. It made Professor Rigaud stiffen as he sat on the edge of the little side-table. It caused a twitch through Dr Fell's vast bulk, so that his eyeglasses tumbled off his nose and the pieces of the sword-cane slowly slid to the floor. All three men were motionless, not lifting a hand.

It was the sound of a pistol-shot.

CHAPTER 10

PROFESSOR RIGAUD spoke first, kicking his heels. The sardonic expression flickered in his face before it was veiled, and he looked at Miles.

'Yes, my friend?' he suggested politely. 'I beg of you to continue this interesting statement! Your sister is amused, much amused, when she thinks of ...' But he could not keep on in this strain. His gruff voice grew shaky as he glanced at Dr Fell. 'Are you, dear doctor, thinking what *I* am thinking?'

'No!' thundered Dr Fell, and broke the tensity. 'No, no, no, no!'

Professor Rigaud shrugged his shoulders.

'For myself, I find it seldom helpful to call a thing improbable after it has actually happened.' He looked at Miles. 'Does your sister own a revolver?'

'Yes! But ...'

Miles got to his feet.

He wouldn't, he said to himself, make a disgraceful exhibition of himself by starting to run: though Rigaud's countenance was a mottled white and even Dr Fell had closed his hands suddenly round the arms of the tapestry chair. Miles walked out of the room into the dark reception-hall. It was on the staircase, the enclosed staircase leading to the upstairs hall, that he did begin to run.

'*Marion!*' he shouted.

Ahead of him upstairs lay the very long, narrow hall, touched by the yellow speck of a night-light, with its line of mute-looking closed doors on either side.

'*Marion! Are you all right?*'

There was no reply.

As he faced the rear of the hall, the door of Marion's bedroom was the last door down or the left. Again Miles started to run. He stopped long enough to pick up the night-light, another little lamp with a cylindrical glass shade, from the top of the radiator half-way down. As he patiently fumbled with the wheel of the wick to make it burn brighter, he discovered that his hands were trembling. He turned the knob of the door, pushed it open, and held the lamp high.

'*Marion!*'

Marion was in bed, partly reclining upwards with her head and shoulders pressed back against the headboard of the bed, in an otherwise empty room. The lamp shook crazily, but it showed him that.

There were two lines of little windows in this room. One line faced eastwards, opposite Miles as he stood in the doorway, and these were still covered by drawn curtains. The other line of windows faced south, towards the back of the house, and white moonlight poured in. As Marion lay in bed – or half lay in bed, shoulders uphunched – she was facing straight towards these southern windows across the length of the room.

'*Marion!*'

She didn't move.

Miles went forward, edged forward with little slow steps. As the line of light shook and crept on, farther and farther into a blur of gloom, it brought out one detail after another.

Marion, wearing light-blue silk pyjamas in a tumbled bed, had not quite drawn up to a sitting position against the head-board of the bed. At first glance her face was almost unrecognizable. The hazel eyes were partly open, glassy and unblinking when the light touched them. The face was chalk white. Moisture glimmered on her forehead under the lamp. Her lips were drawn back over her teeth for the scream she had never been able to utter.

And in her right hand Marion clutched a .32 calibre Ives-Grant revolver. As Miles glanced towards the right, towards the windows Marion faced, he could see the bullet-hole in the glass.

And so Miles stood there mute, a pulse vibrating down his whole arm, when a rather hoarse voice spoke behind him.

'You will permit me?' it said.

Georges Antoine Rigaud, pale but stolid, bounced in with little pigeon-toes steps, holding up the sitting-room lamp from downstairs.

At Marion's right hand there was a bedside table: its drawer partly open, as though the revolver had come from there. On this little table

– Miles noticed such details with a kind of maniacal abstraction – stood Marion's own bedside lamp, turned out long ago, and beside the water-bottle a tiny one-ounce bottle of French perfume with a red-and-gold label. Miles could catch the scent of perfume. It made him half sick.

Professor Rigaud put down the sitting-room lamp on this table.

'I am an amateur of medicine,' he said. 'You will permit?'

'Yes, yes, yes!'

Circling round to the other side of the bed, catlike of movement, Professor Rigaud picked up Marion's limp left wrist. Her whole body looked limp, limp and flat-weighted. Delicately he pressed his hand under her left breast, high up against the region of the heart. A spasm went across Professor Rigaud's face. He had lost all his sardonic air; he showed only deep and genuine distress.

'I am sorry,' he announced. 'This lady is dead.'

Dead.

This wasn't possible.

Miles could not hold up the lamp any longer; his arm trembled too violently; in another second he would let the whole thing fall. Hardly conscious of his own legs, he moved over towards a chest-of-drawers at the right-hand side of the southern windows, and set down the lamp with a bang.

Then he turned back to face Professor Rigaud across the bed.

'What' – he swallowed – 'what did it?'

'Shock.'

'Shock? You mean ...'

'It is medically correct,' said Professor Rigaud, 'to speak of death from fright. The heart (you follow me?) is suddenly deprived of its power to pump blood up to the brain. The blood sinks into, and remains stagnant in, the large veins of the abdomen. You note the pallor? And the perspiration? And the relaxed muscles?'

Miles was not listening.

He loved Marion, really loved her in that thoughtless way we feel towards those we have known for twenty-eight out of our thirty-five years. He thought of Marion, and he thought of Steve Curtis.

'What follows,' said Professor Rigaud, 'is collapse and death. In severe cases ...' Then an almost frightful change came over his face, making the patch of moustache stand out. 'Ah, God!' he shouted, with a cry which was no less heartfelt for being accompanied by a melodramatic gesture. 'I forgot! I forgot! I forgot!'

Miles stared at him

'This lady,' said Professor Rigaud, 'may NOT be dead.'

'*What's that?*'

'In severe cases,' gabbled the professor, 'there is no perceptible pulse. And there may not be any cardiac impulse – no! – even when you put your hand over the heart.' He paused. 'It is not a good hope; but it is possible. How far away is the nearest doctor?'

'About six miles.'

'Can you phone him? Is there a phone here?'

'Yes! But in the meantime …!'

'In the meantime,' replied Professor Rigaud, his eyes feverish as he rubbed at his forehead, 'we must stimulate the heart. That is it! Stimulate the heart!' He squeezed up his eyes, thinking. 'Elevate the limbs, pressure on the abdominal cavity, and … Have you got any strychnine in the house?'

'Great Scott, no!'

'But you have salt, yes? Ordinary table-salt? And a hypodermic needle?'

'I think Marion *did* once have a hypodermic somewhere. I think …'

Where before everything had gone in a rush, now time seemed to have stopped. Every movement seemed intolerably slow. When it was vitally necessary to hurry, you could not hurry.

Miles turned back to the chest-of-drawers, yanked open the topmost drawer, and began to rummage. On top of the maplewood chest, brilliantly lighted now by the lamp he had put down there, stood a folding leather photograph-frame containing two large photographs. One side showed Steve Curtis, with a hat on to conceal his baldness; the other side showed Marion broad-faced and smiling, far away from the pitiable mass of flesh now vacant-eyed on the bed.

It seemed to Miles minutes, and was probably fifteen seconds, before he found the hypodermic syringe in two pieces in its neat leather case.

'Take it downstairs,' his companion was gabbling at him, 'and sterilize it in boiling water. Then heat some other water with a little pinch of salt in it, and bring them both up here. But first of all phone the doctor. I will take the other measures. Hurry, hurry, hurry!'

In the doorway of the bedroom, as Miles ran for it, stood Dr Gideon Fell. He had one last glimpse of those two, Dr Fell and Professor Rigaud, as he hurried out into the hall.

Rigaud, who was taking off his coat and rolling up his sleeves, spoke with a pounce.

'You see this, dear doctor?'

'Yes. I see it.'

'Can you guess what *she* saw outside the window?'

Their voices faded away.

Downstairs in the sitting-room it was dark except for a splendour of moonlight. At the telephone Miles snapped on pocket lighter, finding the address-pad Marion kept there along with two London telephone directories, and dialled Cadnam 4321. He had never met Dr Garvice, even in his uncle's time; but a voice over the wire asked quick questions and got reasonably clear replies.

A minute later he was in the kitchen: which was situated on the west side of the house, across a long enclosed passage like the one upstairs, in the middle of a line of silent bed-rooms. Miles lit several lamps in the big scrubbed room. He set the gas hissing in the new white-enamel range. He ran water into saucepans and banged them on the fire, dropping in the two parts of the hypodermic, while a big white-faced clock ticked on the wall.

Twenty minutes to two o'clock.

Eighteen minutes to two o'clock ...

Lord in heaven, wouldn't that water *ever* boil?

He refused to think of Fay Seton, sleeping on the ground floor in a bedroom not twenty feet away from him now.

He refused to think of her, that is, until he abruptly swung round from the stove and saw Fay standing in the middle of the kitchen behind him, with her finger-tips on the table.

Behind her the door to the passage gaped open on blackness. He hadn't heard her move on the stone floor with the linoleum over it. She was wearing a very thin white night-dress with a pink quilted wrap drawn over it, and white slippers. Her fleecy red hair lay tumbled about her shoulders. Her pink finger-nails tapped, softly and shakily, on the scrubbed top of the table.

What warned Miles was a kind of animal instinct, a *nearness*, a physical sense he always experienced with her. He turned with such suddenness

88

that he knocked against the handle of one saucepan, which spun round on the gas-ring. The heating water hissed slightly at its edges.

And he surprised on Fay Seton's face a look of sheer hatred.

The blue eyes had a shallow blaze; the colour was high against the white skin; the lips were dry and a little drawn back. It was hatred mingled with – yes! with wild anguish. Even when he turned round she couldn't quite control it, couldn't smooth it away: though her breast rose and fell in a kind of gasp, and her finger-tips twitched together.

But she spoke gently.

'What ... happened?'

Tick – tick, went the big clock on the wall, *tick – tick*, four times in measured beats against the silence, before Miles answered her. He could hear the hiss of the steaming water in the saucepan.

'My sister may be dead or dying.'

'Yes. I know.'

'You know?'

'I heard something like a shot. I was only dozing. I went up and looked in there.' Fay breathed this very rapidly, and gave another gasp; she seemed to be making an effort, as though force of will might control blood and nerves, to keep the colour out of her face. 'You must forgive me,' she said. 'I've just seen something I hadn't noticed before.'

'Seen something?'

'Yes. What – happened?'

'Marion was frightened by something outside the window. She fired a shot at it.'

'What was it? A burglar?'

'No burglar on earth could scare Marion. She isn't what you could call a nervous type. Besides ...'

'Please tell me!'

'The windows of that room' – Miles saw it vividly, with its blue, gold-figured curtains, and its yellow-brown carpet, and its big wardrobe and its dressing-table and its chest-of-drawers, and the easy-chair by the fireplace in the same wall as the door – 'the windows of that room are more than fifteen feet above ground. There's nothing underneath but the blank back-wall of the library. I don't see how any burglar could have got up there.'

The water began to boil. Through Miles's mind flashed the word 'salt'; he had completely forgotten that salt. He plunged across to the

89

line of kitchen cupboards, and found a big cardboard container. Professor Rigaud had said only a 'pinch' of salt; and he had said to heat the water, not boil it. Miles dropped a little into the second saucepan just as the first boiled over.

It was as though Fay Seton's knees had started to give way.

There was a kitchen chair by the table. Fay put her hand, on the back of it and slowly sat down; not looking at him, one white knee a little advanced, and the line of her shoulders tense.

The sharp teeth marks in the neck where the life-blood had been drained away …

Miles struck at the tap of the gas-range, extinguishing it. Fay Seton sprang to her feet.

'I – I'm awfully sorry! Can I help you?'

'No! Stand back!'

Question and answer were flung across that quiet kitchen, under the ticking clock, in a way that was unspoken acknowledgement. Miles wondered whether his hands were steady enough to handle the saucepans; but he risked it and caught them up.

Fay spoke softly.

'Professor Rigaud is here, isn't he?'

'Yes. Would you mind standing to one side, please?'

'Did you – did you believe what I said to you to-night? Did you?'

'Yes, yes, yes!' he shouted at her. 'But will you please for the love of heaven stand to one side? My sister …'

Scalding water splashed over the edge of the saucepan. Fay was now standing with her back to the table, pressed against it: all her self-effacement and timidity of manner gone, straight and magnificent, breathing deeply.

'This can't go on,' she said.

Miles did not look into her eyes at that moment; he dared not. For his sudden impulse, very nearly irresistible, had been to take her in his arms. Harry Brooke had done that, young Harry since dead and rotted. And how many others, in the quiet families where she had gone to live?

Meanwhile …

He left the kitchen without looking back at her. From the kitchen the back stairs, opening off this passage, led to the upstairs hall very close to Marion's room. Miles went upstairs in the moonlight, carefully carrying the saucepans. The door of Marion's room stood open about an inch, and he almost barged slap into Professor Rigaud in the aperture.

'I vass coming' – Professor Rigaud's English pronunciation slipped for the first time – 'to see what delayed you.'

Something about Rigaud's expression made Miles's heart contract.

'Professor Rigaud! Is she …?'

'No, no, no! I have brought her to what is called the "reaction". She is breathing and I think her pulse is stronger.'

More scalding water slopped over.

'But I cannot tell, yet, whether this will last. Did you phone the doctor?'

'Yes. He's on his way now.'

'Good. Give me the kettles there. No, no, no!' said Professor Rigaud, whom emotion inclined towards fussiness. 'You will not come in. Recovery from shock is not a pretty sight and besides you will get in my way. Keep out until I tell you.'

He took the saucepans and put them inside on the floor. Then he closed the door in Miles's face.

With a violent uneasy hope welling up even more strongly – men do not talk like that unless they expect recovery – Miles stood back. Moonlight changed and shifted at the hack of the hall; and he saw why.

Dr Gideon Fell, smoking a very large meerschaum pipe, stood beside the window at the end of the hall. The red glow of the pipe-bowl pulsed and darkened, touching Dr Fell's eyeglasses; a mist of smoke curled up ghostlike past the window.

'You know,' observed Dr Fell, taking the pipe out of his mouth, 'I like that man.'

'Professor Rigaud?'

'Yes. I *like* him.'

'So do I. And God knows I'm grateful to him.'

'He is a practical man, a thoroughly practical man. Which,' observed Dr Fell, with a guilty air and several furious puffs at the meerschaum, 'it is to be feared you and I are not. A thoroughly practical man.'

'And yet,' said Miles, 'he believes in vampires.'

'Harrumph. Yes. Exactly.'

'Let's face it. What do *you* believe?'

'My dear Hammond,' returned Dr Fell, puffing out his cheeks and shaking his head with some vehemence, 'at the moment I'm dashed if

I know. That is what depresses me. Before this present affair,' he nodded towards the bedroom, 'before this present affair came to upset my calculations, I believed I was beginning to have more than a glimmer of light about the murder of Howard Brooke ...'

'Yes,' said Miles, 'I thought you were.'

'Oh, ah?'

'When I was giving you Fay Seton's account of the murder on the tower, the look on your face once or twice was enough to scare anybody. Horror? I don't know! Something like that.'

'Was it?' said Dr Fell. The pipe pulsed and darkened. 'Oh, ah! I remember! But what upset me wasn't the thought of an evil spirit. It was the thought of a motive.'

'A motive for murder?'

'Oh, no,' said Dr Fell. 'But it led to murder. A motive so damnably evil and cold-hearted that ...' He paused. Again the pipe pulsed and darkened. 'Do you think we could have a word, now, with Miss Seton?'

CHAPTER 11

'MISS SETON?' Miles repeated sharply.

He could make nothing of Dr Fell's expression now. It was a mask, fleshy and colourless against the moonlight, veiled by smoke which got into Miles's lungs. Yet the ring in Dr Fell's voice, the ring of hatred about that motive, had been unmistakable.

'Miss Seton? I suppose so. She's downstairs now.'

'Downstairs?' said Dr Fell.

'Her bedroom is downstairs.' Miles explained the circumstances and narrated the events of that afternoon. 'It's one of the pleasantest rooms in the house; only just re-decorated, with the paint hardly dry. But she is up and about, if that's what you mean. She – she heard the shot.'

'Indeed!'

'As a matter of fact, she slipped up here and glanced into Marion's room. Something upset her so much that she isn't quite ... quite ...'

'Herself?'

'If you want to put it like that.'

And then Miles rebelled. With human nature as resilient as it is, with Marion (as he conceived) out of danger, it seemed to him that values were re-adjusting themselves and that common sense could burst out of its prison.

'Dr Fell,' he said, 'let's not be hypnotized. Let's not have a spell thrown over us by Rigaud's ghouls and vampires and witch-women. Granting – even granting! – it would have been very difficult for someone to have climbed up outside the windows of Marion's room ...'

'My dear fellow,' Dr Fell said gently, 'I *know* nobody climbed up there. See for yourself!'

And he indicated the window beside which they stood.

Unlike most of the windows in the house, which, were of the French-casement style, this was an ordinary sash-window. Miles pushed it up, put his head out, and looked towards the left.

The illuminated windows of Marion's room – four little windows set together, with two of their lights open – threw out bright light against pale green at the back of the house. Underneath was a blank wall fifteen feet high. Underneath also, which he had forgotten, ran an unplanted flower-bed nearly as broad as the wall was high: a flower-bed smooth and newly watered, of earth finely crushed and hoed, on which a cat could not have walked without leaving a trace.

But a fury of doggedness persisted in Miles Hammond.

'I still say,' he declared, 'we'd better not be hypnotized.'

'How so?'

'We know Marion fired a shot, yes. But how do we know she fired it at something *outside* the window?'

'Aha!' chortled Dr Fell, and a kind of glee breathed towards Miles out of pipe-smoke. 'My compliments, sir. You *are* waking up.'

We don't know it at all,' said Miles. 'We only assume it because it came after all this talk of faces floating outside windows. Isn't it much more natural to think she fired at something *inside* the room? Something perhaps standing in front of her at the foot of the bed?'

'Yes,' Dr Fell assented gravely, 'it is. But don't you see, my dear sir, that this doesn't in the least explain our real problem?'

'What do you mean?'

'Something,' replied Dr Fell, 'frightened your sister. Something which – without Rigaud's timely aid – would quite literally have frightened her to death.'

Dr Fell spoke with slow, fiery emphasis, stressing every word. His pipe had gone out, and he put it down on the sill of the open window. Even his wheezing breath snorted louder with earnestness.

'Now I want you to think for a moment just what that means. Your sister is not, I take it, a nervous woman?'

'Good Lord, no!'

Dr Fell hesitated.

'Let me – harrumph – be more explicit. She's not one of those women who *say* they're not nervous, and laugh at the supernatural in daylight, and then show very different feelings by night?'

A very vivid memory returned to Miles.

'I remember,' he said, 'when I was in hospital, Marion and Steve used to come there as often as they could' – how good they'd been, both of them

– 'with any jokes or stories they thought would amuse me. One was a haunted house. A friend of Steve's (that's Marion's fiancé) found it while he was on Home Guard duty. So they made up a party to go there.'

'With what result?'

'It seems they did find a lot of unexplained disturbances; poltergeist disturbances, not very pleasant. Steve freely confessed *he* had the wind up, and so did one or two others. But Marion only enjoyed it.'

'Oh, my eye!' breathed Dr Fell.

He picked up the dead pipe, and put it down again.

'Then again I ask you,' Dr Fell went on earnestly, 'to remember the circumstances. Your sister was not touched or physically attacked in any way. All the evidence shows she collapsed of nervous shock because of something she *saw*.

'Now suppose,' argued Dr Fell, 'this business was not supernatural. Suppose, for example, I wish to scare someone by playing ghost. Suppose I clothe myself in white robes, and daub my nose with phosphorescent paint, and stick my head through a window and thunderously say, "Boo!" to a group of old ladies in a Bournemouth boarding house.

'It may, perhaps, give them quite a start. They may think that dear old Dr Fell is getting some extraordinary ideas of humour. But would it really *scare* anyone? Would any rigged-up contrivance, any faked ingenuity of the supernatural, produce nowadays more than a momentary jump? Would it induce that shattering effect which – as we know – drains the blood from the heart and can be as deadly as a knife or a bullet?'

Beating his fist into the palm of his left hand, Dr Fell broke off apologetically.

'I beg your pardon,' he added. 'I did not wish either to make ill-timed jokes or alarm you with fears about your sister. But ... Archons of Athens!'

And he spread out his hands.

'Yes,' admitted Miles, 'I know.'

There was a silence.

'So you observe,' pursued Dr Fell, 'that the previous point you made ceases to be of importance. Your sister, in an excess of terror, fired a shot at something. It may have been outside the window. It may have been inside the room. It may have been anywhere. The point is: *what frightened her as much as that?*'

Marion's face …

'But you don't fall back on the assumption,' cried Miles 'that the whole thing comes back to a vampire after all?'

'I don't know.'

Putting his finger-tips to his temples, Dr Fell ruffled the edges of the thick mop of grey-streaked hair which had tumbled over one ear.

'Tell me,' he muttered, 'is there *anything* your sister is afraid of?'

'She didn't like the blitzes or the V-weapons. But then neither did anyone else.'

'I think we may safely rule out,' said Dr Fell, 'the entrance of a V-weapon. A threatening burglar wouldn't do? Something of that sort?'

'Definitely not.'

'Having seen something, and partly raised up in bed, she … by the way, that revolver in her hand: it does belong to her?'

'The Ives-Grant .32? Oh, yes.'

'And she kept it in the drawer of the bedside table?'

'Presumably. I never noticed where she kept it.'

'Something tells me,' said Dr Fell, rubbing his forehead, 'that we want the emotions and reactions of human beings – if they are human beings. We are going to have an immediate word with Miss Fay Seton.'

It was not necessary to go and find her. Fay, who had dressed herself in the same grey frock as she had worn earlier in the evening, was coming towards them now. In the uncertain light it seemed to Miles that she had put on a great deal of lipstick, which she did not ordinarily use.

Her white face, composed now, floated towards them.

'Ma'am,' said Dr Fell in a curious rumbling voice, 'good evening.'

'Good evening.' Fay stopped short. 'You are …?'

'Miss Seton,' introduced Miles, 'this is an old friend of mine. Dr Gideon Fell.'

'Oh. Dr Gideon Fell.' She was silent for a moment, and then she spoke in a slightly different tone. 'You caught the Six Ashes murderer,' she said. 'And the man who poisoned all those people at Sodbury Cross.'

'Well …!' Dr Fell seemed embarrassed. 'I'm an old duffer, ma'am, who *has* had some experience with the ways of crime.'

Fay turned to Miles.

'I – wanted to tell you,' she said in her usual soft voice of sincerity. 'I made rather an exhibition of myself downstairs. I'm sorry. I was – upset.

And I didn't even sympathize with what happened to poor Marion. Can't I be of service in any way?'

She moved tentatively towards the bedroom door not far behind her, but Miles touched her arm.

'Better not go in there. Professor Rigaud is acting as amateur doctor. He won't let anybody in.'

Slight pause.

'How – how is she?'

'A bit better, Rigaud thinks,' said Dr Fell. 'And that, ma'am, brings us to a matter I should rather like to discuss with you.' He picked up his pipe from the window-sill. 'If Miss Hammond recovers, this matter will of course be no concern of the police ...'

'Won't it?' murmured Fay. And across her lips, in that unreal moonlit hall outside the bedroom door, flicked a smile which struck cold to the heart.

Dr Fell's voice sharpened. 'You believe the police *should* be concerned in this, ma'am?'

The curve of that terrifying smile, like a red gash in the face, was gone in a flash along with the glassy turn of the blue eyes.

'Did I say that? How stupid of me. I must have been thinking of something else. What did you want to know?'

'Well, ma'am! As a formality! Since you were the last person presumed to be with Marion Hammond before she lost consciousness ...'

'*I* was? Why on earth should anyone think that?'

Dr Fell regarded her in apparent perplexity.

'Our friend Hammond here,' he grunted, 'has – harrumph – given me an account of a conversation you had with him down in the library earlier to-night. You remember that conversation?'

'Yes.'

'At about half-past eleven, or thereabouts, Marion Hammond came into the library and interrupted you. Apparently you had given her a present of some kind. Miss Hammond said she had a present for you in return. She asked you to go on up to her room ahead of her, and said she would join you after she'd had a word with her brother.' Dr Fell cleared his throat. 'You remember?'

'Oh. Yes! Yes, of course!'

'And therefore, presumably, you did go?'

97

'How stupid of me! – Yes, of course I did.'

'Straight away, ma'am?'

Fay shook her head, rapt and intent on his words.

'No. I supposed Marion would have – personal things to talk over with Mr Hammond there, and I thought it might be a little while before she left him. So first I went to my own room, and put on a nightgown and wrap and slippers. I came up here afterwards.'

'How long afterwards?'

'Ten or fifteen minutes, maybe. Marion had already got there before me.'

'And then?'

The moon was setting, its light grown thin. It was the turn of the night, the hour when to sick people death comes or passes by. All about them, south and east, towered the oaks and beeches of William the Conqueror's hunting forest, a forest old before him, seamed and withered with age; all night quiet, yet now subtly murmurous with a rising breeze. By moonlight the colour red becomes greyish-black, and that was the colour of Fay's moving lips.

'The present I had given Marion,' she explained, 'was a little bottle of French perfume. Jolyeux number three.'

Dr Fell put up a hand to his eyeglasses.

'Oh, ah? The same little red-and-gold bottle that's on the bedside table now?'

'I – I suppose so.' There was that infernal smile again, curling. 'Anyway, she put it on the bedside table by the lamp. She was sitting in a chair there.'

'And then?'

'It wasn't much, but she seemed awfully pleased. She gave me nearly a quarter of a pound of chocolates loose in a box. I have them downstairs in my room now.'

'And then?'

'I – I don't know what you want me to say, really. We talked. I was restless. I walked up and down …'

(Images crowded back into Miles Hammond's mind. As he himself had left the library, hours ago, he remembered glancing up and seeing a woman's shadow pass across the light, lonely against the screen of the New Forest.)

'Marion asked me why I was restless, and I said I didn't know. Mostly she did the talking, about her fiancé and her brother and her plans for the future. The lamp was on the bedside table; did I tell you? And the bottle of perfume. All of a sudden, about midnight it was, she broke off and said there! – it was time we were both turning in and getting some sleep, so I went downstairs to bed. I'm afraid that's all I can tell you.'

'Miss Hammond didn't seem nervous or alarmed about anything?'

'Oh, *no!*'

Dr Fell grunted. Dropping the dead pipe into his pocket, he deliberately removed his eyeglasses and held them a few feet away from his eyes, studying them with screwed-up face like a painter, though in that light he could scarcely have seen them at all. His wheezings and snortings, a sign of deep meditation, grew even louder.

'You know, of course, that Miss Hammond was nearly frightened to death?'

'Yes. It must have been dreadful.'

'Have you any theory, ma'am, to account for what frightened her?'

'I'm afraid not, at the moment.'

'Have you any theory, then,' pursued Dr Fell in exactly the same tone of voice, 'to account for the equally mysterious death of Howard Brooke on Henri Quatre's tower nearly six years ago?'

Without giving her time for a reply, still holding up the eye-glasses and appearing to scrutinize them with intense concentration, Dr Fell added in an offhand tone:

'Some people, Miss Seton, are very curious correspondents. They will pour out in letters to people far away what they wouldn't dream of telling someone in the same town. You have – harrumph – perhaps noticed it?'

To Miles Hammond it seemed that the whole atmosphere of this interview had subtly changed. For Dr Fell spoke again.

'Are you a good swimmer, Miss Seton?'

Pause.

'Fairly good. I daren't do much of it because of my heart.'

'But I should hazard a guess, ma'am, that if necessary you do not object to swimming under water?'

And now a wind came whispering and rustling, sinuously, through the forest; and Miles *knew* the atmosphere had changed. Not subtly, but on Fay Seton's part charged with emotion, perhaps deadly. It was the same silent outburst he had sensed and felt a while ago, in the kitchen, over boiling water. It engulfed the hall in an invisible tide. Fay knew.

Dr Fell knew. Fay's lips were drawn back from her teeth, and the teeth glittered.

It was then, as Fay took a blundering step backwards to get away from Dr Fell, that the door to Marion's bedroom opened.

The opening of the door poured yellow light into the hall. Georges Antoine Rigaud, in his shirt-sleeves, regarded them in a state of near-raving.

'I tell you,' he cried out, 'I cannot keep this woman's heart beating much longer. Where is that doctor? Why does not that doctor arrive? What is delaying …'

Professor Rigaud checked himself.

Past his shoulder, past a wide-open door, Miles by moving a little could see into the bedroom. He could see Marion, his own sister Marion, lying on a still more tumbled bed. The .32 revolver, useless against certain intruders, had slipped off the bed on to the floor. Marion's black hair was spread out on the pillow. Her arms were thrown wide, one sleeve pushed up where a hypodermic injection had been made in the arm. She had the aspect of a sacrifice.

In that moment, by a single gesture, terror rushed on them out of the New Forest.

For Professor Rigaud saw Fay Seton's face. And Georges Antoine Rigaud – Master of Arts, man of the world, tolerant watcher of human foibles – instinctively flung up his hand in the sign against the evil eye.

CHAPTER 12

MILES HAMMOND dreamed a dream.

Instead of being asleep at Greywood, on that Saturday night passing into Sunday morning – which was actually the case – he dreamed that he was downstairs in the sitting-room, at night under a good lamp, seated in an easy-chair and taking notes from a large book.

The passage read:

'*In Slavonic lands popular folklore credits the vampire with existence merely as an animated corpse: that is, a being confined to its coffin by day, and emerging only after nightfall for its prey. In Western Europe, notably in France, the vampire is a demon living outwardly a normal life in the community, but capable during sleep or trance of projecting its soul in the form of straw or spinning mist to take visible bodily shape.*'

Miles nodded as he underscored it.

' "*Creberrima fama est multique se expertos uel ab eis,*" to quote a possible explanation of the origin of these latter, "*qui experto essent, de quorum fide dubitandum non esset audisse confirmant, Siluanos et Panes, quos uulgo incubos uocant, improbos saepe extitisse mulieribus et earum adpetisse ac perigisse concubitum, ut hoc negare impudentiae uideatur.*" '

'I shall have to translate this,' Miles said to himself in his dream. 'I wonder if there's a Latin dictionary in the library.'

So he went into the library in search of a Latin dictionary. But he knew all along who would be waiting there.

During his work at Regency history Miles had for a long time been captivated by the character of Lady Pamela Hoyt, a sprightly court beauty of a hundred and forty years gone by, no better than she should be, and perhaps a murderess. In his dream he knew that in the library he would meet Lady Pamela Hoyt.

There was as yet no sense of fear. The library looked just as usual, with its dusty uneven piles of books round the floor. On one pile of books sat Pamela Hoyt, in a broad-brimmed straw hat and a high-waisted Regency gown of sprigged muslin. Across from her sat Fay Seton. Each one looked just as real as the other; he was conscious of nothing unusual.

'I wonder if you could tell me,' Miles said in his dream, 'whether my uncle keeps a Latin dictionary here?'

He heard their reply soundlessly, if it can be expressed like that.

'I really don't think he does,' replied Lady Pamela politely, and Fay shook her head too. 'But you could go upstairs and ask him.'

There was a flash of lightning outside the windows. Suddenly Miles felt an intense reluctance to go upstairs and ask his uncle about a Latin dictionary. Even in the dream he knew his Uncle Charles was dead, of course; but that wasn't the reason for his reluctance. The reluctance grew into terror, solidifying coldly through his veins. He wouldn't go! He couldn't go! But something impelled him to go. And all the time Pamela Hoyt and Fay Seton, with enormous eyes, sat perfectly motionless like wax dummies. There was a shaking crash of thunder ...

Miles, with bright sunlight in his face, was shocked awake. He sat up, feeling the arms of the chair on either side of him.

He *was* in the sitting-room downstairs, hunched up in the tapestry chair by the fireplace. In a momentary backwash of the dream, wildly, he half expected to see Fay and dead Pamela Hoyt walk out of the library door over there behind him.

But here was the familiar room, with the Leonardo above the mantelpiece, and soft brilliant sunshine. And the telephone was ringing shrilly. The events of last night returned to Miles as he heard it ring.

Marion was safe. Safe, and going to get well. Dr Garvice had said she was out of danger.

Yes! And Dr Fell was asleep upstairs in his own room, and Professor Rigaud in Steve Curtis's: these being the only two other inhabitable bedrooms at Greywood. That was why he had dossed down here in the chair.

Greywood felt hushed, felt empty and new-washed, in a fresh morning stillness, though he could tell by the position of the sun that it must be past eleven o'clock. Still the telephone kept clamouring on the

102

wide window-sill. He stumbled over to it, stretching his muscles, and caught it up.

'May I speak to Mr Miles Hammond?' said a voice. 'This is Barbara Morell.'

Then Miles definitely became awake.

'Speaking,' he answered. 'Are you – I asked you this once before – by any chance a mind-reader?'

'What's that?'

Miles sat down on the floor with his back to the wall under the windows: not a dignified position, but it gave him a sense of sitting across from the speaker for a heart-to-heart talk.

'If you hadn't rung me,' he went on, 'I was going to try to get in touch with you.'

'Oh? Why?'

For some reason it gave him extraordinary pleasure to hear her voice. There was no subtlety, he reflected, about Barbara Morell. Simply *because* she had played that trick with the Murder Club, it showed her as transparent as a child.

'Dr Fell is here ... No, no, he's *not* annoyed about it! He hasn't so much as mentioned the club! ... Last night he tried to make Fay Seton admit something, and he had no success. He says now you're our last hope. He says that if you don't help us we may be dished.'

'I don't think' Barbara's voice said doubtfully, 'you're making yourself very clear.'

'Look here! Listen! If I came in to town this afternoon, could I possibly see you?'

Pause.

'Yes, I suppose so.'

'This is Sunday. I think there's a train,' he searched his memory, 'at half-past one. Yes, I'm sure there's a train at half-past one. It takes roughly two hours. Where could I see you?'

Barbara seemed to be debating.

'I could meet your train at Waterloo. Then we might have tea somewhere.'

'Excellent idea!' All last night's bewilderment swept over him. 'The only thing I can tell you now is that there was a very bad business here last night. Something happened in my sister's room that seems past human belief. If we can only find an explanation ...'

Miles glanced up.

Stephen Curtis – sober-faced, conscientiously correct from his hat to his grey double-breasted suit, carrying a rolled umbrella over his arm – Stephen Curtis, coming in at a jaunty pace from the reception-hall, caught the last words and stopped short.

Miles had dreaded telling Steve, dreaded telling the mental counterpart of Marion. It was all right now, of course. Marion wasn't going to die. At the same time, he spoke hastily to the telephone.

'Sorry I have to ring off now, Barbara. See you later.' And he hung up.

Stephen, his forehead growing faintly worried, contemplated his future brother-in-law sitting on the floor: unshaven, wild, and tousle-headed.

'Look here, old man ...'

'It's all right!' Miles assured him, springing to his feet. 'Marion's had a very bad time of it, but she's going to get well. Dr Garvice says ...'

'Marion?' Steve's voice went high, and all the colour drained out of his face. 'What is it? What's happened?'

'Something or someone got into her room last night, and frightened her very nearly to death. But she'll be as right as rain in two or three days, so you're not to worry.'

For a few seconds, while Miles could not meet his eye, neither of them spoke. Stephen walked forward. Stephen, that self-controlled man, fastened sinewy fingers round the handle of his rolled umbrella; deliberately he lifted the umbrella high in the air; deliberately he brought it down with a smash on the edge of the table under the windows.

The umbrella subsided, bent metal and broken ribs amid black cloth: a useless heap, an inanimate object that for some reason looked pitiful, like the body of a shot bird.

'It was that damned librarian, I suppose?' Stephen asked almost calmly.

'Why should you say that?'

'I don't know. But I knew at the station yesterday, I felt it in my bones, I tried to warn you both, that there was trouble coming. Some people cause something-or-other wherever they go.' A blue, congested vein showed at his temple. '*Marion!*'

'We owe her life, Steve, to a man named Professor Rigaud. I don't think I've told you about him. Don't wake him now; he's had a long night of it; but he's asleep in your room.'

Stephen turned away. He walked over to the line of low white-painted bookshelves along the west wall, with the big framed portraits over them. He stood there with his back to Miles, his hands spread out on the shelf-top. When he turned round a little later Miles saw, with acute embarrassment, that there were tears in his eyes.

Both of them suddenly spoke with desperation of trivialities.

'Did you – er – just get here?' asked Miles.

'Yes. Caught the nine-thirty from town.'

'Crowded?'

'Fairly crowded. Where is she?'

'Upstairs. She's asleep now.'

'Can I see her?'

'I don't know any reason why not. I tell you, she's all right! But go quietly; everybody else is in bed.'

Everybody else, however, was not in bed. As Stephen turned towards the door to the reception hall, there appeared in the doorway the vastness of Dr Fell, carrying a cup of tea on a tray and looking as though he did not quite know how it had got there.

Ordinarily it would have been as startling to Stephen Curtis to find an unexplained guest in the house as to find a new member of the family at breakfast. Now, however, he hardly noticed Dr Fell; the presence of someone else only served as a reminder that he was still wearing his hat. Stephen turned in the doorway. He swept off his hat. He looked at Miles. Nearly bald, even his fair moustache seeming disarranged, Stephen struggled for words.

'You and your damned Murder Club!' he said clearly and viciously.

Then he was gone.

Dr Fell, clearing his throat, lumbered forward hesitantly with the tea on the tray.

'Good morning,' he rumbled. He looked uncomfortable. 'That was –?'

'Steve Curtis. Yes.'

'I – ah – made this tea for you,' said Dr Fell, extending the tray. 'I *made* it all right,' he added argumentatively. 'And then it seems to me I began concentrating on something else, so that some half an hour elapsed before I put in the milk. I greatly fear it may be cold.'

This remark was both made and received in perfect seriousness, since both Dr Fell and Miles were otherwise preoccupied.

'That's all right,' said Miles. 'Thanks very much.'

105

He gulped down the tea, and then put cup and tray on the floor beside him as he sat down in the big chair by the fireplace. Miles was steeling himself for the outburst he knew must come, the admission he was compelled to make.

'This whole situation,' he said, 'is my fault.'

'Steady!' said Dr Fell sharply.

'It's my fault, Dr Fell. I invited Fay Seton here. The good Lord alone knows why I did; but there you are. You heard what Steve said?'

'Which part of what he said?'

' "Some people cause something-or-other wherever they go." '

'Yes. I heard it.'

'We were all worked up and overwrought last night,' Miles went on. 'When Rigaud made that sign against the evil eye, I shouldn't have been surprised to see hell open. In daylight' – he nodded towards the grey and green and sun-gold forest through the eastern windows – 'it's hard to be afraid of vampire-teeth. And yet *something*. Something that troubles the waters. Something that brings pain and disaster to whatever it touches. Do you understand?'

'Oh, ah. I understand. But before you blame yourself –'

'Well?'

'Hadn't we better be sure,' said Dr Fell, 'that Miss Fay Seton *is* the person who troubles the waters?'

Miles sat up straight with a jerk.

Dr Fell, peering sideways at him past the crooked eye-glasses, with a look of Gargantuan distress on his face, fished in the pocket of a baggy alpaca coat. He produced the meerschaum and filled it from an obese pouch. With some effort he lowered himself into a big chair, spreading out over it; he struck a match and lighted the pipe.

'Sir,' he continued, firing up himself as he blew out smoke, 'I could not credit Rigaud's vampire theory from the time I read his manuscript yesterday. I could credit, mind you, a vampire who materialized in the daytime I could even credit a vampire who killed with a sword-stick. But I could not credit, not at any time, a vampire who pinched somebody's brief-case containing money.

'That jarred my sense of the fitness of things. That somehow failed to convince. And late last night, when you told me Fay Seton's own story – including, by the way, a point which is *not* in the manuscript –

106

I had a vision. Through the whole business I saw not real devilishness, but human devilishness.

'Then came the frightening of your sister.

'And that was different, by thunder! That *was* the authentic touch of Satan. It still is.

'Until we know what was in the room, or what was outside the window, we can't give any kind of final verdict on Fay Seton. These two events, the murder on the tower and the frightening of your sister, are connected. They interlock. They depend on each other. And they both in some fashion centre round this odd girl with the red hair.' He was silent for a moment. 'Forgive the personal question; but do you happen to be in love with her?'

Miles looked him in the eyes.

'I don't quite know,' he replied honestly. 'She ...'

'Disturbs you?'

'That's putting it mildly.'

'Supposing her to be − harrumph! − a criminal of some kind, natural or supernatural, would that have any influence on your attitude?'

'For the love of Mike, are you warning me against her too?'

'No!' thundered Dr Fell, and made a hideous face and smote his fist on the arm of the chair with remarkable vehemence. 'On the contrary! If one wool-gathering idea of mine is correct, there are many persons who ought to get down in the dust and beg her pardon. No, sir: I put the question in what Rigaud would call an academic way. Would this (shall we say) make any difference to your attitude?'

'No, I can't say it would. We don't fall in love with a woman because of her good character.'

'That,' said Dr Fell, taking a number of reflective puffs at the meerschaum, 'is an observation none the less true for not being generally admitted. At the same time, this whole situation disturbs me even more. One person's motive (forgive me if I seem cryptic) seems to make nonsense of another person's motive.

'I questioned Miss Seton last night,' he continued, 'and I hinted. To-day I propose to question her without hints. But I fear it won't be any good. The best thing to do is perhaps to get in touch with Miss Barbara Morell ...'

'Wait a minute!' Miles rose to his feet. 'We've got in touch with Barbara Morell! She rang up here not five minutes before you came in!'

'So?' observed Dr Fell, instantly alert. 'What did she want?'

'Come to think of it,' said Miles, 'I haven't the remotest idea. I forgot to ask her.'

Dr Fell eyed him for a long moment.

'My boy,' Dr Fell said with an expansive sigh, 'it is more and more borne in on me that you and I are spiritually kin. I refrain from making frantic comments; that is the sort of thing I always do myself. But what did *you* say? Did you ask her about Jim Morell?'

'No. Steve Curtis came in just then, and I didn't have time. But I remembered you said it might help us to get the information, so I've arranged to see her to-day in town. I might as well,' Miles added bitterly. 'Dr Garvice is getting a nurse for Marion, and everyone claims I'm in the way in addition to being the pigheaded swine who introduced the disturbing element into the house.'

Miles was getting lower and lower, blacker and blacker, in his mind and spirit.

'Fay Seton's not guilty!' he shouted; and he might have gone on to enlarge on this if Dr Laurence Garvice himself, with a bowler hat in one hand and a medicine-case in the other, had not put his head in at the doorway to the reception hall.

Dr Garvice, a middle-aged, pleasant-faced man with a grizzled head and a scrubbed antiseptic manner, obviously had something on his mind. He hesitated before coming in.

'Mr Hammond,' he said, giving a half-smile to Miles and Dr Fell, 'before I see the patient again, I wonder if I could have a word with you?'

'Yes, of course. Don't hesitate to speak in front of Dr Fell.' Dr Garvice closed the door behind him and turned round.

'Mr Hammond,' he said, 'I wonder whether you would mind telling me what frightened the patient?'

Then he held up his hand with the bowler hat.

'I ask,' he went on, 'because this is the worst case of plain nervous shock in my experience. That's to say, there's often, nearly always, severe shock attendant on physical injury. But there's no physical injury of any kind.' He hesitated. 'Is the lady of a highly strung type?'

'No,' said Miles. He felt his throat contract.

'No, I shouldn't have thought so myself. Medically she's as sound as a bell.' There was a little pause, faintly sinister. 'Apparently someone tried to get at her from outside the window?'

'That's the trouble, Doctor. We don't know what happened.'

'Oh. I see. I was hoping you could tell me. – There's no other sign of ... burglars being here?'

'None that I've noticed.'

'Have you informed the police?'

'Good God, no!' Miles blurted this out, and then steadied himself to casualness. 'You can understand, Doctor, that we don't want the police mixed up in this.'

'Yes. No doubt.' With his eye on the pattern of the carpet, Dr Garvice slowly tapped his bowler hat against his leg. 'The lady doesn't suffer from – hallucinations?'

'No. Why do you ask?'

'Well,' and the physician lifted his eyes, 'she keeps on muttering, over and over, about something whispering to her.'

'*Whispering?*'

'Yes. It rather worries me.'

'But "whispering", someone whispering to her, couldn't have caused ...?'

'No. Exactly what I thought myself.'

Whispering ...

The eerie word, with its sibilant note, seemed to hang in the air between them. Dr Garvice still tapped his bowler hat slowly against his leg.

'Well!' He woke up and looked at his wrist-watch. 'I dare say we shall find out soon enough. In the meantime, as I told you last night, there's nothing to worry about. I was lucky enough to get a nurse, who's outside now.' Dr Garvice turned towards the door. 'It's very disturbing, though,' he added. 'I'll look in again when I've seen the patient. And I'd better look in on the other lady too – Miss Seton, isn't it? *She* didn't seem, last night, to have as much blood-colour in her as she should have. Excuse me.'

And the door closed after him.

CHAPTER 13

'I SUPPOSE,' Miles remarked mechanically, 'I'd better go and see about breakfast for all of us.' But he took only two steps towards the dining-room. 'Whispering!' he said. 'Dr Fell, what *is* the answer to all this?'

'Sir,' returned Dr Fell, 'I don't know.'

'Does it give you a clue of any kind?'

'Unfortunately, no. The vampire –'

'Need we use that word?'

'The vampire, in folk-lore, whispered softly to her victim at the beginning of the influence that threw the victim into a trance. But the point is that no vampire, real or faked, *no* sort of imitation bogy at all, would have had the least effect on your sister. That is correct?'

'I'd swear to it. Last night I gave you an instance to prove it. For Marion' – he tried to find the right words – 'such things just didn't enter her mind.'

'You'd call her completely unimaginative?'

'That's a strong word to use about anybody. But certainly she's completely contemptuous of *that*. When I tried to talk to her about the supernatural, she made me sound foolish even to myself. And when I talked about Count Cagliostro …'

'Cagliostro?' Dr Fell blinked at him. 'Apropos what? Oh, ah! I see! Rigaud's book?'

'Yes. According to Fay Seton, Marion seems to have got a quite sincere if hazy idea that Cagliostro was a personal friend of mine.'

Dr Fell's scatterbrain had been set off again. He leaned back in the chair, his pipe gone out, and dreamily contemplated a corner of the ceiling for so long a time that Miles thought he must be a victim of catalepsy until Miles saw the far-away twinkle which began in the doctor's eye, the vast sleepy beam which overspread his face, the series of chuckles which gradually ran up the ridges of his waistcoat.

'It's a fascinating subject, you know,' mused Dr Fell.

'Vampires?' said Miles bitterly.

'Cagliostro,' replied Dr Fell.

He gestured with his pipe.

'Now there is a historical character,' he continued, 'whom I have always detested and yet obscurely admired. The tubby little Italian, the eye-roller, "Count Front-of-Brass", who claimed to be two thousand years old from drinking his own elixir of life! The wizard, the alchemist, the healer! Moving across the screen of the late eighteenth century in a red waistcoat covered with diamonds! Aweing kings' courts from Paris to St Petersburg! Founding his cult of Egyptian Masonry, to which women were admitted, and addressing his female disciples with everybody *in puris naturalibus*! Making gold! Prophesying the future! And, incredibly, getting away with it!

'The man was never exposed, you remember. His ruin came about through that business of Marie Antoinette's diamond necklace, in which the count had no concern whatever.

'But I think his most intriguing exploit was his Banquet of the Dead, at the mysterious house in the rue St Claude, where the ghosts of six great men were gravely summoned from the shadows to sit down at dinner with six living guests.

' "*At first*," writes one biographer, "*conversation did not flow freely.*" This seems to me one of the classic understatements. My own conversation would have dried up, would positively have petrified, if I found myself at a dinner-table requesting Voltaire to pass the salt or asking the Duc de Choiseul how he liked the quality of the spam. And at this dinner the ghosts themselves seem to have been rather embarrassed as well, to judge by the quality of their talk.

'No, sir. Let me repeat that I don't like Count Cagliostro; I dislike his swagger as I dislike any man's swagger. But I will concede that he had a notion of doing things handsomely. England too, that home of quacks and impostors, has a great claim on him.'

Miles Hammond, professionally interested in spite of himself, interjected a protest.

'*England?*' Miles repeated. 'Did you say England?'

'I did.'

'If I remember correctly, Cagliostro did visit London on two occasions. They were very unfortunate occasions for him ...'

111

'Ah!' agreed Dr Fell. 'But it was in London that he was initiated into the secret society which gave him the idea for his own secret society later. The present-day Magic Circle ought to go round to Gerrard Street, to what used to he the King's Head Tavern, and put up a plaque. Gerrard Street! Oh, ah! Yes! Very close, by the way, to Beltring's Restaurant where we were to meet two nights ago, and Miss Barbara Morell said …'

Suddenly Dr Fell paused.

His hands went to his forehead. The meerschaum pipe dropped unheeded out of his mouth, bounced against his knee, and rolled to the floor. Afterwards he seemed to congeal into a figure so motionless that not even a wheeze of breath could be heard.

'Pray forgive me,' he said presently, and took his hands away from his forehead. 'Absence of mind has some use in this world after all. I think I've got it.'

'Got what?' Miles shouted.

'I know what frightened your sister. – Let me alone for a moment!' Dr Fell pleaded, with a wild look and an almost piteous voice. 'Her body was relaxed! Completely relaxed! We saw it for ourselves! And yet at the same time …'

'Well? What about it?'

'Done by design,' Dr Fell said. 'Done by deliberate, brutal design.' He looked startled. 'And that must mean, God help us, that –!'

Again realization came into his mind, realization of something else, this time slowly, like an exploring light from room to room. It was as though Miles could follow the workings of his brain, read the moving eyes (for Dr Fell has not a poker face) without seeing quite past that last nightmarish door to what lay beyond.

'Let's go upstairs,' Dr Fell said at length, 'and see if there is any proof that I'm right.'

Miles nodded. In silence he followed Dr Fell, who now leaned heavily on his crutch-handled stick, up to Marion's bedroom. From the doctor radiated a shaggy glow of certainty, a fiery energy, which made Miles sure that a barrier *had* been passed. Henceforward, Miles felt, there was danger. Henceforward they were racing towards trouble. Here's a malignant force, and Dr Fell knows what it is; we'll kill it, or it will kill us, but look to yourself! – because the game has begun.

112

Dr Fell tapped at the bedroom door, which was opened by a youngish nurse in uniform.

Inside the room was dim and a little stuffy, despite sunlight and clean air. The thin blue, gold-figured curtains had been drawn across both sets of windows; and, with black-out curtains removed weeks ago, a faint dazzle of sun showed beyond. Marion, asleep, lay tidily in a tidy bed and room which showed already the touch of the professional nurse. The nurse herself, carrying a hand wash-basin, moved back from opening the door. Stephen Curtis, a pitiable man, stood with hunched shoulders by the chest-of-drawers. And Dr Garvice, who was just on the point of leaving after his examination, looked round surprised.

Dr. Fell walked up to him.

'Sir,' he began in a voice which arrested the attention of everyone there, 'last night you did me the honour to say you were familiar with my name.'

The other bowed, faintly inquiring.

'I am not,' said Dr Fell, 'a physician; nor have I any medical knowledge beyond that which might be possessed by any man in the street. You may refuse the request I am about to make. You would have every right to do so. But I should like to examine your patient.'

And now showed the inner, troubled state of Dr Laurence Garvice's mind. He glanced towards the bed.

'Examine the patient?' Dr Garvice repeated.

'I should like to examine her neck and her teeth.'

Pause.

'But, my dear sir!' protested the physician, his voice going up loudly before he checked it. 'There isn't a wound or a mark anywhere on the lady's body!'

'Sir,' replied Dr Fell, 'I am aware of that.'

'And if you're thinking of a drug, or something like that ...!'

'I know,' announced Dr Fell carefully, 'that Miss Hammond was not physically hurt. I know that no question arises of a drug or any kind of toxic agent. I know her condition is caused by fear and nothing else. But still I should like to examine her neck and teeth.'

The physician made a half-helpless gesture with his bowler hat.

'Go ahead,' he said. 'Miss Peters! You might open the curtains just a little. Please excuse *me*. I'm off to look in on Miss Seton downstairs.'

Yet he lingered in the doorway as Dr Fell approached the bed. It was Stephen Curtis, after glancing in bewilderment at Miles and receiving only a shrug for reply, who twitched back a few inches one of the curtains on the south windows. A little light ran lengthways across the bed. Otherwise they stood in a bluish-coloured dusk, motionless, with birds bickering outside, while Dr Fell bent over.

Miles couldn't see what he was doing. His broad back hid all that was visible of Marion above the blanket and the neat fold of the top sheet. Nor was there any sign of movement from Marion.

Somebody's watch – in fact, Dr Garvice's wrist-watch – could be heard ticking distinctly.

'Well?' Dr Garvice prompted. He stirred with impatience in the doorway. 'Have you found anything?'

'No! said Dr Fell despairingly, and straightened up and put his hand on the crutch-handled stick propped against the bed. He turned round. He began, muttering to himself and holding fast his eyeglasses with his left hand, to peer at the carpet round the edges of the bed.

'No,' he added, 'I haven't found anything.' He stared straight ahead of him 'Stop a bit, though! There *is* a test! I can't remember the name of it offhand; but, by thunder, there *is* a test! It will prove definitely ...'

'Prove what?'

'The presence of an evil spirit,' said Dr Fell.

There was a slight rattle as Nurse Peters handled the washbasin. Dr Garvice kept his composure.

'You're joking, of course. And in any case' – his voice became brisk – 'I'm afraid I can't allow you to disturb the patient any longer. You'd better come along too, Mr Curtis!'

And he stood to one side like a shepherd while Dr Fell, Miles, and Stephen filed out. Then he closed the door.

'Sir,' said Dr Fell, impressively lifting his crutch-handled stick and tapping it against the air, 'the whole joke is that I am not joking. I believe – harrumph – you said you were on your way down to see Miss Fay Seton. *She* isn't by any chance ill, is she?'

'Oh, no. The lady was a bit nervy early this morning and I gave her a sedative.'

'Then I wonder if you will ask Miss Seton, at her convenience, to come and join us here in the upstairs hall? Where,' said Dr Fell, 'we had a very interesting talk last night. Will you convey that message?'

Dr Garvice studied him from under grizzled eyebrows.

'I don't understand what's going on here,' he stated slowly. He hesitated. 'Maybe it's just as well I don't understand.' He hesitated again. 'I'll convey your message. Good day.'

Miles watched him go at his unhurried pace down the hall. Then Miles shook the arm of Stephen Curtis.

'Hang it all, Steve!' he said to a man who was standing against the wall hump-shouldered, like an object hung on a hat-peg, 'you've got to brace up! There's no sense in taking this so hard as all that! You must have heard the doctor say Marion's in no danger! After all, she's my sister!'

Stephen straightened up.

'No,' he admitted in his slow voice. 'I suppose not. But then after all she's only your sister. And she's my ... my ...'

'Yes. I know.'

'That's the whole point, Miles. You don't know. You never have been very fond of Marion, have you? But, speaking of being concerned about people, what about you and this girlfriend of *yours*? The librarian?'

'Well, what about us?'

'She poisoned somebody, didn't she?'

'What do you mean, she poisoned somebody?'

'When we were having tea at Waterloo yesterday,' said Stephen, 'it seems to me Marion said this Fay What's-her-name was guilty of poisoning somebody.' Here Stephen began to shout. 'You wouldn't give two hoots about your own sister, would you? No! But you *would* care everything in the world, you *would* upset everything and everybody, for an infernal little slut you picked up out of the gutter to –'

'*Steve! Take it easy! What's wrong?*'

A shocked, startled look passed slowly over Stephen Curtis's face, showing consternation in the eyes.

His mouth fell open under the fair moustache. He put up a hand to his necktie, fingering it. He shook his head as though to clear something away. When he spoke again it was in a voice of contrition.

'Sorry, old man,' Stephen muttered, and punched in an embarrassed way at Miles's arm. 'Can't think what came over me. Wouldn't have said that for worlds! But you know how it is when something funny happens and you can't understand any of it. I'm going to go and lie down.'

'Wait a minute! Come back! Not in that room!'

'What do you mean, not in that room?'

'Not in your own bedroom, Steve! Professor Rigaud's trying to get some sleep in there, and ...'

'Oh, so-and-so to Professor Rigaud!' said Stephen, and bolted down the back stairs like a man pursued.

The troubling of the waters again!

Now, Miles thought, it had reached out and touched Steve as well. It seemed to colour every action and inspire every thought here at Greywood. He still refused, fiercely refused, to believe anything whatever against Fay Seton. But what had Dr Fell meant by that remark about an evil spirit? Surely to heaven it wasn't intended to be taken quite literally? Miles swung round, to find Dr Fell's gaze fixed on him.

'You are wondering,' inquired Dr Fell, 'what I want with Miss Seton? I can tell you very simply. I want the truth.'

'The truth about what?'

'The truth,' returned Dr Fell, 'about Howard Brooke's murder and the fright-bogy of last night. And she can't, for her soul's sake she daren't, evade questions now. I think we shall have it settled in a very few minutes.'

They heard quick footsteps on the distant front stairs. A figure appeared at the other end of the long, narrow hall. When Miles saw that it was Dr Laurence Garvice, when he saw Dr Garvice's hastened stride, he had one of those inspired premonitions which can fly to the heart of truth.

It seemed a very long time before the physician reached them.

'I thought I'd better come up and tell you,' he announced. 'Miss Seton has gone.'

Dr Fell's crutch-handled stick dropped with a clatter on the bare boards.

'*Gone?*' His voice was so husky that he had to clear his throat.

'She – er – left this for Mr Hammond,' said Garvice. 'At least,' he amended hastily, 'I assume she's gone. I found this,' he held up a sealed envelope, 'propped up against the pillow in her bedroom.'

Miles took the envelope, which was addressed to him in a fine, clear, sharp-pointed handwriting. He turned it over in his fingers, momentarily without the courage to open it. But when he did grit his teeth and tear open the envelope, he was little reassured by the contents of the folded note inside.

DEAR MR HAMMOND,

I am sorry to say I shall have to be absent in London to-day on a matter that compels attention. I think now I *was* wise to keep my little room in town. And a brief-case *is* so useful, isn't it? But don't worry. I shall return after nightfall.

Yours sincerely,
FAY SETON.

The sky, which had been fine, was clouding over with little smoky wisps of black: a moving sky, an uneasy sky. Miles held the letter close to the window, and read it aloud. That was when the ominous word 'brief-case' struck out at him.

'Oh, my *God!*' breathed Dr Fell. He said this very simply, as a man might witness ruin or tragedy. 'And yet I ought to have guessed it. I ought to have guessed it. I ought to have guessed it!'

'But what's wrong?' demanded Miles. 'Fay says she'll be back after nightfall.'

'Yes. Oh, ah. Yes.' Dr Fell rolled his eyes. 'I wonder what time she left here? I WONDER what time she left here?'

'*I* don't know,' said Garvice hastily. 'Don't look at me!'

'But somebody must have seen her go!' bellowed Dr Fell, in an enclosed passage which was beginning to feel very warm. 'A conspicuous girl like that! Tall, red-haired, probably wearing ...'

The door to Marion's bedroom opened. Miss Peters, putting her head out in protest against the noise, saw Dr Garvice and stopped short.

'Oh. I didn't know *you* were here, Doctor,' the nurse said pointedly, in a small reproving voice. Afterwards, moved by human curiosity, she wavered. 'Pardon me. If you're looking for a woman of that description ...'

Dr Fell wheeled round in vastness.

'Yes?'

'I think maybe I saw her,' the nurse informed him.

'When?' roared Dr Fell. The nurse shied back. 'Where?'

'Nearly – nearly three-quarters of an hour ago, when I was coming here on my bicycle. She was getting on the bus out in the main road.'

'A bus,' demanded Dr Fell, 'that would take her to Southampton Central railway station? Oh, ah! And what train to London could she catch by taking that bus?'

'Well, there's the one-thirty,' replied Garvice. 'She could make that one comfortably?'

'The one-thirty?' echoed Miles Hammond. 'But that's the train I'm taking! *I* intended to get the bus that would ...'

'You mean that wouldn't,' corrected Garvice with a rather strained smile. 'You'll never make that train by bus, or even by private car unless you drove like Sir Malcolm Campbell. It's ten minutes past one now.'

'Listen to me,' said Dr Fell in a voice he very seldom used. His hand fell on Miles's shoulder. 'You are going to catch that one-thirty train.'

'But that's impossible! There's a man who does a car-hire service to and from the station – Steve always uses him – but it would take too long to get him here. It's out of the question!'

'You forget,' said Dr Fell, 'that Rigaud's illegally borrowed car is still outside in the drive.' There was a wild, strained look in his eyes. 'Listen to me!' he repeated. 'It is absolutely vital for you to overtake Fay Seton. Absolutely vital. Are you willing to have a shot at catching the train?'

'Hell yes. I'll drive her at ninety an hour. But suppose I do miss the train?'

'I don't know!' roared Dr Fell as though physical pain, and hammered his fist against his temple. 'This "little room in town" she speaks about. She's going there – yes, of course she is! Have you got her London address?'

'No. She came straight to me from the employment agency.'

'In that case,' said Dr Fell, 'you have simply *got* to catch the train. I'll explain as much as possible while we run. But something damnable is going to happen, I warn you here and now, if that woman tries to carry out her plans. It is quite literally a matter of life and death. You have *got* to catch that train!'

CHAPTER 14

THE guard's whistle piped shrilly.

Two or three last doors slammed. The one-thirty train to London, smoothly gliding, drew out of Southampton Central Station and gathered speed so that its windows seemed to flash past.

'You can't do it, I tell you!' panted Stephen Curtis.

'Want to bet?' Miles said through his teeth. 'Drive the car back, Steve. I'm all right now.'

'Never jump on a train when it's going as fast as that!' yelled Stephen. 'Never ...'

The voice receded. Miles was running blindly beside the door of a first-class smoking compartment. He dodged a luggage-truck, with someone shouting at him, and laid hold of the door-handle. Since the train was on his left-hand side as he ran, the jump wasn't going to be easy.

He yanked open the door, felt through his back the terrifying crick-crack twinge of overbalancement as he jumped, saved himself by a reeling catch at the side of the door, and, with the dizziness of his old illness pouring through his head, slammed the door behind him.

He had made it. He was on the same train with Fay Seton. Miles stood at the open window, panting and half-blind, staring out and listening to the click of the wheels. When he had partly got his breath he turned round.

Ten pairs of eyes regarded him with barely concealed loathing.

The first-class compartment, nominally built to seat six persons, now held five squeezed in on each side. To railway travellers there is always something infuriating about a late arrival who gets in at the last moment, and this was a particularly bad case. Though no one said anything, the atmosphere was glacial except for a stoutish Waaf who gave him a glance of encouragement.

'I – er – beg your pardon,' said. Miles.

He wondered vaguely whether he ought to add a maxim from the letters of Lord Chesterfield, some little apophthegm of this sort; but he sensed the atmosphere and in any case he had other things to worry about.

Miles stumbled hastily across feet, gained the door to the corridor, went out and closed it behind him amid a general wave of thankfulness. Here he stood considering. He was reasonably presentable, having sloshed water on his face and scraped himself raw with a dry razor, though his empty stomach cried aloud. But this wasn't important.

The important thing was to find Fay immediately.

It was not a long train, and not very crowded. That is to say, people were packed into seats trying to read newspapers with their hands flat against their breasts like corpses; dozens stood in the corridor amid barricades of luggage. But few were actually standing inside the compartments except those fat women with third-class tickets who go and stand in first-class compartments, radiating reproachfulness, until some, guilty-feeling male gives them his seat.

Working his way along the corridors, tripping over luggage, becoming entangled with people queueing for lavatories, Miles tried to work out a philosophical essay in his mind. He was watching, he said to himself, a whole cross-section of England as the train rattled and swayed, and the green countryside flashed by, and he peered into one compartment after another.

But, in actual fact, he wasn't feeling philosophical.

After a first quick journey he was apprehensive. After a second he was panicky. After a third …

For Fay Seton was not aboard the train.

Steady now! Don't get the wind up!

Fay's got to be here!

But she wasn't.

Miles stood in a corridor midway along the length of the train, gripping the window-railing and trying to keep calm. The afternoon had grown warmer and darker, in black smoky clouds that seemed to mix with the smoke of the train. Miles stared out of the window until the moving landscape blurred. He was seeing Dr Fell's frightened face, and hearing Dr Fell's voice.

That 'explanation', delivered by the doctor in a vacant undertone while engaged in cramming biscuits into Miles's pockets to take the place of breakfast, had not been very coherent.

120

'Find her and stay with her! Find her and stay with her!' That had been the burden of it. 'If she insists on coming back to Greywood to-night, that's all right – in fact, it's probably the best thing – but stay with her and don't leave her side for a minute!'

'Is she in danger?'

'In my opinion, yes,' said Dr Fell. 'And if you want to see her proved innocent of' – he hesitated – 'of at least the worst charge against her, for the love of heaven don't fail me!'

The worst charge against her?

Miles shook his head. The jerk of the train swayed and roused him. Fay had either missed the train – which seemed incredible, unless the bus had broken down – or, more probably, she had turned back after all.

And here he was speeding away in the opposite direction, away from whatever might be happening. But ... hold on! here was a hopeful point! ... the 'something damnable' Dr Fell had predicted seemed to concern what would occur if Fay *went to London* and returned to carry out her plans. That meant there was nothing to worry about. Or did it?

Miles could never remember a longer journey. The train was an express; he couldn't have got out to turn back if he had wanted to. Rain-whips stung the windows. Miles got entangled with a family party which overflowed from compartment into corridor like a camp-fire group, and remembered that its sandwiches were in a suitcase under a mountainous pile of somebody else's luggage, and for a time created the general wild aspect of moving-day. It was twenty minutes to four when the train drew in at Waterloo.

Waiting for him, just outside the barrier, stood Barbara Morrell.

The sheer pleasure he felt at seeing her momentarily drove out his anxieties. Round them the clacking torrent from the train poured through the barrier. From the station loud-speaker, a refined voice hollowly enunciated.

'Hello,' said Barbara.

She seemed more aloof than he remembered her.

'Hello,' said Miles. 'I – er – hardly liked to drag you over here to the station.'

'Oh, that's all right,' said Barbara. He well remembered, now, the grey eyes with their long black lashes. 'Besides, I have to be at the office later this evening.'

'At the office? On Sunday night?'

'I'm in Fleet Street,' said Barbara. 'I'm a journalist. That's why I said I didn't "exactly" write fiction.' She brushed this away. The grey eyes studied him furtively. 'What's wrong?' she asked suddenly. 'What is it? You look …'

'There's the devil and all to pay,' Miles burst out. He felt somehow that he could let himself go in front of this girl. 'I was supposed to find Fay Seton at any cost. Everything depended on it. We all thought she'd be in this train. Now I don't know what in blazes to do, because she wasn't in the train after all.'

'Wasn't in the train?' Barbara repeated. Her eyes opened wide. 'But Fay Seton *was* in the train! She walked through that barrier not twenty seconds before you did!'

'*Will pass-en-gers for Hon-i-ton,*' sang the dictatorial loud-speaker, *'join the queue outside Platform Num-ber Nine! Will pass-en-gers for Hon-i-ton …'*

It blattered above every other noise in the station. And yet the realm of nightmare had returned.

'You must have been seeing things!' said Miles. 'I tell you she wasn't aboard that train!' He looked round wildly as a new thought occurred to him. 'Stop a bit! So you do know her after all?'

'No! I'd never set eyes on her before in my life!'

'Then how do you know it was Fay Seton?'

'From the photograph. The coloured photograph Professor Rigaud showed us on Friday night. After all, I … I thought she was with you. And so I wasn't going to keep the appointment. Or at least – I didn't quite know. What's *wrong?*'

This was disaster fine and full.

He wasn't mad, Miles told himself; and he wasn't drunk, and he wasn't blind; and he could take his oath Fay Seton had not been aboard that train. Fantastic images occurred to him, of a white face and a red mouth. These images were exotic plants which withered in the atmosphere of Waterloo Station, certainly in the atmosphere of the train he had just left.

Yet he looked down at Barbara's fair hair and grey eyes; he thought of her normalness – that was it! a lovable normalness – in this murky affair; and at the same time he thought of all that had happened since he saw her last.

Marion *was* lying in a stupor at Greywood, and not from the effects of poison or a knife. Dr Fell *had* spoken of an evil spirit. These things were not fancies; they were facts. Miles remembered his impression of that morning: here's a malignant force, and Dr Fell knows what it is; we'll kill it, or it will kill us; and, in sober God's truth, the game had begun now.

All this went through his head in the split-second of Barbara's remark.

'You saw Fay Seton come through the gates,' he said. 'In which direction did she go?'

'I couldn't tell. There are too many people.'

'Wait a minute! We're not beaten yet! Professor Rigaud told me last night ... yes, he's at Greywood too! ... that you phoned him yesterday, and that you knew Fay's address. She's got a room in town somewhere, and according to Dr Fell she'll go straight to it. *Do* you know the address?'

'Yes!' Barbara, in a tailored suit and white blouse, with a mackintosh draped over her shoulders and an umbrella hung across her arm, fumblingly opened her handbag and took out an address-book. 'This is it. Five Bolsover Place, NW1. But ...!'

'Where's Bolsover Place?'

'Well, Bolsover Street is off Camden High Street in Camden Town. I – I looked it up when I wondered whether I ought to go and see her. It's rather a dingy neighbourhood, but I imagine she's even more hard up than the rest of us.'

'What's her quickest way to get there?'

'By Underground, easily. You can go straight through from here without a change.'

'Then that's what she's done, you can bet a fiver! She can't be two minutes ahead of us! Probably we can catch her! Come on!'

Give me some luck! he was praying under his breath. Give me just one proper hand to play, one card higher than a deuce or a three! And not long afterwards, when they burst out of a ticket-queue and penetrated down into the airless depths where a maze of lines join, he got his card.

Miles heard the rumble of the approaching train as they emerged on the platform of the Northern Line. They were at one end of the platform, and people straggled for more than a hundred yards along its curve. Vision was blurred in this half-cylinder cavern, once brave with white tiling, now sordid and ill-lighted.

The red train swept out of its tunnel in a gale of wind, and streamed past to a stop. And he saw Fay Seton.

He saw her by the bright flash of windows now unscaled from blast-netting. She was standing at the extreme other end of the platform, the front of the train; and she moved forward as the doors rolled open.

'Fay!' he yelled. *'Fay!'*

It went completely unheard.

'Edgware train!' the guard was bellowing. 'Edgware train!'

'Don't try to run up there!' warned Barbara. 'The doors will close and we'll lose her altogether. Hadn't we better go in here?'

They dived into the rear car of the train, a non-smoker, just before the doors did close. Its only other occupants were a policeman, a somnolent-looking Australian soldier, and the guard at his panel of control-buttons. Miles had got only a faint glimpse of Fay's face; but it had looked fierce, preoccupied, with that same curious smile of last night.

It was maddening to be so close to her, and yet ...

'If I can get through to the front of the train –!'

'Please!' urged Barbara. She indicated the sign, 'Do Not Pass From One Car To Another Whilst the Train is In Motion'; she indicated the guard, and she indicated the policeman. 'It wouldn't do much good, would it, if you got yourself arrested now?'

'No, I suppose not.'

'She'll get out at Camden Town. So will we. Sit down here.'

In their ears was a soft, streaming thunder as the train rocketed through the tunnel. The car swayed and creaked round a curve; lights behind opaque glass jolted on the upholstery of the seats. Miles, all his nerves twitching with doubt, sank down beside Barbara on a double-seat facing forward.

'I don't like to ask too many questions,' continued Barbara, 'but I've been half mad with curiosity ever since I talked to you on the phone. What is all the urgency about overtaking Fay Seton?'

The train ground to a stop, and the sliding doors rolled open.

'Charing Cross!' yelled the guard conscientiously. *'Edgware train!'*

Miles sprang to his feet.

'Really it's all right,' Barbara pleaded. 'If Dr Fell says she's going to that place of hers, she's bound to get out at Camden Town. What can happen in the meantime?'

124

'I don't know,' admitted Miles. 'Look here,' he added, sitting down again and taking her hand in both of his. 'I've known you only a very short time; but do you mind me saying I'd rather talk to you now than almost anyone else I can think of?'

'No,' answered Barbara, looking away from him, 'I don't mind.'

'I can't say how you've been spending the week-end,' pursued Miles, 'but we've been having nothing but a Grand Guignol of vampires and near-murders, and ...'

'What did you Say?' She drew back her hand quickly.

'Yes! And Dr Fell claims you may be able to supply one of the most important pieces of information, whatever that is.' He paused. 'Who is Jim Morell?'

Clank-thud went the rush of the train, hollow-streaming through its tunnel; a breeze touched their hair from the ventilator-windows.

'You can't connect him with this,' said Barbara, and her fingers tightened round her handbag. 'He doesn't know, he never did know, anything about the death of Mr Brooke! He ...'

'Yes! But do you mind telling me who he is?'

'He's my brother.' Barbara moistened her very smooth, pink lips; not as attractive, perhaps, not as heady, as those of the passive blue-eyed woman now in the first car of the train. Miles shook this thought out of his mind as Barbara asked quickly: 'Where did you hear about him?'

'From Fay Seton.'

'Oh?' She started a little.

'I'll tell you the whole story in just a minute. But there are certain things to straighten out first. Your brother ... where is he now?'

'He's in Canada. For three years he was a prisoner of war in Germany, and we thought he was dead. He's been sent out to Canada for his health. Jim's older than I am; he was quite a well-known painter, before the war.'

'And I understand he was a friend of Harry Brooke.'

'Yes.' Then Barbara spoke, softly but very clearly. 'He was a friend of that utterly unspeakable swine Harry Brooke.'

'Strand!' shouted out the guard. *'Edgware train!'*

Subconsciously Miles was listening hard for that voice; listening for every slowing-down of the rumbling wheels, every sigh and jolt as the doors rolled open. The one thing he mustn't miss, on his soul's life, were those words, 'Camden Town'.

But – utterly unspeakable swine? Harry Brooke?

'There's just one thing,' continued Miles, with discomfort stirring through him but with a fierce determination to face it. 'I'd better mention before I tell you what happened. And that's this:

'I believe in Fay Seton. I've got into trouble with practically everyone for saying that: with my sister Marion, with Steve Curtis, with Professor Rigaud, even perhaps with Dr Fell, though I'm not quite so sure where he stands. And, since you were the first person who warned me against her ...'

'I warned you against her?'

'Yes. Didn't you?'

'Oh!' breathed Barbara Morell.

She had drawn back a little from him, with the dark cylinder-curved walls flying past outside the windows. She breathed that monosyllable in a tone of utter stupefaction, as though she could not believe her ears.

Miles had an instinct that the whole situation was going to change again; that something was not only wrong, but deadly wrong. Barbara stared at him, her mouth open. He saw comprehension come into the grey eyes, slow incredulous comprehension as they searched his face; then half-laughter, a wild helpless gesture ...

'You thought,' she insisted, 'that I –?'

'Yes! Didn't you?'

'Listen.' Barbara put her hand on his arm, and spoke with clear-eyed sincerity. 'I wasn't trying to warn you against her. I was wondering if you could *help* her. Fay Seton is ...'

'Go on!'

'Fay Seton is one of the most completely wronged, bedevilled, and – and *hurt* persons I've ever heard of. All I was trying to find out was whether she might have committed the murder, because I didn't know any details about the murder. She'd have been justified, you know, if she *had* killed someone! But you could tell, from what Professor Rigaud said, she hadn't done that, either. And I was at my wits' end.'

Barbara made a short, slight gesture.

'If you remember, at Beltring's, I wasn't even so much as interested in anything except the murder. The things that went before it, the charges of immorality and – and the other ridiculous thing that almost got her stoned by the country people, didn't matter. Because they were a deliberate, cruel frame-up against her from start to finish.'

126

Barbara's voice rose.

'I *knew* that. I can prove it. I've got a whole packet of letters to prove it. That woman's been in hell from lying gossip that prejudiced her in the eyes of the police, and may have ruined her life. I could have helped her. I *can* help her. But I'm too much of a coward! I'm too much of a coward! I'm too much of a coward!'

CHAPTER 15

'LEICESTER SQUARE!' sang the guard.

One or two persons got in. But the long, hot Underground car was still almost empty. The Australian soldier snored. A button tinkled, in communication with the driver far away at the front; the doors rolled shut. It was still a good distance to Camden Town.

Miles didn't notice. He was again in the upstairs room at Beltring's Restaurant, watching Barbara Morell as she faced Professor Rigaud across the dinner-table: watching the expression of her eyes, hearing that curious exclamation under her breath – incredulity or contempt – dismissing as of no importance the statement that Howard Brooke had cursed Fay Seton aloud in the Crédit Lyonnais Bank.

Miles was fitting every word, every gesture, into a pattern that hitherto had baffled him.

'Professor Rigaud,' continued Barbara, 'is very observant at seeing and describing the outside of things. But he never once realizes, he really doesn't, what's *inside*. I could have wept when he said jokingly that he was a blind bat and owl. Because in a sense that's perfectly true.

'For a whole summer Professor Rigaud stood at Harry Brooke's shoulder. He preached at Harry; he moulded him, he influenced him. Yet he never guessed the truth. Harry, for all his athletic skill and his good looks – and,' said Barbara with contempt, 'they must have been rather pretty-boy good looks – was simply a cold-hearted fish determined to get his own way.'

(Cold-hearted. Cold-hearted. Where had Miles heard that same term before?)

Barbara bit her lip.

'You remember,' she said, 'that Harry's heart was set on becoming a painter?'

'Yes. I remember.'

'And he would argue with his parents about it? And then, as Professor Rigaud described it, he would hit a tennis-ball like a streak or go out on the lawn and sit with a "white-faced brooding swearing look"?'

'I remember that too.'

'Harry knew it was the one thing on earth his parents would never consent to. They really did idolize him, but just because they idolized him they'd never consent. And he wasn't — wasn't man enough to leave a lot of money and strike out for himself. I'm sorry to talk like this,' Barbara added helplessly, 'but it's true. So Harry, long before Fay Seton came there, set about scheming in his horrible little mind for a way to *compel* them to consent.

'Then Fay arrived there to be his father's secretary, and he did see a way at last.

'I — I've never met the woman,' Barbara confessed broodingly. 'I can only judge her through letters. I may be all wrong. But I see her as passive and good-natured; *really* inexperienced; a bit of a romantic, and without much sense of humour.

'And Harry Brooke thought of a way. First he would pretend to fall in love with Fay ...'

'Pretend to fall in love with her?'

'Yes.'

Dimly Miles began to see the design take form. And yet it was inevitable. As inevitable as ...

'Tottenham Court Road!'

'Stop a bit,' Miles muttered. 'The old proverb says that there are two things which will be believed about any man, and one of them is that he has taken to drink. We might add that there are two things which will be believed about any woman, and both of them are ...'

'Both of them,' admitted Barbara, 'are that she has a horribly bad character' — the colour went up in her face — 'and probably carries on with every man in the district. The more quiet and unobtrusive she is, especially if she won't look you straight in the eye or enthuse over a lot of silly games like golf or tennis, then the more people are convinced there must be something in it.

'Harry's scheme was as cold-blooded as that. He would write his father a lot of vilely phrased anonymous letters about her ...'

'Anonymous letters!' said Miles.

'He would start a whispering campaign against her, connecting her name with Jean This and Jacques That. His parents – they weren't too keen already about his marrying anyone – would get alarmed at the scandal and beg him to break it off.

He'd already prepared the way by inventing a story, absolutely false, that she'd refused him the first time he proposed marriage with the hint that there was some terrible secret reason why she couldn't marry him. He told that tale to Professor Rigaud, and poor old Professor Rigaud retailed it to us. Do you recall that?'

Miles nodded.

'I also recall,' he said, 'that when *I* mentioned the same story to her last night, she ...'

'She – what?'

'Never mind! Go on!'

'So the scandal would gather, and Harry's parents would beg him to break off the marriage. Harry would only look noble and refuse. The more he refused, the more frantic they would be. Finally he would be crushed, practically in tears, and he would say: "All right, I'll give her up. But if I do consent to give her up, will you send me to Paris for two years to study painting so that I can forget her?" '

'Would they have agreed *then*? Don't we all know what families are? Of course they would have! They'd have seized at it in blessed relief.

'Only,' added Barbara, 'Harry's little plan didn't work out quite like that, you see.

'The anonymous letters horribly worried his father, who wouldn't even so much as mention them to his mother. But Harry's whispering campaign in the district almost failed completely. You know that French shrug of the shoulder, and the *"Et alors?"* which just about corresponds to, "So what?" They were busy people; they had crops to harvest; such things harmed no one if they didn't interfere with work; so what?'

Barbara began to laugh hysterically, but she checked herself.

'It was Professor Rigaud, always preaching to Harry about crime and the occult – he told us so himself – who in all innocence put Harry on to the thing these people really did fear. The thing that *would* make them talk and even scream. It's silly and it's horrible and of course it worked straight away. Harry deliberately bribed that sixteen-year-old boy to counterfeit marks in his own throat and start a story about a vampire ...

'You do see now, don't you?'

'*Goodge Street!*'

'Harry knew, of course, that his father wouldn't believe any nonsense about vampires. Harry didn't want his father to believe that. What Mr Brooke would hear, what he couldn't help hearing in every corner round Chartres, was a story about his son's fiancée visiting Pierre Fresnac so often at night, and ... and all the rest of it. That would be enough. That would be more than enough.'

Miles Hammond shivered.

Clank-thud went the train, roaring on in its fusty tunnel. Lights jolted on metal and upholstery. In Barbara's story Miles could see tragedy coming as clearly as though he did not already know of its existence.

'I don't question what you tell me,' he said, and he took a key-ring out of his pocket and twisted it fiercely as though he wanted to tear it in two. 'But how do you know these details?'

'Harry wrote them all to my brother!' cried Barbara.

She was silent for a moment.

'Jim's a painter, you see. Harry admired him tremendously. Harry thought – honestly thought! – that Jim as a man of the world would approve of his scheme to get away from a stuffy family atmosphere and call him no end of a clever fellow for thinking this up.'

'Did you know all about it at the time?'

Barbara opened her eyes wide.

'Good heavens, no! That was six years ago. I was only twenty at the time. I remember Jim did keep getting letters from France that worried him, but he never made any remark about it. Then ...'

'Go on!'

She swallowed hard.

'About the middle of August in that year, I remember Jim with his beard suddenly getting up from the breakfast table with a letter in his hand and saying, "My God, the old man's been murdered." He referred once or twice to the Brooke case, and tried to find out all he could from anything that was published in the English newspapers. But afterwards you couldn't get him to say a word about it.

'Then the war. Jim was reported dead in forty-two; we believed he was dead. I – I went through his papers. I came across this awful story spread out from letter to letter. Of course there wasn't anything I could do. There wasn't much I could even *learn*, except a few scanty things in the back files of the papers: that Mr Brooke had been stabbed and the police rather thought Miss Fay Seton had killed him.

'It was only in this last week … Things never do come singly, do they? They always heap up on you all at once!'

'Yes. I can testify to that.'

'*Warren Street!*'

'A press photograph came into the office, showing three Englishwomen who were returning from France, and one of them was, "Miss Fay Seton, whose peacetime profession is that of librarian". And a man at the office happened to tell me all about the famous Murder Club, and said that the speaker on Friday night was to be Professor Rigaud, giving an eyewitness account of the Brooke case.'

There were tears in Barbara's eyes now.

'Professor Rigaud loathes journalists. He wouldn't ever before speak at the Murder Club, even, because he was afraid they'd bring in the press. I couldn't go to him in private unless I produced my bundle of letters to explain why I was interested; and I *couldn't* – do you understand that? – I *couldn't* have Jim's name mixed up in this if something dreadful came out of it. So I …'

'You tried to get Rigaud to yourself at Beltring's?'

'Yes.'

She nodded quickly, and then stared out of the window.

'When you mentioned that you were looking for a librarian, it did occur to me, "Oh, Lord! Suppose …?" You know what I mean?'

'Yes.' Miles nodded. 'I follow you.'

'You were so fascinated by that coloured photograph, so much under its spell, that I thought to myself, "Suppose I confide him? If he wants to find a librarian, suppose I ask him to find Fay Seton and tell her there's someone who *knows* she's been the victim of a filthy frame-up? It's possible he'll meet her in any case; but suppose I ask him to find her?"'

'And why didn't you confide in me?'

Barbara's fingers twisted round her handbag.

'Oh, I don't know.' She shook her head rapidly. 'As I said to you at the time, it was only a silly idea of mine. And maybe I resented it, a little, that you were so obviously smitten.'

'But, look here! –'

Barbara flung this away and rushed on.

'But the main thing was: what could you or I actually *do* for her? Apparently they didn't believe she was guilty of murder, and that was the main thing. She'd been the victim of enough foul lying stories to poison anyone's life, but you can't un-ruin a reputation. Even if I weren't such a coward, how could I help? I told you, the last thing I said before I jumped out of that taxi, I don't see how I can be of any use now!'

'The letters don't contain any information about the murder of Mr Brooke, then?'

'No! Look here!'

Winking to keep back tears, her face flushed and her ash-blonde head bent forward, Barbara fumbled inside the hand-bag. She held out four folded sheets of notepaper closely written.

'This,' she said, 'is the last letter Harry Brooke ever wrote to Jim. He was writing it on the afternoon of the murder. First it goes on – gloating! – over the success of his scheme to blacken Fay and get what he wanted. Then it breaks off suddenly. Look at the end bit!'

'Euston!'

Miles dropped the key-ring back in his pocket and took the letter. The end, done in a violent agitated scrawl for an afterthought, was headed, '6.45 p.m.' Its words danced in front of Miles's eyes as the train quivered and roared.

JIM, something terrible has just happened. Somebody's killed Dad. Rigaud and I left him on the tower, and somebody went up and stabbed him. Must get this in the post quickly to ask you for God's sake, old man, don't ever tell anybody what I've been writing to you. If Fay went scatty and killed the old boy because he tried to buy her off, I won't want anybody to know I've been putting out reports about her. It wouldn't look right and besides I didn't want anything like this to happen. Please, old man. Yours in haste, H. B.

So much raw, unpleasant human nature cried out of that letter, Miles thought, that it was as though he could see the man writing it.

Miles stared straight ahead, lost now to everything.

Rage against Harry Brooke clouded his mind; it maddened him and weakened him. To think he never suspected anything in the character of Harry Brooke ... and yet, obscurely, hadn't he? Professor Rigaud had been wrong in estimating this pleasant young man's motives. Yet Rigaud

133

had drawn, sharply drawn, a picture of nerves and instability. Miles himself had once used the word neurotic to describe him.

Harry Brooke had coolly and deliberately, to get his own way, invented the whole damned ...

But, if Miles had ever doubted whether he himself was in love with Fay Seton, he doubted no longer.

The thought of Fay, completely innocent, sick with bewilderment and fright, was one that neither the heart nor the imagination could resist. He cursed himself for ever having doubts of any kind about her. He had been seeing everything through distorted spectacles; he had been wondering, almost with a sense of repulsion mixed with the attraction he felt for her, what power of evil *might* lie behind the blue eyes. And yet all the time ...

'She isn't guilty,' Miles said. 'She isn't guilty of *anything*.'

'That's right'

'I tell you what Fay feels about herself. And don't think I'm making exaggerated or melodramatic statements when I say so. She feels that she's damned.'

'Why do you think that?'

'I don't think it. I know it.' Intense conviction seized him. That's what was in her whole behaviour last night. Rightly or wrongly, she feels that she can't get away from something, and that she's damned, I don't pretend to explain what's been going on, but I know that much.

'What's more, she's in danger. Something would happen, Dr Fell said, if she tried to carry out her plans. That's why he said I must catch her at any cost and not lose touch with her for a moment. He said it was a matter of life and death. And, so help me, that's what I'm going to do! We owe her that much, after all she's been through. The very split-second we get out of this train ...'

Miles stopped.

Some inner ear, some faint consciousness still alert, had just rung a warning. It warned him that, for the first time since he entered this Underground train, the train had come to a stop before he remembered hearing it stop.

Then, with the bright image of the car leaping out at him, he heard a sound which galvanized him. It was the soft, rolling rumble of the doors as they started to close.

'*Miles!*' cried Barbara – and woke up at exactly the same moment.

The doors closed with a soft bump. The guard's bell-push tinkled Miles, springing up to stare out of the window as the train glided on again, saw the words of the station-sign glaring out at him with white letters on a blue ground, and the words were 'Camden Town'.

He was afterwards told that he shouted something to the guard, but he did not realize this at the time. He only remembered plunging frantically at the doors, wrenching to get his fingers into the joining and tear them open. Someone said, 'Take it easy, mate!' The Australian soldier woke up. The policeman, interested, got to his feet.

It was no good.

As the train whipped past the platform, gathering speed, Miles stood with his face against the glass of the doors.

Half a dozen persons straggled towards the way out. Dingy overhead lights swung with the wind which billowed through this stale-smelling cavern. He clearly saw Fay — in an open tweed coat and black beret, with the same blank, miserable, tortured look on her face — walking towards the way out as the train bore him past into the tunnel.

CHAPTER 16

UNDER a very dark sky, drizzling, the rain splashed into Bolsover Place, Camden Town.

Off the broad stretch of Camden High Street at no great distance from the Underground station, even off the narrow dinginess of Bolsover Street, this was a cul-de-sac seen under a brick arch.

Its surface was of uneven paving-stones now black with rain. Straight ahead were two blitzed houses, looking like ordinary houses until you noticed the state of the windows. On the right was a smallish factory or warehouse bearing the legend, 'J. Mings & Co. Ltd., Artificial Dentures'. On the left lay first a small one-story front, boarded up, whose sign said that it had once served suppers. Next to this were two houses, brick-built of that indeterminate colour between grey and brown, with some glass in their windows and an air not entirely of decay.

Nothing stirred there, not even a stray cat. Miles, heedless of the fact that the rain was soaking him through, gripped Barbara's arm.

'It's all right,' Barbara muttered, moving her shoulders under the mackintosh, and holding her umbrella crookedly. 'We haven't lost ten minutes.'

'No. But we have lost that time.'

Miles knew that she was frightened now. On the way back, where at least they had been able to step instantly into a train going in the other direction at Chalk Farm, he had been pouring out the story of last night's events. It was plain that Barbara no more knew what to make of it than he did; but she was afraid.

'Number Five,' said Miles. 'Number Five.'

It was the last house down on the left, at right angles with the two blitzed houses. Miles noticed something else as he led Barbara over the uneven paving-stones. In a large grimy display-window on the premises of J. Mings & Co. Ltd. was a very large set of artificial teeth.

As an advertising display they might have been considered gruesome or comic, but had they been in a better state of repair they could not have failed to attract attention. Made of metal painted in naturalistic colours as to teeth and gums, loomed there close-shut and disembodied, a giant's teeth in the faint grey light. Miles didn't like them. He felt their presence behind him as he went up to the blistered door of Number Five, on which there was a knocker.

But his hand never reached the knocker.

Instantly a woman's head appeared at the open ground-floor window of the house next door, moving aside what once might have been a lace curtain. She was a middle-aged woman who looked at the newcomers avidly; not at all in suspicion, but with pervading curiosity.

'Miss Fay Seton?' said Miles.

The woman turned round towards the room behind her, evidently to kick at something, before she replied. Then she nodded towards Number Five.

'First-floor-up-left-front.'

'I – er – just walk in?'

''Ow else?'

'I see. Thank you.'

The woman gravely inclined her head in acknowledgement of this, and just as gravely withdrew. Miles turned the knob of the door and opened it. He motioned Barbara ahead of him into a passage with a staircase. The stale mildewy air of the passage went over them in a wave. When Miles closed the door it was so dark that they could barely make out the outline of the stairs. Distantly he could hear rain pattering on a sky-light.

'I don't like it.' Barbara spoke under her breath. 'Why ever does she want to live in a place like this?'

'You know what it is in London nowadays. You can't get anything anywhere for love or money.'

'But why did she keep the room after she'd gone to Greywood?'

Miles wondered that himself. He didn't like the place either. He wanted to shout Fay's name, to be assured she was here after all.

'First-floor-up-left-front,' said Miles. 'Mind the stairs!'

It was a steep staircase, which turned round a steep bend into a narrow passage leading towards the front of the house. At the end of this passage was a window, one of its panes mended with cardboard, which looked down into Bolsover Place. It admitted enough light to show them a closed door on each side of the passage. A few seconds later, when Miles had started for the left-hand door, it admitted still more light as well.

A fairly bright glow sprang up outside that front window, half kindling the little passage with its black linoleum. Miles, his heart in his mouth, had just raised a hand to knock at the left-hand door when the light startled him like an interruption. It startled Barbara too; he heard her heel scrape on the linoleum. Both of them glanced out of the window.

The teeth were moving.

Across the way, in the premises of Messrs J. Mings & Co., a bored caretaker was amusing a Sunday afternoon by switching on a light in the grimy window and setting in motion the electric mechanism which controlled the set of teeth.

Very slowly they opened, very slowly they closed: endlessly opening and closing to catch your eye. Grimy and evil-looking in disuse, sometimes sticking a little, the pink gums and partly darkened teeth gaped wide and shut again. They had an effect at once theatrical and horribly real. They were soundless and inhuman. Through the window, blurred with rain, they reared a shadow of themselves – slowly, very slowly opening and closing – on the wall of the passage.

Barbara said softly:

Of all the …!'

'Sh–h!'

Miles could not have said why he called for silence; to him-self he seemed occupied with the reflexion that the display opposite was damned poor advertising and not very funny. He lifted his hand again, and knocked at the door.

'Yes?' called a calm voice, after a very slight pause.

It was Fay's voice. She was all right.

Miles stood motionless for a second or two, watching out of the corner of his eye that blurred shadow moving on the wall, before he turned the knob. The door was not locked. He opened it.

Fay Seton, still in the tweed coat over her dove-grey dress, stood in front of a chest of drawers looking round inquiringly. Her expression was placid, not even very interested, until she saw who the newcomer was. Then she gave a smothered cry.

138

He could see every detail of the room clearly, since the curtains were drawn and the light was burning. A dim bulb hanging over the chest of drawers showed him the rather broken-down bedroom furniture, the discoloured wall-paper, the frayed carpet. A heavy tin box, painted black and half as big as a trunk, had been hastily drawn out from under the bed; its lid was not quite shut, and a small padlock hung open from the hasp.

Fay's voice went shrilling up.

'What are you doing here?'

'I followed you! I was told to follow you I You're in danger! There's –'

Miles took two steps into the room.

'I'm afraid you startled me,' said Fay, controlling herself. One hand went under her heart, a gesture he had seen her make before. She gave a little laugh. 'I didn't expect –! After all –!' Then, quickly: 'Who's that with you?'

'This is Miss Morell. The sister of – well, of Jim Morell. She wants very much to meet you. She ...'

Then Miles saw what was on top of the chest of drawers, and everything in existence seemed to stop.

First he saw an old brief-case of black leather, dried and dusty and cracked, bulging from something inside; its straps were loosened, and the flap was partly opened. But an old brief-case may belong to anyone. Beside it lay a large, flat packet of banknotes, the topmost one showing the denomination of twenty pounds. The colour of the banknotes might once have been white; they had now a dry blurred, smeary appearance, and were stained in dry patches of rust-brown.

Fay's pale face was paler yet as she saw the direction of his glance. It seemed very difficult for her to draw breath.

'Yes,' she told him. 'Those are bloodstains. Mr Brooke's blood, you see, got on them when they ...'

'For the love of God, Fay!'

'I'm not needed here,' Barbara's voice spoke frantically, but not loudly. 'I didn't really want to come. But Miles ...'

'Please do come in,' Fay said in her gentle voice, while the blue eyes kept roving and roving as though she scarcely saw him 'And close the door.'

Yet she was not calm. This apparent case was the effect of sheer despair, or of some emotion akin to it. Miles's head was spinning. He carefully

139

closed the door, to get even a few seconds in which to think. Gently he put his hand on Barbara's shoulder, for Barbara was on the point of running out of the room. He looked round the bedroom, feeling its close air stifle him.

Then he found his voice.

'But you can't be guilty after all!' he said with desperate reasonableness. It seemed vitally important to convince Fay, logically, that she couldn't be guilty. 'I tell you, it's impossible! It's ... Listen!'

'Yes?' said Fay.

Beside the chest of drawers there was an old armchair with patches of its back and arms frayed to threads. Fay sank down into it, her shoulders drooping. Though her expression hardly changed, the tears welled out of her eyes and ran unheeded down her cheeks. He had never seen her cry before, and this was worse than anything else.

'We know now,' said Miles, feeling numb, 'that you weren't guilty of anything at all. I've, heard ... I've just heard, I tell you! ... that all those accusations against you were a fake deliberately trumped up by Harry Brooke –'

Fay raised her head quickly.

'So you know that,' she said.

'What's more' – he suddenly realized something else, and stood back and pointed his finger at her– 'you knew it too! You knew they were trumped up by Harry Brooke! You've known it all along!'

It was more than the flash of illumination which sometimes comes from strung-up emotion: it was a fitting-together of facts.

'*That's* why, last night, you started to laugh in that crazy way when I asked you whether you and Harry Brooke had got married after all. *That's* why you brought up the subject of anonymous letters against you, though Rigaud had never mentioned any. *That's* why you talked about Jim Morell, the great friend Harry wrote to every week; though Rigaud never heard of him either. – You've known all along! Haven't you?'

'Yes. I've known all along.'

It was little more than a whisper. The tears still welled out of her eyes, and her lips had begun to shake as well.

'Are you insane, Fay? Have you gone completely off your head? Why didn't you ever speak out and say so?'

'Because ... oh, God, what difference does it make now?'

'What difference does it make?' Miles swallowed hard. 'With this damned thing – !' He strode over to the chest of drawers and picked up the packet of banknotes, feeling repulsion in the touch of them. 'There are three more packets in the brief-case, I suppose?'

'Yes,' said Fay. 'Three more. I only stole them. I didn't spend them.'

'Come to think of it, what else is in that brief-case? What makes it bulge like that?'

'Don't touch that brief-case! Please!'

'All right. I've got no right to badger you like this. I know that. I'm only doing it because – because it's necessary. But you ask what difference it makes? When for nearly six years the police have been trying to find out what happened to this case and the money inside it?'

The footsteps outside in the passage, which they had been too preoccupied to hear until now, approached the door with a casual air. But the tap on the door, though not loud, had a peremptory sound which could not be disregarded.

It was Miles who spoke; neither of the two women were capable of it. *'Who's there?'*

'I'm a police-officer,' said the voice outside, with that same combination of the casual and the peremptory. 'Mind if I come in?'

Miles's hand, still holding the banknotes, moved as fast as a striking snake when he thrust those notes into his pocket. It was, he thought to himself, just as well. For the person outside did not wait for an invitation.

Framed in the doorway, as he swung the door wide open, stood a tall square-shouldered man in a raincoat and a bowler hat. All of them, perhaps, had been expecting a uniform; to Miles at least this was rather more ominous. There was something vaguely familiar about the newcomer's face: the close-cropped moustache turning grey, the square jaw, with muscles conspicuous at the corners, the suggestion of the military.

He stood looking from one to the other of the persons in front of him, his hand on the knob; and, in the passage behind him, the light reared and lowered a shadow of the opening and closing of teeth.

Twice those teeth opened and closed before the newcomer cleared his throat.

'Miss Fay Seton?'

141

Fay rose to her feet, turning out her wrist by way of reply. Superbly graceful, unconscious of the tear-stains on her face; drained of violence, past caring.

'My name is Hadley,' the stranger announced. 'Superintendent Hadley. Metropolitan C.I.D.'

And now Miles realized why this face was vaguely familiar. Miles had moved over to the side of Barbara Morell. It was Barbara who spoke.

'I interviewed you once,' said Barbara shakily, 'for the *Morning Record*. You talked a good deal, but you wouldn't give me permission to print much of it.'

'Right,' agreed Hadley, and looked at her. 'You're Miss Morell, of course.' He looked thoughtfully at Miles. 'And you must be Mr Hammond. You seem to have got yourself pretty thoroughly soaking wet.'

'It wasn't raining when I left home.'

'Always wise,' said Hadley, shaking his head, 'to take a raincoat when you go out in these days. I could lend you mine, only I'm afraid I'm going to need it myself.'

The studiedly social air of all this, with its element of deadly danger and tension underneath, couldn't go on for long. Miles broke it.

'Look here, Superintendent!' he burst out. 'You didn't come here to talk about the weather. The main thing is – you're a friend of Dr Fell.'

'That's right,' agreed Hadley. He came in, removed his hat, and closed the door.

'But Dr Fell said the police weren't going to be brought into this!'

'Into what?' Hadley asked politely, with a slight smile.

'Into anything!'

'Well, that depends on what you mean,' said Hadley.

His eyes wandered round the room: at Fay's handbag and black beret on the bed, at the big dusty tin box drawn out from under the bed, at the drawn curtains on the two little windows. His gaze rested, without apparent curiosity, on the brief-case lying there conspicuously under the light over the chest of drawers.

Miles, his right hand tightly clutching the sheaf of banknotes in his pocket, watched him as you might watch a tame tiger.

The fact is,' Hadley pursued easily, 'I've had a very long phone conversation with the maestro ...'

'With Dr Fell?'

'Yes. And a good deal of it wasn't quite clear. But it seems, Mr Hammond, your sister had a very bad and dangerous scare last night.'

Fay Seton moved round the big tin box and picked up her handbag from the bed. She went to the chest of drawers, tilted the mirror above it so as better to catch the light, and set about with handkerchief and powder to remove the traces of tears. Her eyes in the mirror were blank, like blue marbles; but her elbow quivered frantically.

Miles clutched the banknotes.

'Dr Fell told you what happened at Greywood?' he asked.

'Yes.'

'So the police have to be called in?'

'Oh, no. Not unless we're asked. And in any case you'd approach the police of the district; not London. No,' said Hadley in a leisurely way, 'what Fell really wanted was to know the name of a certain test.'

'Certain test?'

'A scientific test to determine ... well, what he wanted to determine. And whether I could tell him anyone who knew how to carry it out. He said he couldn't remember the name of the test, or anything much about it except that you used melted paraffin.' Hadley smiled slightly. 'He meant the Gonzalez test, of course.'

Then Superintendent Hadley moved forward.

'Dr Fell also asked me,' he went on, 'whether we had any means of finding out Miss Seton's address, in case you? – he looked at Miles – 'in case you by any chance missed her. I said naturally we had, since she must have taken out an identity card.' Hadley paused. 'By the way, Miss Seton, have you got your identity card?'

The reflexion of Fay's eyes regarded him in the mirror. She had almost finished making up; her hands were steady.

'Yes,' answered Fay.

'As a matter of form, may I see it?'

Fay took the card out of her handbag, gave it to him without comment, and turned back to the mirror. For some reason the look of wild strain was returning to her eyes as she picked up the powder compact again.

(What, thought Miles, is going on under all this?)

'I notice, Miss Seton, that this doesn't give any last address.'

'No. I've been living for the past six years in France.'

'So I understand. You've got a French identity card, of course?'

'I'm afraid not. I lost it.'

'What was your means of employment in France, Miss Seton?'

'I had no fixed means of employment.'

'Is that so?' Hadley's dark eyebrows went up, in contrast to the polish of his steel-grey hair. 'Must have been a bit difficult to get rations there, wasn't it?'

'I had no – fixed means of employment.'

'But I understand you've trained professionally both as librarian and as secretary?'

'Yes. That's true.'

'In fact, come to think of it, you were employed as secretary by a Mr Howard Brooke before his death in nineteen thirty-nine. Now there,' observed Hadley, as though suddenly struck by a new idea, 'there's a case where we *should* be glad of a bit of help, to pass on to our French colleagues.'

(Watch the immense cat approach! Watch its devious courses!)

'But I was forgetting,' said Hadley, dismissing this so instantly that all three of his listeners jumped, 'I was forgetting the real reason why I came here!'

'The real reason why you came here?'

'Yes, Miss Seton. Er – your identity card. Don't you want it back?'

'Thank you.'

Fay was compelled to turn round. She took the card from him; and then, in her grey dress and long damp tweed coat, she stood with her back to the chest of drawers. Her body now hid the brief-case, which seemed to shout to heaven. If Miles Hammond had been a thief with every seam of his pockets lined with stolen property, he could not have felt guiltier.

'Dr Fell asked me,' pursued Hadley, 'in a strictly unofficial way, to keep an eye on you. It seems that you ran away from him ...'

'I don't think I quite understand. I didn't run away.'

'With the intention of coming back again, of course! That's understood!'

Fay's eyes closed spasmodically, and opened again.

'Just before then, Miss Seton, Dr Fell was going to ask you something very important.'

'Oh?'

144

'He instructed me to tell you that he hadn't put the question last night,' continued Hadley, 'because he didn't guess then what he guesses at the present time. But he wants very much to have an answer to that question.' Hadley's tone changed only slightly; it was still polite, still casually inquiring; but the whole room seemed to grow warmer as he added:

'May I ask that question now?'

CHAPTER 17

THE hanging light over the chest of drawers shone down on Fay's hair, and brought out the warmth of it in contrast to the apparent coldness of her face and body.

'A question about …?' Her hand – Miles could have shouted warning – instinctively moved towards the brief-case behind her.

'A question,' said Hadley, 'in connexion with the frightening of Miss Marion Hammond last night.' (Fay's hand darted back again; she straightened up.)

'And I'm afraid,' continued Hadley, 'I must preface it by getting the situation clear. Don't mind my notebook, Miss Seton! It's not official. I've only put down what Fell asked me to put down.' His eyes strayed to the identity card in her hand. 'Or do you refuse to answer questions, Miss Seton?'

'Do I ever – refuse?'

'Thank you. Now then: with regard to the frightening of Miss Marion Hammond …'

'*I* didn't do it!'

'You may not be always conscious,' said Hadley, 'of what you do or the effect it has.'

Hadley's voice remained quiet when he said this.

'However!' he added quickly, and there was a penetrating quality about his gaze which made the eyes seem to grow larger. 'We're not talking now about your conscious guilt or innocence in anything. I'm only trying (What shall I say?) to get this picture clear. As I understand it, you were the last person *known* to be with Marion Hammond before she was – frightened?'

Fay gave a quick, hypnotized nod.

'You left her alone in the bedroom in good health and spirits, at … about what time?'

'About midnight. I told Dr Fell so.'

'Ah, yes. So you did. – Had Miss Hammond undressed at this time?'

'Yes. She was in blue silk pyjamas. Sitting in a chair by the bedside table.'

'Now, Miss Seton! Considerably later, a shot was fired in Miss Hammond's room. Do you remember what time that was?'

'No. I'm afraid I haven't the remotest idea.'

Hadley swung round to Miles.

'Can you help us, Mr Hammond? Everyone, including Dr Fell himself, seems vague about times.'

'I can't help you,' answered Miles, 'except in this one thing.' He paused, with the scene coming back to him. 'After the shot, I ran up to Marion's bedroom. Professor Rigaud joined me, and a few minutes later Dr Fell. Professor Rigaud asked me to go downstairs, to sterilize a hypodermic and do some other things in the kitchen. When I got to the kitchen, the time was twenty minutes to two. There's a big clock on the wall, and I remember noticing it.'

Hadley nodded. 'So the time of the shot, roughly, was round about half-past one or a little later?'

'Yes. I should think so.'

'You agree with that, Miss Seton?'

'I'm afraid' – Fay lifted her shoulders – 'I simply don't remember. I never paid any attention to the time.'

'But you did *hear* this shot?'

'Oh, yes. I was dozing.'

'And afterwards, I understand, you slipped upstairs and looked in at the bedroom door? – Excuse me, Miss Seton? I'm afraid I didn't quite catch that answer?'

'I said: yes.' Fay's lips shaped themselves with rounded distinctness. Something of last night's atmosphere returned to her, of heightened breathing and expression of eye.

'Your room is on the ground floor?'

'Yes.'

'When you heard this shot in the middle of the night, what made you think the noise came from upstairs? And from that room in particular?'

'Well! Soon after the shot I heard people running in the upstairs hall. Every sound carries at night.' For the first time Fay seemed honestly puzzled. 'So I wondered what was wrong. I got up and put on a wrap and slippers, and lighted a lamp, and went upstairs. The door of Miss Hammond's room was wide open, and there was a light inside. So I went there and peeped in.'

'What did you see?'

Fay moistened her lips.

'I saw Miss Hammond lying half up in bed, holding a gun. I saw a man named Professor Rigaud – I'd known him before – standing on the far side of the bed. I saw,' she hesitated, 'Mr Miles Hammond. I heard Professor Rigaud say this was shock, and that Miss Hammond wasn't dead.'

'But you didn't go in? Or call out to them?'

'No!'

'What happened then?'

'I heard someone who sounded awfully heavy and clumsy start to walk up the front stairs at the other end of the hall,' answered Fay. 'I know now it must have been Dr Fell on his way to the bedroom. I turned out the lamp I was carrying, and ran down the back stairs. He didn't see me.'

'What was it that upset you, Miss Seton?'

'Upset me?'

'When you looked into that room,' Hadley told her with careful slowness, 'you saw something that upset you. What was it?'

'I don't understand!'

'Miss Seton,' explained Hadley, putting away the notebook he had taken out of his inside breast pocket, 'I've had to make all these elaborate inquiries to ask you just one question. You saw something, and it upset you so much that later you apologized to Mr Hammond in Dr Fell's presence for making what you called a disgraceful exhibition of yourself. You weren't frightened; the feeling wasn't in the least connected with fear. What upset you?'

Fay whirled round towards Miles. 'Did you tell Dr Fell?'

And Miles stared at her. 'Tell him what?'

'What I said to you last night,' Fay retorted, her fingers twitching together, 'when we were there in the kitchen and I – I wasn't quite myself.'

'I didn't tell Dr Fell anything,' Miles snapped, with a violence he could not understand. 'And in any case what difference does it make?'

Miles took a step or two away from her. He bumped into Barbara, who also moved back. For a fraction of a second, as Barbara's head turned, he surprised on Barbara's face a look which completed his demoralization.

Barbara's eyes had been fixed steadily on Fay for some time. In her eyes, slowly growing, was an expression of wonder; and of something else which was not dislike, but very near dislike.

If Barbara turns against her too, Miles thought, we might as well throw up the brief for the defence and retire. But Barbara of all people couldn't be turning against Fay! And Miles still fought back.

'I shouldn't answer any questions,' he said. 'If Superintendent Hadley isn't here officially, he's got no blasted right to come barging in and hint that there'll be sinister consequences if you don't answer. Upset! Anybody would have been upset after what happened last night.' He looked at Fay again. 'In any case, all you said to me was that you'd just seen something you hadn't noticed before, and ...'

'Ah!' breathed Hadley, and rapped his bowler hat against the palm of his left hand. 'Miss Seton had just seen something she hadn't noticed before! That's what we thought.'

Fay let out a cry.

'Why not tell us, Miss Seton?' suggested Hadley, in a tone of great persuasiveness. 'Why not make the full confession you intended to make? If it comes to that, why not hand over the brief-case' – casually he pointed in the direction of it – 'and the two thousand pounds and the other things as well? Why not ...'

That was the point at which the light over the chest of drawers went out.

Nobody was prepared for danger. Nobody was alert. Everything was concentrated in that little space where Fay Seton faced Hadley and Miles and Barbara.

And, though nobody had touched the electric switch by the door, the light went out. With heavy black-out curtains drawn on the little windows, a weight of darkness descended on them like a hood over the face, blotting out rational thoughts as it blotted out images. There *was* a faint flicker of light from the passage outside as the door swiftly opened. And something rushed at them out of the passage.

Fay Seton screamed.

They heard the noise of it go piercing up. They heard a cry like, 'Don't, don't, don't!' and a crashing sound as of someone falling over the big tin box in the middle of the floor. In the few seconds when Miles had forgotten a certain malignant influence, that influence had caught up with them. He lunged out in the darkness, and felt somebody's shoulder

149

slip past him. The door to the passage banged. Somewhere there were running footsteps. Miles heard a rattle of rings as someone – it was Barbara – drew back the curtain off one window.

Grey rain-filtered light entered from Bolsover Place, along with the light from the moving teeth across the way. Superintendent Hadley ran to the window, flung it up, and blew a police-whistle.

Fay Seton, unhurt, had been thrown back against the bed. She clutched at the counterpane to save herself from falling, and dragged it with her as she sank to her knees.

'Fay! Are you all right?'

Fay hardly heard him. She whipped round, her eyes going instinctively towards the top of the chest of drawers.

'Are you all right?'

'It's gone,' said Fay in a choked voice. 'It's gone. It's gone.'

For the brief-case was no longer there. Ahead of anyone else, ahead of either Miles or Hadley, Fay jumped over the heavy tin box and ran towards the door. She ran with a headlong madness and an agility which carried her half-way down the passage, in the direction of the stairs, before Miles went racing after her.

And even the brief-case could not stop that crazy flight.

For Miles found the brief-case lying discarded on the floor of the passage, dimly seen in the light of the opening and shutting teeth. Fay must have run straight across it; she could not even have noticed it. Miles shouted to her as she gained the top of the steep stairs leading down to the ground floor. He snatched up the brief-case, holding it upside down as though to gain her eye by pantomime. From inside the gaping leather there fell out three white packets of banknotes like the other in the bedroom. These landed on the floor, along with a pouring of some dry gritty substance like mortar-dust. There was nothing else in the brief-case.

Miles flung himself at the head of the stairs.

'It's here, I tell you! It's not gone! It's been dropped! It's here!'

Did she hear him? He could not be sure. But, at least briefly, she paused and looked up.

Fay was about half-way down the stairs, steep stairs covered with ragged linoleum. The front door of the house stood wide open, so that light from the window across the street filtered weirdly up the staircase.

Miles, leaning perilously over the balustrade along the passage and holding up the brief-case, was looking down into her face as she raised it.

'Don't you understand?' he shouted. 'There's no need to run like that! Here *is* the brief-case! It's ...'

Now he could have sworn she hadn't heard. Fay's left hand rested lightly on the stair-rail. Her neck was arched, the red hair thrown back as she looked up. On her face was a faintly wondering look. Her heightened colour, even the glitter of her eyes, seemed to fade into a deathly bluish pallor which put a gentle expression on her mouth and then took away all expression at all.

Fay's legs gave way at the knees. Softly, like a dress falling from a hook, so bonelessly that it could not even have caused a bruise, she fell sideways and rolled over and over to the foot of the stairs. Yet the crash of the fall, in contrast to that terrifying limpness ...

Miles Hammond stood still.

The stifling, mildewy air of the passage had got into his lungs like the sudden suspicion in his mind. He seemed to have been breathing that air for a very long time, with the bloodstained banknotes in his pocket and the cracked brief-case in his hand.

Out of the corner of his eye Miles saw Barbara come up beside him and look down over the railing. Superintendent Hadley, muttering something under his breath, bounded past them and went downstairs with long strides which shook and thumped on every tread. He jumped over the figure lying at the foot of the stairs with its cheek against the dirt of the floor. Hadley went down on one knee to examine that figure. Presently he raised his head to look up at them. His voice sounded hollowly up the stairs.

'Wasn't this woman supposed to have a weak heart?'

'Yes,' said Miles calmly. 'Yes. That's right.'

'We'd better ring for an ambulance,' the hollow voice replied. 'But she shouldn't have got worked up and run like that. I think it's finished her.'

Miles walked slowly downstairs.

His left hand rested on the balustrade where Fay's hand had rested. He dropped the brief-case as he walked. Across the street, seen now through an open front door, the ugly bodiless teeth very slowly opened and closed, opened and closed throughout all eternity, as he bent over Fay's body.

CHAPTER 18

It was half-past six o'clock on that same Sunday evening, though it might have been days later as regards the apparent passage of time, when Miles and Barbara sat in Fay Seton's bedroom up on the first floor.

The electric light was burning again over the chest of drawers. Barbara sat in the frayed armchair. Miles sat on the edge of the bed, beside Fay's black beret. He was looking down at the battered tin box when Barbara spoke.

'Shall we go out and see if there's a Lyons or an A.B.C. open on Sunday? Or a pub where they might have a sandwich?'

'No. Hadley told us to stay here.'

'How long has it been since you last had anything to eat?'

'One of the greatest gifts with which a woman can be endowed' – Miles tried to manage a smile, though he felt the smile stretch like a sick leer – 'is the gift of not mentioning the subject of food at inconvenient times.'

'Sorry,' said Barbara, and was silent for a long time. 'Fay *may* recover, you know.'

'Yes. She may recover.'

And then the silence went on for a very long time, while Barbara plucked at the edges of the chair-arms.

'Does this mean so very much to you, Miles?'

'That isn't the main point at all. I simply feel that this woman has been given the worst possible raw deal from life. That things ought to be put right somehow! That justice ought to be done! That ...'

He picked up Fay's black beret from the bed, and hastily put it down again.

'Anyway,' he added, 'what's the use?'

'In the short time you've known her,' said Barbara, evidently after another struggle to keep silent, 'did Fay Seton become as real as Agnes Sorel or Pamela Hoyt?'

'I beg your pardon? What's that?'

'At Beltring's,' answered Barbara without looking at him, 'you said a historian's work was to take distant people, dead and gone people, and bring them to life by thinking of them as real people. When you first heard Fay's story, you said she was no more real than Agnes Sorel or Pamela Hoyt.'

In an inconsequential way, still plucking at the edges of the chair-arm, Barbara added:

'Agnes Sorel I'd heard of, of course. But I never heard of Pamela Hoyt. I – looked her up in the encyclopaedia, but she wasn't there.'

'Pamela Hoyt was a Regency beauty, suspected of evil courses. A captivating character, too; I read quite a lot about her at one time. By the way: in Latin, what does *panes* mean beside the plural of bread? It couldn't have meant bread, from the context.'

It was Barbara's turn to blink at him in surprise.

'I'm afraid I'm not enough of a Latinist to know. Why do you ask?'

'Well, I had a dream.'

'A dream?'

'Yes.' Miles pondered this in the heavy, dully insistent way with which the mind will seize on trifles at a time of emotional disturbance. 'It was a passage in medieval Latin; you know the sort of thing: peculiar verb-endings and u's instead of v's.' He shook his head. 'All about something and *panes*; but all I can remember now is the *ut* clause at the end, that it would be most foolish to deny something.'

'I still don't understand.'

(Why wouldn't that infernally sickish feeling leave his chest?)

'Well, I dreamed I went into the library looking for a Latin dictionary. Pamela Hoyt and Fay Seton were both there, sitting on dusty mounds of books and assuring me my uncle hadn't got a Latin dictionary.' Miles started to laugh. 'Funny thing, too; I just remembered it. I don't know what Dr Freud would have made of that one.'

'*I* do,' said Barbara.

'Something sinister, I imagine. It would appear to be something sinister no matter what you dream.'

'No,' said Barbara slowly. 'Nothing like that.'

For some time she had been regarding Miles in the same hesitant, baffled, helpless way, the luminous whites of her eyes shining in sympathy.

Then Barbara sprang to her feet. Both windows had been opened to the drizzling afternoon, admitting clean damp air. At least, Miles reflected, they had shut off the advertising lights and that dental horror across the street. Barbara turned at the window.

'Poor woman!' Barbara said, and he knew she was not referring to a dead Pamela Hoyt. 'Poor, silly, romantic …!'

'Why do you call Fay silly and romantic?'

'She knew those anonymous letters, and all the rumours about her, were the work of Harry Brooke. But she never said so to anybody. I suppose,' Barbara shook her head slowly, 'she may still have been in love with him.'

'After *that*?'

'Of course.'

'I don't believe it!'

'It might have been that. We all – we all are capable of awfully funny things. Or,' Barbara shivered, 'there may have been some other reason for keeping silent, even after she knew Harry was dead. I don't know. The point is …'

'The point is,' said Miles, 'why is Hadley keeping us here? And what's going on?' He considered. 'Is it very far to this What's-its-name Hospital where they've taken her?'

'A goodish distance, yes. Were you thinking of going there?'

'Well, Hadley can't keep us here indefinitely for no apparent reason at all. We've got to get *some* kind of news.'

They received some kind of news. Professor Georges Antoine Rigaud – they heard his distinctive step long before they saw him – came slowly up the stairs, along the passage, and in at the open door.

Professor Rigaud seemed an older and even more troubled man than when he had voiced his theory about a vampire. Only a few drops of rain fell now, so that he was comparatively dry. His soft dark hat was jammed down all round his head. His patch of moustache worked with the movement of his mouth. He leaned heavily on the yellow sword-cane which acquired such evil colour in this dingy room.

'Mees Morell,' he said. His voice was husky. 'Mr Hammond. Now I will tell you something.'

He moved forward from the door.

'My friends, you are no doubt familiar with the great Musketeer romances of the elder Dumas. You will recall how the Musketeers went

154

to England. You will recall that the only two words of English known to D'Artagnan were "Come" and "God damn".' He shook a thick arm in the air. 'Would that my knowledge of the English language were confined to the same harmless and uncomplicated terms!'

Miles sprang from the edge of the bed.

'Never mind D'Artagnan, Professor Rigaud. How did *you* get here?'

'Dr Fell and I,' said the other, 'have arrived back by car from the New Forest. We have telephoned his friend the police superintendent. Dr Fell goes to the hospital, and I come here.'

'You've just come from the New Forest? How's Marion?'

'In health,' returned Professor Rigaud, 'she is excellent. She is sitting up and eating food and talking what you call twenty to the dozen.'

'Then in that case,' cried Barbara, and swallowed before she went on, 'you know what frightened her?'

'Yes, mademoiselle. We have heard what frightened her.'

And Professor Rigaud's face slowly grew pale, paler than it had been when he talked of vampires.

'My friend,' he pounced out at Miles, as though he guessed the direction of the latter's thoughts, 'I gave you theories about a certain supernatural agency. Well! It would appear that in this case I was misled by facts intended to mislead. But I do not put myself in ashes and sackcloth for that. No! For I would say to you that one case of an agency proved spurious no more disproves the existence of such supernatural agencies than a forged banknote disproves the existence of the Bank of England. Do you concede this?'

'Yes, I concede it. But ...'

'No!' reiterated Professor Rigaud, wagging his head portentously and rapping the ferrule of the cane against the floor. 'I do not put myself in ashes and sackcloth for that. I put myself in ashes and sackcloth because – in fine, because this is worse.'

He held up the sword-cane.

'May I make to you, my friend, a small present? May I give you this treasured relic? I do not, now, find as much satisfaction in it as others find in the headstone of Dougal or a penwiper made of human flesh. I am human. My gorge can rise. May I give it to you?'

'No, I don't want the infernal thing! Put it away! What we're trying to ask you ...'

155

'*Justement!*' said Professor Rigaud, and flung the sword-cane on the bed.

'Marion *is* all right?' Miles insisted. 'There can't be any relapse of any kind?'

'There cannot.'

'Then this thing that frightened her.' Miles braced himself. 'What did she see?'

'She saw,' replied the other concisely, 'nothing.'

'*Nothing?*'

'Exactly.'

'Yet she was frightened as much as that without being harmed in any way?'

'Exactly,' assented Professor Rigaud, and made angry little frightened noises in his throat. 'She was frightened by something she heard and something she felt. Notably by the whispering.'

The whispering ...

If Miles Hammond had hoped to get away from the realm of monsters and nightmares, he found that he had not been permitted to move very far. He glanced at Barbara, who only shook her head helplessly. Professor Rigaud was still making the little seething noises in his throat, like a kettle boiling; but the noises were not funny. His eyes had a strangled, congested look.

'This thing,' he cried, 'is a thing that could be managed by you or me or Jacques Bonhomme. Its simplicity horrifies me. And yet –'

He broke off.

Outside in Bolsover Place, with a squeal of brakes and a bumping on the uneven paving-stones, a motor-car drew up. Professor Rigaud stumped over to one window. He flung up his arms.

'Dr Fell,' he added, turning round from the window again, 'arrives back from the hospital sooner than I expected him. I must go.'

'Go? Why must you go? Professor Rigaud!'

The good professor was not permitted to go very far. For the bulk of Dr Gideon Fell, hatless but in his box-pleated cape, impelled mightily on the crutch-handled stick, had the effect of filling up the stairs, filling up the passage, and finally filling up the doorway. It had the effect of preventing any exit except by way of the window, which presumably was not Professor Rigaud's intention. So Dr Fell stood there with a gargantuan swaying motion rather like a tethered elephant, still rather wild-eyed and with his

156

eyeglasses coming askew, controlling his breathing for Johnsonesque utterance to Miles.

'Sir,' he began, 'I bring you news.'

'*Fay, Seton —?*'

'Fay Seton is alive,' replied Dr Fell. Then, with a clatter you could almost hear, he swept that hope away. 'How long she lives will depend on the care she takes of herself. It may be months; it may be days. I fear I must tell you she is a doomed woman, as in a sense she has always been a doomed woman.'

For a little time nobody spoke.

Barbara, Miles noted in an abstracted way, was standing just where Fay had stood: by the chest of drawers, under the hanging lamp. Barbara's fingers were pressed to her lips in an expression of horror mingled with overwhelming pity.

'Couldn't we,' said Miles, clearing his throat, 'couldn't we go over to the hospital and see her?'

'No, sir,' returned Dr Fell.

For the first time Miles noticed that there was a police-sergeant in the hall behind Dr Fell. Motioning to this sergeant, Dr Fell squeezed his way through and closed the door behind him.

'*I* have just come from talking to Miss Seton,' he went on. 'I have heard the whole pitiful story.' His expression was vaguely fierce. 'It enables me to fill in the details of my own guesses and half-hits.' As Dr Fell's expression grew more fierce, he put up a hand partly to adjust his eyeglasses and partly perhaps to shade his eyes. 'But that, you see, causes the trouble.'

Miles's disquiet had increased.

'What do you mean, trouble?'

'Hadley will be here presently, with — harrumph — a certain duty to perform. Its result will not be pleasant for one person now in this room. That's why I thought I had better come here first and warn you. I thought I had better explain to you certain matters you may not have grasped even yet.'

'Certain matters? About — ?'

'About those two crimes,' said Dr Fell. He peered at Barbara as though noticing her for the first time. 'Oh, ah!' 'breathed Dr Fell with an air of enlightenment. 'And you must be Miss Morell!'

'Yes! I want to apologize ...'

'Tut, tut! Not for the famous fiasco of the Murder Club?'

'Well … yes.'

'A small matter,' said Dr Fell, with a massive gesture of dismissal.

He lumbered to the frayed armchair, which had been pushed near one window. With the aid of his crutch-handled stick he sat down, the armchair accommodating him as best it could. After rolling back his shaggy head to take a reflective survey of Barbara, of Miles, and of Professor Rigaud, he reached into his inside breast pocket under the cape. From this he produced Professor Rigaud's sheaf of manuscript, now much crumpled and frayed at the edges.

And he produced something else which Miles recognized. It was the coloured photograph of Fay Seton, last seen by Miles at Beltring's Restaurant. With the same air of ferocity overlying bitter worry and distress, Dr Fell sat studying the photograph.

'Dr Fell,' said Miles. 'Hold on! Half a minute!'

The doctor rolled up his head.

'Eh? Yes? What is it?'

'I suppose Superintendent Hadley's told you what happened in this room a couple of hours ago?'

'H'mf, yes. He's told me.'

'Barbara and I came in here and found Fay standing where Barbara is now, with *the* brief-case and a bundle of bloodstained banknotes. I – er – shoved those notes into my pocket just before Hadley arrived. I needn't have bothered. After asking a lot of questions which seemed to tend towards Fay's guilt, he showed he knew about the brief-case all along.'

Dr Fell frowned. 'Well?'

'At the height of the questioning, this light went out. Somebody must have thrown the main-switch in the fuse-box just outside in the passage. Someone or something rushed in here …'

'Someone,' repeated Dr Fell, 'or something. By thunder, I like the choice of words!'

'Whoever it was, it threw Fay to one side and ran out of here with the brief-case. We didn't see anything. I picked up the brief-case outside a minute later. It had nothing in it but the three other packets of notes and a little gritty dust. Hadley took the whole lot away with him, including my concealed notes, when he left with Fay in the – in the ambulance.'

Miles gritted his teeth.

158

'I mention all this,' he went on, 'because so many hints have been made about her guilt that I'd like to see justice done in one respect. Whatever reason you had for asking me, Dr Fell, you did ask me to get in touch with Barbara Morell. And I did, with sensational results.'

'Ah!' murmured Dr Fell in a vaguely distressed way. He would not meet Miles's eye.

'Did you know, for instance, that it was Harry Brooke who wrote a series of anonymous letters accusing Fay of having affairs with men all over the district? And then, when that charge fell flat, Harry stirred up superstition by bribing young Fresnac to slash marks in his own neck and start this nonsense about vampirism? Did you know that?'

'Yes,' assented Dr Fell. 'I know it. It's true enough.'

'We have here' – Miles gestured to Barbara, who opened her handbag – 'a letter written by Harry Brooke on the very afternoon of the murder. He wrote it to Barbara's brother, who,' Miles added hastily, 'isn't at all concerned in this. If you still have any doubts …'

Dr Fell reared up his shoulders with sudden acute interest.

'You have that letter?' he demanded. 'May I see it?'

'With pleasure. Barbara?'

Rather reluctantly, Miles thought, Barbara handed over the letter. Dr Fell took it, adjusted his eyeglasses, and slowly read it through. His expression had grown even more lowering when he put it down on one knee on top of the manuscript and the photograph.

'It's a pretty story, isn't it?' Miles asked bitterly. 'A very fine thing to hound her with! But let's leave Harry's ethics out of this, if nobody gives a curse about Fay's side of it. The point is, this whole situation came about through a trick played by Harry Brooke …'

'No!' said Dr Fell, in a voice like a pistol-shot.

Miles stared at him.

'What do you mean by that?' Miles demanded. 'You're not saying that Pierre Fresnac and this grotesque charge of vampirism – ?'

'Oh, no,' said Dr Fell, shaking his head. 'We may leave young Fresnac and the manufactured teeth-marks entirely out of the picture. They are irrelevant. They don't count. But …'

'But what?'

Dr Fell, after contemplating the floor, slowly raised his head and looked Miles in the eyes.

'Harry Brooke,' he said, 'wrote a lot of anonymous letters containing accusations in which he didn't believe. That is the irony! That is the tragedy! For, although Harry Brooke didn't know it – didn't dream of it, wouldn't have believed it if you'd told him – the accusations were nevertheless perfectly true.'

Silence.

A silence which stretched out unendurably ...

Barbara Morell put her hand softly on Miles's arm. It seemed to Miles that between Dr Fell and Barbara flashed a glance of understanding. But he wanted time to assimilate the meaning of those words.

'Behold now,' said Dr Fell, rounding the syllables with thunderous emphasis, 'an explanation which presently will fit so many puzzling factors in this affair. Fay Seton *had* to have men. I wish to put this matter with delicacy, so I will merely refer you to the psychologists. But it is a form of psychic illness which has tortured her since youth.

'She is no more to be blamed for it than for the heart-weakness which accompanied it. In women so constituted – there are not a great number of them, but they do appear in consulting-rooms – the result does not always end in actual disaster. But Fay Seton (don't you see?) was emotionally the wrong kind of woman to have this quirk in her nature. Her outward Puritanism, her fastidiousness, her delicacy, her gentle manners, were *not* assumed. They are real. To have relations with casual strangers was and is torture to her.

'When she went out to France as Howard Brooke's secretary in nineteen-thirty-nine, she was resolved to conquer this. She would: she would, she would! Her behaviour at Chartres was irreproachable. And then ...'

Dr Fell paused.

Again he took up the photograph and studied it.

'Do you begin to understand now? The atmosphere which always surrounded her was an air of ... well, look into your own memory! It went with her. It haunted her. It clung round her. *That* was the quality which touched and troubled everywhere the people with whom she came in contact, even though they did not understand it. It was a quality sensed by nearly all men. It was a quality sensed, and bitterly resented, by nearly all women.

'Think of Georgina Brooke! Think of Marion Hammond! Think of ...' Dr Fell broke off, and blinked at Barbara. 'I believe you met her a while ago, ma'am?'

Barbara made a helpless gesture.

'I only met Fay for a very few minutes!' she protested quickly. 'How on earth could I tell anything? Of course not! I ...'

'Will you think again, ma'am?' said Dr Fell gently.

'Besides,' said Barbara, 'I liked her!'

And Barbara turned away.

Dr Fell tapped the photograph. The pictured eyes – with their faint irony, their bitterness under the far-away expression – made Fay Seton's presence live and move in this room as strongly as the discarded handbag still on the chest of drawers, or the fallen identity card, or the black beret on the bed.

'That is the figure, good-natured and well-meaning, we must see walking in bewilderment – or apparent bewilderment – through the events that follow.' Dr Fell's big voice was raised. 'Two crimes were committed. Both of them were the work of the same criminal ...'

'The same criminal?' cried Barbara.

And Dr Fell nodded.

'The first,' he said, 'was unpremeditated and slap-dash; it became a miracle in spite of itself. The second was planned and careful, bringing a bit of the dark world into our lives. Shall I continue?'

CHAPTER 19

ABSENTLY Dr Fell was filling his meerschaum pipe as he spoke, the manuscript and the photograph and the letter still on his knee, and his eye fixed drowsily on a corner of the ceiling.

'I should like, with your permission, to take you back to Chartres on the fateful twelfth of August when Howard Brooke was murdered.

'Now I am no orator, as Rigaud is. He could describe for you, in stabbing little phrases clustered together, the house called Beauregard, and the winding river, and Henri Quatre's tower looming over the trees, and the hot thundery day when it wouldn't quite rain. In fact, he has done so.' Dr Fell tapped the manuscript. 'But I want you to *understand* that little group of people at Beauregard.

Archons of Athens! It couldn't have been worse.

'Fay Seton had become engaged to Harry Brooke. She had really fallen in love – or had convinced herself she had – with a callow, coldhearted young man who had nothing to recommend him except his youth and his good looks. Do you remember that scene, described by Harry to Rigaud, in which Harry proposes marriage and is at first rejected?'

Again Barbara protested.

'But that incident,' she cried, 'wasn't true! never happened!'

'Oh, ah,' agreed Dr Fell, nodding with some violence. 'It never happened. The point being that it might well have happened in every detail. Fay Seton must have known, in her heart of hearts, that with all her good intentions she couldn't marry anybody unless she wanted to wreck the marriage in three months by her ... well, let it pass.

'But this time – no! This time is different. We have changed all that. This time she is really in love, romantically as well as physically, and it will work out. After all, nobody has been able to say a word against her since she has come to France as Mr Brooke's secretary.

'And all this time Harry Brooke – never seeing anything, drawing on what Harry thinks is his imagination – had been driving his father to distraction with anonymous letters against Fay. Harry's only concern was to get his own way; to get to Paris and study painting. What did *he* care for a rather silent, passive girl, who tended to draw away from his embraces and remained half cold when he kissed her? Thunderation, no! Give him somebody with a bit of life!

'Irony? I rather think so.

'And then the figurative storm burst. On the twelfth of August, somebody stabbed Mr Brooke. Let me show you how.'

Miles Hammond turned round abruptly.

Miles walked over and sat down beside Professor Rigaud on the edge of the bed. Neither of these two, though for different reasons, had spoken a word for some time.

'Yesterday morning,' pursued Dr Fell, putting down his filled pipe to pick up the sheaf of manuscript and weigh it in his hand, 'my friend Georges Rigaud brought me this account of the case. If I quote from it at any time, you two others will perhaps recognize that Rigaud used exactly the same words when telling it to you verbally.

'He also showed me a certain sword-stick of evil memory.' Dr Fell blinked across at Professor Rigaud. 'Have you – harrumph – by any chance got the same weapon here now?'

With an angry, half-frightened gesture Professor Rigaud picked up the sword-cane and flung it across the room. Dr Fell caught it neatly. But Barbara, as though it had been an attack, backed away against the closed door.

'Ah, zut!' cried Professor Rigaud, and shook his arms in the air.

'You doubt my remarks, sir?' inquired Dr Fell. 'You did not doubt when I gave you a very short sketch earlier to-day.'

'No, no, no!' said Professor Rigaud. 'What you say about this woman Fay Seton is *right*, is absolutely right. I claim a point when I said to you that the characteristics of the vampire are also in folklore the characteristics of eroticism. But I kick me the pants because I, the old cynic, do not see all this for myself!'

'Sir,' returned Dr Fell, 'you acknowledge yourself that you are not much interested in material clues. That is why, even when you were writing about it, you failed to observe ...'

'Observe what?' said Barbara. 'Dr Fell, *who killed Mr Brooke?*'

Outside there was a distant crash of thunder, which made the window-frames vibrate and startled them all. The rain, in this wet June, was going to return.

'Let me,' said Dr Fell, 'simply outline to you the events of that afternoon. You will see for yourselves, when you dovetail the story of Professor Rigaud with the story of Fay Seton herself, what deductions are to be drawn from them.

'Mr Howard Brooke returned to Beauregard from the Crédit Lyonnais bank about three o'clock, carrying the brief-case with the money. The events of the murder properly begin then, and we can follow them from there. Where were the other members of the household at this time?

'At just before three o'clock Fay Seton left the house, carrying bathing-dress and towel, to go for a walk northwards along the river bank. Mrs Brooke was in the kitchen, speaking to the cook. Harry Brooke was – or had been – upstairs in his own room, writing a letter. We know now that it was *this* letter.'

Dr Fell held up the letter.

With a significant grimace he continued:

'Mr Brooke, then, returned at three and asked for Harry. Mrs Brooke replied that Harry was upstairs in his own room. Harry in the meantime, believing his father would be at the office (as Rigaud did too; see testimony) and never dreaming he might be on his way home, had left the letter unfinished and gone to the garage.

'Mr Brooke went up to Harry's room, and presently came down again. Now we see – just here! – the curious change in Howard Brooke's behaviour. He wasn't frantically angry then, as he had been before. Listen, from the evidence, to his wife's description of his manner as he came down the stairs: "So *pitiful* he looked, and so aged, and walking slowly as though he were ill."

'What had he found, up there in Harry's room?

'I will anticipate the evidence and tell you.

'On Harry's desk he saw an unfinished letter. He glanced at it; he glanced at it again, startled; he picked it up and read it through. And his whole honest, comfortable universe crashed down in ruins.

'Carefully outlined, in closely written pages to Jim Morell, was a résumé of Harry's whole scheme to blacken Fay Seton. The anonymous letters; the

164

discreditable rumours; the vampire hoax. And all this was written down by his son Harry – his absolute idol, that hearty innocent – so that the father should be filthily tricked into giving Harry his own way.

'Do you wonder that it struck him dumb? Do you wonder that he looked like that as he walked downstairs, and slowly – how very slowly! – out along the river-bank towards the tower? He had made an appointment with Fay Seton for four o'clock. He was going to keep that appointment. But I see Howard Brooke as a thoroughly honest man, a straight-forward man who would loathe this worse than anything Harry could have done. He would meet Fay Seton at the tower, all right. But he was going there to apologize.'

Dr Fell paused.

Barbara shivered. She glanced at Miles, who sat in a kind of trance, and checked herself from speaking.

'Let us return, however,' pursued Dr Fell, 'to the known facts. Mr Brooke, in the tweed cap and raincoat he had been wearing at the Crédit Lyonnais, went towards the tower. Five minutes later, who turned up? Harry, by thunder! – hearing that his father had been there, and asking where he was now. Mrs Brooke told him. Harry stood for a moment "thinking to himself, muttering". Then he followed his father.'

Here Dr Fell bent forward with great earnestness.

'Now for a point which isn't mentioned by Rigaud or in the official records. It isn't mentioned because nobody bothered with it. Nobody thought it was important. The only person who has mentioned it is Fay Seton, though she wasn't there when it happened and couldn't have known it at all unless she had special reason for knowing.

'But this is what she told Miles Hammond last night. She said that, when Harry Brooke left the house in pursuit of Mr Brooke, *Harry Brooke snatched up his raincoat.*'

Dr Fell glanced over at Miles.

'You remember that, my boy?'

'Yes,' said Miles, conquering a shaky throat. 'But why shouldn't Harry have taken a raincoat? After all, it *was* a drizzling day!'

Dr Fell waved him to silence.

'Professor Rigaud,' Dr Fell continued, 'followed both father and son to the tower some considerable time afterwards. At the door of the tower, unexpectedly, he met Fay Seton.

165

'The girl told him that Harry and Mr Brooke were upstairs on top of the tower, having an argument. She declared she hadn't heard a word of what father and son were saying; but her eyes, testifies Rigaud, were the eyes of one who remembers a horrible experience. She said she wouldn't interrupt at that moment, and in a frantic state of agitation she ran away.

'On top of the tower Rigaud found Harry and his father, also very agitated. Both were pale and worked up. Harry seemed to be pleading, while his father demanded to be allowed to attend to "this situation" – whatever it was – in his own way, and harshly told Rigaud to take Harry away.

'At this time Harry certainly wore no raincoat; he was hatless and coatless, in a corduroy suit described by Rigaud. The sword-stick, untouched with blade screwed into sheath, rested against the parapet. So did the brief-case, but for some reason it had become a *bulging* brief-case.

'That extraordinary word struck me when I first read the manuscript.

'Bulging!

'Now the brief-case certainly hadn't been like that when Howard Brooke showed its contents to Rigaud at the Crédit Lyonnais. Inside, "in solitary state" – I quote Rigaud's own words – were four slender packets of banknotes. Nothing else! But now, when Rigaud and Harry left Mr Brooke alone on the tower, there was something stuffed away inside it ...

'Look here!' added Dr Fell.

And he held up the yellow sword-cane.

Treating it with extraordinary care, he unscrewed the handle, took the thin blade from the hollow stick, and held it up.

'This weapon,' he said, 'was found after the murder of Mr Brooke lying in two halves: the blade near the victim's foot, the sheath rolled away against the parapet. The two halves were not joined together until long afterwards, days after the murder. The police took them away, for expert examination, just as they were found.

'In other words,' explained Dr Fell with thunderous fierceness, 'they were not joined together until long after the blood had dried. Yet there are stains of blood *inside* the scabbard. *O tempora! O mores!* Doesn't that mean anything to you?'

Raising his eyebrows in hideous pantomime, Dr Fell peered round at his companions as though urging them on.

'I've got a horrible half-idea I do know what you mean!' cried Barbara. 'But I – I don't quite see it yet. All I can think of is ...'

'Is what?' asked Dr Fell.

'Is Mr Brooke,' said Barbara. 'Walking out of the house after he'd read Harry's letter. Walking slowly towards the tower. Trying to realize what his son had done. Trying to make up his mind what to do.'

'Yes,' Dr Fell said quietly. 'Let us follow him.'

'Harry Brooke, I dare swear, must have felt a trifle sick when he learned from his mother about Mr Brooke's unexpected return home. Harry remembered his own unfinished letter lying upstairs, where Mr Brooke had just been. Had the old man read it? That was the important point. So Harry put on a raincoat – let's believe he did – and ran out after his father.

'He reached the tower. He found that Mr Brooke, for that solitude we want when we're hurt, had climbed up to the top. Harry followed him there. One look at his father's face, in that dark, windy, drizzling light, must have shown him that Howard Brooke knew everything.

'Mr Brooke would hardly have been slow to pour out what he had just learned. And Fay Seton, on the stairs, heard the whole thing.

'She had returned from her stroll northwards along the river-bank, as she tells us, about half-past three. She had not yet gone in for a swim; her costume was still over her arm. She wandered into the tower. She heard frantic voices coming from above. And softly, on her openwork rubber-soled sandals, she crept up the stairs.

'Fay Seton, poised on that curving staircase in the gloom, not only heard but saw everything that went on. She saw Harry and his father, each wearing a raincoat. She saw the yellow cane propped against the parapet, the brief-case lying on the floor, while Howard Brooke gesticulated.

'What wild recriminations did the father pour out then? Did he threaten to disown Harry? Possibly. Did he swear that Harry should never see Paris or painting as long as *his* life lasted? Probably. Did he repeat, with a kind of incredulous disgust, all that beautiful Harry had done against the reputation of the girl who was in love with him? Almost certainly.

'And Fay Seton heard it.

'But, sick as that must have made her, she was to hear and see worse.

'For such scenes sometimes get out of control. This one did. The father suddenly turned away, past speech; turned his back on Harry as he was to

167

do later. Harry saw the ruin of all his plans. He saw no soft life for himself now. And something snapped in his head. In a child's fury he snatched up the sword-stick, twisted it out of its scabbard, and stabbed his father through the back.'

Dr Fell, uneasy through all his bulk at his own words, fitted together the two halves of the sword-stick. Then he put it down quietly on the floor.

Neither Barbara nor Miles nor Professor Rigaud spoke, during a silence while you might have counted ten. Miles slowly rose to his feet. The torpor was leaving him. Gradually he saw ...

'The blow,' Miles said, 'was struck just *then*?'

'Yes. The blow was struck just then.'

'And the time?'

'The time,' returned Dr Fell, 'was nearly ten minutes to four. Professor Rigaud there was very close to the tower.

'The wound made by the blade was a deep, thin wound: the sort, we find in medical jurisprudence, that makes the victim think he is not at all badly hurt. Howard Brooke saw his son standing there white-faced and stupid, hardly realizing what he had done. What were the father's reactions to all this? If you know men like Mr Brooke, you can prophesy exactly.

'Fay Seton, silent and unseen, had fled down the stairs. In the doorway she met Rigaud and ran from him. And Rigaud, hearing the voices upstairs, put his head inside the tower and shouted up to them.

'In his narrative Rigaud tells us that the voices stopped instantly. By thunder, they did!

'For, let me repeat, what were Howard Brooke's feelings about all this? He had just heard the hail of a family friend, Rigaud, who will be up those stairs as soon as a stout man can climb them. Was Mr Brooke's instinct, in the middle of this awkward mess, to denounce Harry? Lord of all domestic troubles, no! Just the opposite! His immediate desperate wish was to hush things up, to pretend somehow that nothing at all had happened.

'I think it was the father who snarled to the son: "Give me your raincoat!" And I am sure it was quite natural for him to do so.

'You – harrumph – perceive the point?

'In the back of his own raincoat, as he saw by whipping it off, was a tear through which blood had soaked. But a good lined raincoat will do more than turn rain from outside. It will also keep blood from showing through from inside. If he wore Harry's coat, and somehow disposed of his own, he could conceal that ugly bleeding wound in his back …

'You guess what he did. He hastily rolled up his own rain-coat, stuffed it into the brief-case, and fastened the straps. He thrust the sword-blade back into its scabbard (hence the blood inside); he tightened its threads and propped it up again. He put on Harry's raincoat. By the time Rigaud had toiled to the top of the stairs, Howard Brooke was ready to prevent scandal.

'But, my eye! How that whole tense shivery scene on top of the tower takes on a different aspect if you read it like this!

'The pale-faced son stammering, "But, sir −!" The father in a cold buttoned-up voice, "For the last time, will you allow me to deal with this matter in my own way?" This matter! And then, flaring out: "Will you take my son away from here until I have adjusted certain matters to my own satisfaction? Take him anywhere!" And the father turns his back.

'There was a chill in the voice, a chill in the heart. You sensed it, my dear Rigaud, when you spoke of Harry, beaten and deflated, being led dumbly down those stairs. And Harry's sullen shining eye in the wood, while Harry wondered what in God's name the old man was going to do.

'Well, what was the old man going to do? He was going to get home, of course, with that incriminating raincoat decently hidden in his brief-case. There he could hide scandal. My son tried to kill me! That was the worst revulsion of all. He was going to get home. And then …'

'Continue, please!' prompted Professor Rigaud, snapping his fingers in the air as Dr Fell's voice died away. 'This is the part I have not followed. He was going to get home. And then −?'

Dr Fell looked up.

'He found he couldn't,' Dr Fell said simply. 'Howard Brooke knew he was fainting. And he suspected he might be dying.

'He saw quite clearly he couldn't get down that steep spiral stair, forty feet above ground, without pitching forward into space. He would be found fainting here − if nothing worse − wearing Harry's raincoat, and his own pierced bloodstained raincoat in the brief-case. Questions would be asked. The facts, properly interpreted, would be utterly damning to Harry.

'Now that man really loved his son. He had got two dazing revelations that afternoon. He meant to be very severe with the boy. But he wouldn't see Harry, poor idolized Harry, really in serious trouble. So he did the

169

obvious thing, the only possible thing, to show he must have been attacked after Harry left.

'With his last strength he took his own raincoat out of the brief-case, and put it on again. Harry's, now bloodstained too, he thrust into the case. He *must* get rid of that brief-case somehow. In a sense that was easy, because there was water just below.

'But he couldn't simply drop it over the edge, though the police of Chartres in their suicide theory thought he might accidently have knocked it over. He couldn't drop it, for the not-very-abstruse reason that the brief-case would float.

'However, on the battlements of the parapet facing the river-side were big crumbling fragments of loose rock. These could be wrenched loose and put into the brief-case, fastened in with the straps, and the weighted case would sink.

'He managed to drop it over. He managed to take the sword-cane from its scabbard, wipe its handle free from any trace of Harry's touch – that of course was why only his own fingerprints were found on it – and throw the two halves on the floor. Then Howard Brooke collapsed. He was not dead when the screaming child found him. He was not dead when Harry and Rigaud arrived. He died in Harry's arms, clinging pathetically to Harry and trying to assure his murderer it would be all right.

'God rest the man's soul,' added Dr Fell, slowly putting up his hands to cup them over his eyes.

For a time Dr Fell's wheezing breaths were the only sound in that room. A few drops of rain spattered outside the windows.

'Ladies and gentlemen,' said Dr Fell, taking his hands away from his eyes and regarding his companions soberly, 'I submit this to you now. I submit it, as I could have submitted it last night after reading the manuscript and hearing the report of Fay Seton's story, as the only feasible explanation of how Howard Brooke met his death.

'The stains *inside* the sword-stick, showing the blade must have been put back in the sheath and then taken out again before it was found! The bulging brief-case! Harry's disappearing coat! The missing fragments of rock from the parapet! The curious question of fingerprints!

'For the secret of this apparent miracle – which was not intended to be a mystery at all – lies in a very simple fact. It is the fact that one man's raincoat looks very much like another man's raincoat.

'We don't write our names in raincoats. They are not of a distinctive colour. They are made only in a few stock sizes; and we know that Harry Brooke "in height and weight", as Rigaud says, was like his father. Among Englishmen especially it is a point of pride, even of caste and gentlemanliness, for his raincoat to be as old and disreputable as possible without becoming an actual eyesore. When next you go into a restaurant, observe the line of bedraggled objects hanging on coat-pegs and you will understand.

'Our friend Rigaud here never dreamed he had seen Mr Brooke in two different coats at two different times. Since Mr Brooke was actually found dying in his own coat, nobody else ever suspected. Nobody, that is, except Fay Seton.'

Professor Rigaud got to his feet and took little short steps up and down the room.

'*She* knew?' he demanded.

'Undoubtedly.'

'But after I saw her for a moment at the door of the tower, and she ran away from me, what did she do?'

'*I* can tell you,' Barbara said quietly.

Professor Rigaud, fussed and fussy, made gestures as though he would try to shush her.

'You, mademoiselle? And how would it occur to you to know?'

'I can tell you,' answered Barbara simply, 'because it's what I should have done myself.' Barbara's eyes were shining with a light of pain and sympathy. 'Please let me go on! I can *see* it!

'Fay went for a swim in the river, just as she said she did. She wanted to feel cool; she wanted to feel clean. She'd really – really fallen in love with Harry Brooke. In circumstances like that it'd be easy,' Barbara shook her head, 'to convince yourself ... well! that the past was the past. That this was a new life.

'And then she'd just crept up to the tower, and heard. She heard what Harry had said about her. As though instinctively he knew it was true! As though the whole world could look at her and know it was true. She'd seen Harry stab his father, but she didn't think Mr Brooke was seriously hurt.

'Fay dived into the river, and floated down towards the tower. There were no witnesses on that side, remember! And – of course!' cried Barbara.

171

'Fay saw the brief-case fall from the tower!' Barbara, afire with this new realization, turned to Dr Fell. 'Isn't that true?'

Dr Fell inclined his head gravely.

'That, ma'am, is whang in the gold.'

'She dived down and got the brief-case. She carried it with her when she left the river, and hid it in the woods. Fay didn't know what was going on, of course; she didn't realize until later what must have happened.' Barbara hesitated. 'Miles Hammond told me, on the way here, what her own story was. I think she never realized what was going on until ...'

'Until,' supplied Miles, with an intensity of bitterness, 'until Harry Brooke came rushing up to her, exuding hypocritical shock, and cried out, "My God, Fay, somebody's killed Dad." No wonder Fay looked a trifle cynical when she told me!'

'One moment!' said Professor Rigaud.

After giving the impression of hopping up and down, though in fact he did not move, Professor Rigaud raised his forefinger impressively.

'In this cynicism,' he declared, 'I begin to see a meaning for much. Death of all lives, yes! This woman,' – he shook his forefinger – 'this woman now possesses evidence which can send Harry Brooke to the guillotine!' He looked at Dr Fell. 'Is it not so?'

'For you also,' assented Dr Fell, 'whang in the gold.'

'In this brief-case,' continued Rigaud, his face swelling, 'are the stones used to weight it and Harry's raincoat stained with blood inside where his father has worn it. It would convince any court. It would show the truth.' He paused, considering. 'Yet Fay Seton does not use this evidence.'

'Of course not,' said Barbara.

'Why do you say of course, mademoiselle?'

'Don't you see?' cried Barbara. 'She'd got to a state of – of tiredness, of bitterness, where she could practically laugh? It didn't *affect* her any longer. She wasn't even interested in showing up Harry Brooke for what he was.

'She, the amateur harlot! He, the amateur murderer and hypocrite! Let's be indulgent to each other's foibles, and go our ways in a world where nothing will ever come right anyway. I – I don't want to sound silly, but that's how you really *would* feel about a situation like that.

172

'I think,' said Barbara, 'she told Harry Brooke. I think she told him she wasn't going to expose him unless the police arrested her. But, in case the police did arrest her, she was going to keep that brief-case with its contents hidden away where nobody could find it.

'And she did keep the brief-case! That's it! She kept it for six long years! She brought it to England with her. It was always where she could find it. But she never had any reason to touch it, until … until …'

Barbara's voice trailed off.

Her eyes looked suddenly and vaguely frightened, as though Barbara wondered whether her own imagination had carried her too far. For Dr Fell, with wide-eyed and wheezing interest, was leaning forward in expectancy.

'Until –?' prompted Dr Fell, in a hollow voice like wind along the Underground tunnel. 'Archons of Athens! You're doing it! Don't stop there! Fay Seton never had any reason to touch the brief-case until …?'

But Miles Hammond hardly heard this. Sheer hatred welled up in his throat and choked him.

'So Harry Brooke,' Miles said, 'still got away with it?'

Barbara swung round from Dr Fell. 'How do you mean?'

'His father protected him,' Miles made a fierce gesture, 'even when Harry bent over a dying man and mouthed out, "Dad, who did this?" Now we learn that even Fay Seton protected him.'

'Steady, my boy! Steady!'

'The Harry Brookes of this world,' said Miles, 'always get away with it. Whether it's luck, or circumstance, or some celestial gift in their own natures, I don't pretend to guess. That fellow ought to have gone to the guillotine, or spent the rest of his life on Devil's Island. Instead it's Fay Seton, who never did the least harm to anybody, who …' His voice rose up. 'By God, I wish I could have met Harry Brooke six years ago! I'd give my soul to have a reckoning with him!'

'That's not difficult,' remarked Dr Fell. 'Would you like to have a reckoning with him now?'

An enormous crash of thunder, rolling in broken echoes over the roof-tops, flung its noise into the room. Raindrops blew past Dr Fell as he sat by the window: not quite so ruddy of countenance now, with his unlighted pipe in his hand.

Dr Fell raised his voice.

'*Are you out there, Hadley?*' he shouted.

Barbara jumped away from the door; staring, she groped back to stand at the foot of the bed. Professor Rigaud used a French expletive not often heard in polite society.

And then everything seemed to happen at once.

As a rain-laden breeze came in at the windows, making the hanging lamp sway over the chest of drawers, some heavy weight thudded against the outside of the closed door to the passage. The knob twisted only slightly, but frantically, as though hands fought for it. Then the door banged open, rebounding against the wall. Three men, who were trying to keep their feet while fighting, lurched forward in a wrestling-group which almost toppled over when it banged against the tin box.

On one side was Superintendent Hadley, trying to grip somebody's wrists. On the other side was a uniformed police-inspector. In the middle ...

'Professor Rigaud' – Dr Fell's voice spoke clearly – 'will you be good enough to identify that chap for us? The man in the middle?'

Miles Hammond looked for himself at the staring eyes, the corners of the mouth drawn back, the writhing legs that kicked out at his captors with vicious and sinewy strength. It was Miles who answered.

'*Identify him?*'

'Yes,' said Dr Fell.

'Look here,' cried Miles, 'what is all this? That's Steve Curtis, my sister's fiancé! What are you trying to do?'

'We are trying,' thundered Dr Fell, 'to make an identification. And I think we have done it. For the man who calls himself Stephen Curtis *is* Harry Brooke.'

174

CHAPTER 20

FREDÉRIC, the head-waiter at Beltring's Restaurant – which is one of the few places in the West End where you can get food on a Sunday – was always glad to oblige Dr Fell, even when Dr Fell wanted a private room at short notice.

Frédéric's manner froze to ice when he saw the doctor's three guests: Professor Rigaud, Mr Hammond, and small fair-haired Miss Morell, the same three who had been at Beltring's two nights before.

But the guests did not seem happy either, especially at what Frédéric considered a very tactful gesture on his part; for he ushered them into the same private dining-room as before, the room used by the Murder Club. He noticed that they seemed to eat rather from a sense of duty than any appreciation of the menu.

He did not see that their looks were even stranger afterwards, when they sat round the table.

'I will now,' groaned Professor Rigaud, 'take my medicine. Continue.'

'Yes,' said Miles, without looking at Dr Fell. 'Continue.' Barbara was silent.

'Look here!' protested Dr Fell, making vast and vague gestures of distress which spilled ash from his pipe down his waistcoat. 'Wouldn't you rather wait until …?'

'No,' said Miles, and stared hard at a salt-cellar.

'Then I ask you,' said Dr Fell, 'to take your mind back to last night at Greywood, when Rigaud and I had arrived on Rigaud's romantic mission to warn you about vampirism.'

'I also wished,' observed the professor a trifle guiltily, 'to have a look at Sir Charles Hammond's library. But in all the time I am at Greywood the one room I do not see is the library. Life is like that.'

'You and Rigaud and I,' he pursued, 'were in the sitting-room, and you had just told me Fay Seton's own account of the Brooke murder.

'Harry Brooke, I decided, was the murderer. But his motive? That was where I had the glimmer of a guess – based, I think on your description of Fay's hysterical laughter when you asked if she had married Harry – that these anonymous letters, these slanderous reports, were a put-up job managed by the unpleasant Harry himself.

'Mind you! I never once suspected the reports were really true after all, until Fay Seton told me so herself in the hospital this evening. It made blazing sense of so much that was obscure; it completed the pattern; but *I* never suspected it.

'What I saw was an innocent woman traduced by the man who pretended to be in love with her. Suppose Howard Brooke found this out, from the mysterious letter Harry was writing on the afternoon of the murder? In that case the person we must find was the equally mysterious correspondent, Jim Morell.

'This hypothesis would explain why Harry killed his father. It would show Fay as innocent of everything except – for some reason of her own! – hiding the brief-case that was dropped into the river, and never denouncing Harry. In any case the charge of vampirism was nonsense. I was just announcing this to you when ...

'We heard a revolver-shot upstairs. We found what had happened to your sister.

'And I didn't understand *anything*.

'However! Let me now put together certain points I saw for myself, certain information you gave me, and certain other information given by your sister Marion when she was able to make a statement before we left Greywood. Let me show you how the whole game was played out under your eyes.

'On Saturday afternoon, at four o'clock, you met your sister and "Stephen Curtis" at Waterloo Station. In the tea-room you flung your hand-grenade (though of course you didn't know it at the time) by announcing you had engaged Fay Seton to come to Greywood. Is that correct?'

'Steve! Steve Curtis!' Resolutely Miles shut out of his mind the face that kept appearing between him and the candle-flames.

'Yes,' Miles agreed. 'That's correct.'

'How did the alleged Stephen Curtis receive the news?'

'In the light of what we know now,' Miles replied dryly, 'it would be a strong understatement to say he didn't like it. But he

176

announced that he couldn't go back to Greywood with us that evening.'

'Had you known he couldn't go back to Greywood with you that evening?'

'No! Now you mention it, it surprised Marion as much as it did me. Steve began to talk rather hastily about a sudden crisis at the office.'

'Was the name of Professor Rigaud mentioned at any time? Was "Curtis" aware you'd met Rigaud?'

Miles pressed a hand against his eyes, reconstructing the scene. He saw, in blurred colours which sharpened to such ugliness, 'Steve' fiddling with his pipe and 'Steve' putting on his hat and 'Steve' somewhat shakily laughing.

'No!' Miles responded. 'Come to think of it, he didn't even know I'd gone to a meeting of the Murder Club, or what the Murder Club was. I did say something about "the professor", but I'll swear I never mentioned Rigaud's name.'

Dr Fell bent forward, with a pink-faced and terrifying benevolence.

'Fay Seton,' Dr Fell said softly, *'still held the evidence which could send Harry Brooke to the guillotine. But, if Fay Seton were disposed of, there would apparently be nobody to connect "Stephen Curtis" with Harry Brooke?'*

Miles started to push back his chair.

'God Almighty!' he said. 'You mean ...?'

'So-oftly!' urged Dr Fell, waving a mesmeric hand before eyeglasses coming askew. 'But here – oh, here! – is the point at which I want you to jog your memory. During that conversation, when you and your sister and the so-called Curtis were present, was anything said about rooms?'

'About rooms?'

'About bedrooms!' persisted Dr Fell, with the air of a monster lurking in ambush. 'About bedrooms! Eh?'

'Well, yes. Marion said she was going to put Fay in her bedroom, and move downstairs herself to a better ground-floor room we'd just been redecorating.'

'Ah!' said Dr Fell, nodding several times. 'It did seem to me I heard you talking at Greywood about the bedroom situation. So your sister wanted to put Fay Seton in *her* bedroom! Oh, ah! Yes! But she didn't do it?'

'No. She wanted to do it that evening, but Fay refused. Fay preferred the ground-floor room because of her heart. Fewer stairs to climb.'

177

Dr Fell pointed with his pipe.

'But suppose,' he suggested, 'you believe Fay Seton will be in the upstairs bedroom at the back of the house. Suppose, to make dead sure of this, you keep a watch on the house. You hide yourself among the trees at the rear of the house. You look up at a line of uncurtained windows. And, at some time before midnight,, what do you see?

'You see Fay Seton – wearing nightgown and wrap – slowly walking back and forth in front of those windows.

'Marion Hammond can't be seen at all. Marion is sitting in a chair over at the other side of the room, by the bedside table. She can't even be seen through the side or eastern windows, because they're curtained. But Fay Seton *can* be seen.

'And further suppose, in the black early hours of the morning, you creep into that dark bedroom intent on a neat and artistic murder. You are going to kill someone asleep in that bed. And, as you approach, you catch a very faint whiff of perfume: a distinctive perfume always associated with Fay Seton.

'You can't know, of course, that Fay has made the present of a little bottle of this perfume to Marion Hammond. The perfume bottle stands now on the bedside table. But you can't know that. You can only breathe the scent of that perfume. Is there any doubt in your mind now?'

Miles had seen it coming, seen it coming ever since Dr Fell's first remark. But now the image seemed to rush out at him.

'Yes!' said Dr Fell with emphasis. 'Harry Brooke, alias Stephen Curtis, planned a skilful murder. And he got the wrong woman.'

There was a silence.

'However!' added Dr Fell, sweeping out his arm in a gesture which sent a coffee cup flying across the little dining-room, but which nobody noticed. 'However! I am again indulging in my deplorable habit of anticipating the evidence.

'Last night, let it be admitted, I was royally stumped. With regard to the Brooke murder, I *believed* Harry had done the deed. I *believed* Fay Seton had afterwards got the brief-case, with its damning raincoat, and still had it; in fact, I hinted as much to her with a question about underwater swimming. But nothing seemed to explain this mysterious attack on Marion Hammond.

'Even an incident on the following morning did not quite unseal these eyes. It was the first time I ever saw "Mr Stephen Curtis".

'He had returned, very brisk and jaunty, apparently from London. He strolled into the sitting-room while you' – Dr Fell again looked very hard at Miles – 'were speaking on the phone to Miss Morell. Do you remember?'

'Yes,' said Miles.

'*I* remember the conversation,' said Barbara. 'But ...'

'As for myself,' rumbled Dr Fell, 'I was just behind him, carrying a cup of tea on a tray.' Dr Fell furrowed up his face with intense concentration. 'Your words to Miss Morell, in "Stephen Curtis's" hearing, were (harrumph) almost exactly as follows.

' "There was a very bad business here last night," you said to Miss Morell. "Something happened in my sister's room that seems past human belief." You broke off at the beginning of another sentence as "Stephen Curtis" came in.

'Instantly you got up to reassure him, in a fever of care that he shouldn't worry. "It's all right," you said to him; "Marion's had a very bad time of it, but she's going to get well." You recall that part of it too?'

Very clearly Miles could see 'Steve' standing there, in his neat grey suit, with the rolled-up umbrella over his arm. Again he saw the colour slowly drain out of 'Steve's' face.

'I couldn't see his face,' – it was as though Dr Fell, uncannily, were answering Miles's thoughts – 'but I heard this gentleman's voice go up a couple of octaves when he said "Marion?" Just like that!

'Sir, I tell you this: if my wits worked better in the morning (as they do not) that one word would have given the whole show away. "Curtis" was completely thunderstruck. But why should he have been? He had just heard you announce that something very bad had occurred in your sister's room.

'Suppose I return home, and hear someone saying over the telephone that something very bad has occurred in my wife's room? Don't I naturally assume that the accident, or whatever it is, has occurred to my wife? Am I bowled over with utter astonishment when I hear that the victim *is* my wife, and not my Aunt Martha from Hackney Wick?

'That tore it.

'Unfortunately, I failed at the moment to see.

'But do you remember what he did immediately afterwards? He deliberately lifted his umbrella, and very coolly and deliberately smashed

179

it to flinders across the edge of the table. "Stephen Curtis" is supposed to be – he pretends to be – a stolid kind of person. But that was Harry Brooke hitting the tennis-ball. That was Harry Brooke not getting what he wanted.'

Miles Hammond stared at memory.

'Steve's' personable face: Harry Brooke's face. The fair hair: Harry Brooke's hair. Harry, Miles reflected, hadn't gone prematurely grey from nerves, as Professor Rigaud said he would; he had lost the hair, and it was for some reason grotesque to think of Harry Brooke as nearly bald.

That was why they thought of him as older, of course. 'Steve' might have been in his late thirties. But they had never heard his age.

They: meaning himself and Marion ...

Miles was roused by Dr Fell's voice.

'This gentleman,' the doctor went on grimly, 'saw his scheme dished. Fay Seton was alive; she was there in the house. And you gave him, unintentionally, almost as bad a shock a moment afterwards. You told him that *another* person who knew him as Harry Brooke, Professor Rigaud, was at Greywood; and was, in fact, upstairs asleep in "Curtis's" own room.

'Do you wonder he turned away and went over towards the bookshelves to hide his face?

'Disaster lurked ahead of every step he took now. He had tried to kill Fay Seton, and nearly killed Marion Hammond instead. With that plan gone ...'

'Dr Fell!' said Barbara softly.

'Hey?' rumbled Dr Fell, drawn out of obscure meditation. 'Oh, ah! Miss Morell! What is it?'

'I know I'm an outsider.' Barbara ran her finger along the edge of the tablecloth. 'I have no real concern in this, except as one who wants to help and can't. But' – the grey eyes lifted pleadingly – 'but please, *please*, before poor Miles goes crazy and maybe the rest of us as well, will you tell us what this man did that frightened Marion so much?'

'Ah!' said Dr Fell.

'Harry Brooke,' said Barbara, 'is a poisonous worm. But he's not clever. Where did he get the idea for what you call an "artistic" murder?'

'Mademoiselle,' said Professor Rigaud, with an air of powerful gloom like Napoleon at St Helena, 'he got it from ME. And I have received it from an incident in the life of Count Cagliostro.'

'Of course!' breathed Barbara.

'Madernoiselle,' said Professor Rigaud in a fever, beginning to hammer the flat of his hand on the table, 'will you oblige me by not saying "of course" on the wrong occasions? Explain, if you please' – the rapping grew to a frenzy – 'how you mean "of course" or how you could possibly mean "of course"!'

'I'm sorry.' Barbara looked round helplessly. 'I only meant you told us yourself you kept lecturing to Harry Brooke about crime and the occult …'

'But what's occult about this?' asked Miles. 'Before you arrived this afternoon, Dr Fell, our friend Rigaud talked a lot of gibberish about that business. He said that what frightened Marion was something she had heard and felt, but not seen. But that's impossible on the fate of it.'

'Why impossible?' asked Dr Fell.

'Well! Because she must have seen something! After all, she did fire a shot at it …'

'Oh, no, she didn't!' said Dr Fell sharply.

Miles and Barbara stared at each other.

'But a shot,' insisted Miles, '*was* fired in that room when we heard it?'

'Oh, yes.'

'Then at whom was it fired? At Marion?'

'Oh, no,' answered Dr Fell.

Barbara put a soothing hand gently on Miles's arm.

'Maybe it would be better,' she suggested, 'if we let Dr Fell tell it in his own way.'

'Yes,' Dr Fell sounded fussed. He looked at Miles. 'I think – harrumph – I am perhaps puzzling you a little,' he said in a tone of genuine distress.

'Odd as it may sound, you are.'

'Yes. But there was no intention to puzzle. You see, I should have realized all along your sister could never have fired that shot. She was *relaxed*. Her whole body, as in all cases of shock, was completely limp and nerveless. And yet, when we first saw her, her fingers were clutched round the handle of the revolver.

'Now that's impossible. If she *had* fired a shot before collapsing, the mere weight of the revolver would have dragged it out of her hand. Sir, it meant that her fingers were carefully *placed* round the revolver afterwards, in a very fine bit of misdirection, to throw us all off the track.

'But I never saw this until this afternoon when, in my scatterbrained way, I was musing over the life of Cagliostro. I found myself touching lightly on various incidents in his career. I remembered his initiation into the lodge of a secret society at the King's Head Tavern in Gerrard Street.

'Frankly, I am very fond of secret societies myself. But I must point out that initiations in the eighteenth century were not exactly tea-parties at Cheltenham to-day. They were always unnerving. They were sometimes dangerous. When the Grand Goblin issued an order of life-or-death, the neophyte could never be sure he didn't mean business.

'So let us see!

'Cagliostro – blindfolded and on his knees – had already had something of an unnerving time. Finally they told him he must prove his fidelity to the order, even if it meant his death. They put a pistol into his hand, and said it was loaded. They told him to put the pistol to his own head, and pull the trigger.

'Now the candidate believed, as anyone would, that this was only a hoax. He *believed* the hammer would fall on an empty gun. But in that one second, stretching out to eternity, when he pulled the trigger ...

'Cagliostro pulled the trigger. And instead of a click there was a thunderous report, the flash of the pistol, the stunning shock of the bullet.

'What had happened, of course, was that the pistol in his hand *was* empty after all. But, at the very instant he pulled the trigger, someone else holding another pistol beside his ear – pointing away from him – had fired a real shot and rapped him sharply over the head. He never forgot that single instant when he felt, or thought he felt, the crash of the bullet into his own head.

'How would that do as an idea for murder? The murder of a woman with a weak heart?

'You creep up in the middle of the night. You gag your victim, before she can cry out, with some soft material that will leave no traces afterwards. You hold to her temple the cold muzzle of a pistol, an empty pistol. And for minutes, dragging terrible minutes in the small hours of the night, you whisper to her.

'You are going to kill her, you explain. Your whispering voice goes on, telling her all about it. She does not see a second pistol loaded with real bullets.

'At the proper time (so runs your own plan) you will fire a bullet close to her head, but not so close that the expansion of gases will leave powder-marks on her. You will then put the revolver into her own hand. After her death it will be believed that *she* fired at some imaginary burglar or intruder or ghost, and that no other person was there at all.

'So you keep on whispering, multiplying terrors in the dark. The time, you explain, is at hand now. Very slowly you squeeze the trigger of the empty gun, to draw back the hammer. She hears the oily noise of the hammer moving back . . slowly, very slowly ... the hammer creaking farther ... the hammer at its peak before it strikes, and then ...'

Whack!

Dr Fell brought his hand down sharply on the table. It was only that, the noise of a hand striking wood; and yet all three of his listeners jumped as though they had seen the flash and heard the shot.

Barbara, her face white, got up and backed away from the table. The candle-flames, too, were still shaking and jumping.

'Look here!' said Miles. 'Damn it all!'

'I – harrumph – beg your pardon,' said Dr Fell, making guilty gestures and fixing his eyeglasses more firmly on his nose. 'It was not really meant to upset anyone. But it was necessary to make you understand the *diablerie* of the trick.

'On a woman with a weak heart it was not at all problematical; it was certain. Forgive me, my dear Hammond; but you saw what happened in the case of a sound woman like your sister.

'None of us (let us face it) has too-steady nerves nowadays, especially where bumps or bangs are concerned. You said your sister didn't like the blitzes or the V-weapons. That was the only sort of thing that might have frightened her, as it did.

'And, by thunder, sir! – if you are worrying about your sister, if you are feeling sorry for things, if you are wondering how she will take it when she hears of all this, just ask yourself what she would have been let in for if she *had* married "Stephen Curtis".'

'Yes,' said Miles. He put his elbows on the table and his temples in his hands. 'Yes, I see. Go on.'

'Harrumph, ha!' said Dr Fell.

'Once having tumbled to the trick early this afternoon,' he continued, 'the whole design unrolled itself at once. Why should anyone have attacked Marion Hammond like that?

'I remembered the interesting reaction of "Mr Curtis" to the announcement that it was *Marion* who had been frightened. I remembered your own remarks about bedrooms. I remembered a woman's figure in nightgown and wrap, walking back and forth in front of uncurtained windows. I remembered a perfume bottle. And the answer was that nobody had tried to frighten Marion Hammond. The intended victim was Fay Seton.

'But in that case ...

'First of all, you may remember, I went up to your sister's bedroom. I wanted to see if the assailant might have left any traces.

'There would have been no violence, of course. The murderer wouldn't even have needed to tie his victim. After the first few minutes he wouldn't have needed to hold her at all; he could use his two hands for his revolvers – one empty, one loaded – because the pistol-muzzle at the temple would have been enough.

"But it was just possible that the gag (which he *had* to have) might have left some traces on her teeth or on her neck. There were none, nor were there traces of anything left on the floor round the bed.

'In the bedroom, a study in frightened woe again presented itself in the person of "Mr Stephen Curtis". Why should "Stephen Curtis" be interested in trying to kill a total stranger like Fay Seton, with a trick taken from the life of Cagliostro?

'Cagliostro suggested Professor Rigaud. Professor Rigaud suggested Harry Brooke, whom he had tutored in matters of ...

'O Lord! O Bacchus!

'It wasn't possible "Stephen Curtis" might *be* Harry Brooke?

'No, fantastic! Harry Brooke was dead. A truce to this nonsense!

'At the same time, while I vainly looked round the carpet for traces left by the murderer, some whisk of scatterbrained intelligence kept on working. It suddenly occurred to me that I was overlooking evidence which had been under my nose since last night.

'A shot was fired in here, the would-be murderer using for business gun the .32 Ives-Grant he must have known Marion Hammond kept in the bedside table ("Curtis" again), and for empty gun any old weapon he brought along. Very well!

'At some time following the shot, Miss Fay Seton slipped up to this bedroom and peeped in. She saw something which upset her badly. She wasn't frightened, mind you. No! It was caused by ...'

Miles Hammond intervened.

'Shall I tell you, Dr Fell?' he suggested. 'I talked to Fay in the kitchen, where I was boiling water. She'd just come from the bedroom. Her expression was hatred: hatred, mixed with a kind of wild anguish. At the end of the conversation she burst out with, "This can't go on!"'

Dr Fell nodded.

'And she also told you, as I am now aware,' Dr Fell inquired, 'that she'd just seen something she hadn't noticed before?'

'Yes. That's right.'

'What, then, could she have noticed in Marion Hammond's bedroom? That was what I asked myself in that same bedroom: in the presence of yourself, and Dr Garvice, and the nurse, and "Stephen Curtis".

'After all, Fay Seton bad been in that room for quite a long while on Saturday night, talking to Miss Hammond, evidently without seeing anything strange on her first visit to the room.

'Then I remembered that eerie conversation I had with her later the same night – out at the end of the passage, in the moonlight – when her whole attitude burned with a repressed emotion that made her smile, once or twice, like a vampire. I remembered the queer reply she made to one of my questions, when I was asking her about her visit during which she talked to Marion Hammond.

' "Mostly," said Fay Seton in referring to Marion, "she did the talking, about her fiancé and her brother and her plans for the future." Then Fay, for no apparent reason, added these inconsequential words: *"The lamp was on the bedside table; did I tell you?"*

'Lamp? 'That reference jarred me at the time. And now ...

'After Marion Hammond was found ostensibly dead, there were two lamps taken into the room. One was carried by you' – he looked at Professor Rigaud – 'and the other' – he looked at Miles – 'was carried by you. Think, now, both of you! Where did you set those lamps down?'

'I do not follow this!' cried Rigaud. 'My lamp, of course, I placed on the bedside table beside one that is not burning.'

185

'And you?' demanded Dr Fell of Miles.

'I'd just been told,' replied Miles, staring at the past, 'that Marion was dead. I was holding up the lamp, and my whole arm started to shake so that I couldn't hold it any longer. I went across and put the lamp down – on the chest of drawers.'

'Ah!' murmured Dr Fell. 'And now tell me, if you please, what was also on that chest of drawers?'

'A big leather picture-frame, containing a big photograph of Marion on one side and a big photograph of "Steve" on the other. I remember the lamp threw a strong light on those pictures, though that side of the room had been darkish before, and –'

Miles broke off in realization. Dr Fell nodded.

'A photograph of "Stephen Curtis", brilliantly lighted," said Dr Fell. '*That* was what Fay Seton saw, staring at her from the room as she peeped in at the doorway after the shot. It explained her whole attitude.

'She knew. By thunder, *she knew*!

'Probably she didn't at all guess how the Cagliostro trick had been worked. But she did know the attempt had been made on her and not on Marion Hammond, because she knew who was behind it Marion Hammond's fiancé was Harry Brooke.

'And that finished it. That was the last straw. That really did make her white with hatred and anguish. Once more she had tried to find a new life, new surroundings; she had been decent; she had forgiven Harry Brooke and concealed the evidence against him about his father's murder; and destiny still won't leave off hounding her. Destiny, or some damnable force which has it in for her, has brought Harry Brooke back from nowhere to try to take her life ...'

Dr Fell coughed.

'I have bored you with this at some length,' he apologized, 'though the process of thinking it took perhaps three seconds while I wool-gathered in that bedroom in the presence of Miles Hammond, and the doctor, and the nurse, and "Curtis" himself, who was standing by the chest of drawers then.

'To determine whether I was right about the Cagliostro trick, it further occurred to me, should be very simple. There is a scientific test, called the Gonzalez test or the nitrate test, by which you can infallibly prove whether a given hand did or did not fire a given revolver.

'If Marion Hammond hadn't pulled that trigger, I could write Q.E.D. And if Harry Brooke *did* happen to be dead as they claimed, it looked as though the crime must have been committed by an evil spirit.

'I somewhat imprudently announced this, to the annoyance of Dr Garvice, who responded by slinging us all out of the bedroom. But there were some interesting repercussions immediately afterwards.

'My first move, of course, was to put Miss Fay Seton in a corner and make her admit all this. I asked Garvice, in the presence of "Curtis", whether he would be good enough to send Miss Seton up to see me. There followed, from "Curtis", an outburst of nerves which shocked even you.

'Suddenly he realized he was wasting time; the girl might be up here at any minute. He must get away out of sight. He said he was going to his room to lie down, and — bang! I could have laughed, you know, if the whole thing hadn't been so grotesquely wicked and bitter. No sooner did "Stephen Curtis" touch his bedroom door, than you shouted to him not to go in there, because Professor Rigaud — who also knew Harry Brooke — was asleep and mustn't be disturbed.

'No, by thunder! He *mustn' t* be disturbed!

'Do you wonder, again, that "Curtis" plunged down the back stairs as though the devil were after him?

'But I had little time to speculate about this, because Dr Garvice returned with some information which thoroughly scared me. Fay Seton had gone. The note she left, especially that line, "A brief-case is so useful, isn't it?" let the cat out of the bag: or, more properly, the raincoat out of the brief-case.

'I knew what she was going to do. I had been a prize idiot for not realizing it the night before.

'When I had told Fay Seton that if Miss Hammond recovered this matter would be no concern of the police, *that* was where she had smiled in so terrifying a way and murmured, "Won't it?" Fay Seton was sick and tired and ready to blow up.

'At her room in town she had the evidence which could still send Harry Brooke to the guillotine. She was damned well going to get it, return with it, throw it in our faces, and call for an arrest.

'And so — look out!

'The alleged Stephen Curtis was really desperate. If he used his head, he wasn't dished even yet. When he crept up there in the dark, and played

187

the Cagliostro trick, Marion hadn't seen him and hadn't heard any voice except a whisper. She would never have thought (and didn't, when we talked to her later) that the attacker was her own fiancé. Nobody else had seen him; he had slipped into the house by the back door, up the back staircase, into the bedroom, and down again to get away before you others reached the bedroom after the shot.

'But Fay Seton, returning alone to a solitary forest place, with hanging evidence?

'That was why, my dear Hammond, I sent you after her in such haste and instructed you to stay with her. Afterwards things went *all* wrong.'

'Ha!' said Professor Rigaud, snorting and rapping on the table to call for attention.

'This jolly *farceur,*' continued Rigaud, 'dashes into my bedroom where I am asleep, hauls me from bed, hauls me to the window, and says, "Look!" I look out, and I see two persons leaving the house. "That's Mr Hammond," says he; "but quick, quick, quick, who is the other man?" "My God", I say, "either I am dreaming or it is Harry Brooke". And he plunges away for the telephone.'

Dr Fell grunted.

'What I hadn't remembered,' Dr Fell explained, 'is that Hammond had read the woman's note aloud, in ringing tones which carried to a half-crazed man at the foot of the back stairs. And,' added Dr Fell, turning to Miles, 'he went along with you in the car to the station. Didn't he?'

'Yes! But he didn't get aboard the train.'

'Oh, yes, he did,' said Dr Fell. By the simple process of jumping in after you did. You never noticed him, never thought of him, because you were searching so feverishly for a *woman.* When you searched that train, any man, if he kept a newspaper in front of his face as so many were doing, would never get a second glance.

'You failed to find Fay Seton either, for which you must blame your own overwrought state of mind. There was nothing in the least mysterious about it. She was in a state of mind even less receptive to crowds than yours; she did what many people do nowadays if they are good-looking women and can get away with it; she travelled in the guard's van.

'That is a foolish episode leading to a last tragic episode.

'Fay went to London in a blank hysteria of rage and despair. She was going to end all this. She was going to tell the truth about everything. But

188

then, when Superintendent Hadley was actually in her room urging her to speak ...'

'Yes?' prompted Barbara.

'She still found she couldn't do it,' said Dr Fell.

'You mean she was still in love with Harry Brooke?'

'Oh, no,' said Dr Fell. 'That was all past and gone. That had been only a momentary idea of respectability. No: it was a part, now, of the same evil destiny that kept hounding her whatever she did. You see, the Harry Brooke, who became metamorphosed into Stephen Curtis ...'

Professor Rigaud waved his hands.

'But this,' he interrupted, 'is another thing I do not understand. How did that change come about? When and how did Harry Brooke become Stephen Curtis?'

'Sir,' replied Dr Fell, 'above all things my spirit is wearied by the routine card-indexing necessary to check up on a person's papers. Since you have formally identified the man as Harry Brooke, I leave the rest to Hadley. But I believe' – he looked at Miles – 'you haven't known "Curtis" for a very long time?'

'No; only for a couple of years.'

'And according to your sister, he was invalided out of the Forces comparatively early in the war?'

'Yes. In the summer of nineteen-forty.'

'My own guess,' said Dr Fell, 'is that Harry Brooke in France at the outbreak of the war couldn't endure the threat constantly hanging over him. It wore his temperament to shreds. He couldn't stand the idea of Fay Seton with evidence that would ... well, think of the cold morning at dawn and the blade of the guillotine looming in front of you.

'So he decided to do what many other men have done before him: to cut free, and make a new life for himself. After all, the Germans were over-running France; in his opinion, for good; his father's money, his father's goods were lost to him in any case. In my opinion, there was a real Stephen Curtis who died in the retreat to Dunkirk. And Harry Brooke, in the French Army, was attached to the British as interpreter. In the chaos of that time, I think he assumed the clothes and papers and identity of the real Stephen Curtis.

'In England he built up this identity. He was six years older, a dozen years older as we count time in war, than the boy who thought he wanted to be a painter. He had a reasonably solid position. He was comfortably engaged to a girl who had come into money, and who managed him as in his heart he always wanted to be managed ...'

'It's odd you should say that,' Miles muttered. 'Marion commented on exactly the same thing.'

'This was the position when Fay appeared to wreck him. The poor fellow didn't really *want* to kill her, you know.' Dr Fell blinked at Miles. 'Do you remember what he asked you, in the tea-room at Waterloo, after he'd got over the first nauseating shock?'

'Stop a bit!' said Miles. 'He asked me how long it would take Fay to catalogue the books in the library. You mean ...?'

'If it had taken only a week or so, as he suggested, he might have found some excuse for keeping out of her way. But you swept that away by saying it would take months. So the decision was made like *that*.' Dr Fell snapped his fingers. 'Fay could destroy his new position, even if she didn't denounce him as his father's murderer. And so, remembering the suggestion from the fife of Cagliostro ...'

'I *will* clear my character of this,' said Professor Rigaud in a frenzy. 'I once told him, yes, that a person with a weak heart might be frightened to death like that. But the detail of neatly placing the revolver in the victim's hand, so it will be believed she has fired the shot itself: that I do not think of. That is criminal genius!'

'I quite agree,' said Dr Fell. 'And I sincerely trust no one else will imitate him. You create a murder in which the victim appears to have frightened herself to death, at the sight of some intruder who was never there.'

Professor Rigaud was still in a frenzy.

'Not only was this not my invention,' he declared, 'but – how I hate crime, myself! – with this added detail I do not even recognize the trick when I see it played in from of me.' He paused, drew a handkerchief from his pocket, and mopped his forehead.

'Had Harry Brooke,' he added, 'any other such ingenious plan in his head when he followed Fay Seton to London this afternoon?'

'No,' said Dr Fell. 'He was merely going to kill her and destroy *all* the evidence. I shiver to think what might have happened if he had got to Bolsover Place before Hammond and Miss Morell. But "Curtis" was following *them*, do you see? With Fay Seton in the guard's van, he couldn't find her either. So he had to follow them if he wanted to be led to her.

'Then Hadley arrived. And "Curtis", who could hear everything from the passage outside the room in Bolsover Place, lost his head. His only idea now was to get that raincoat – the blood-stained raincoat, the one thing utterly damning to him – before Fay broke down and exposed him.

'He threw the main electric switch in the fuse-box outside in the passage. He got away in the dark with the brief-case, and dropped it in flight because he was clinging so hard to the raincoat still weighted with heavy stones. He ran straight out of that house into ...'

'Into what?' demanded Miles.

'A policeman,' said Dr Fell. 'You may remember that Hadley didn't even bother to chase him? Hadley merely opened the window and blew a police whistle. We'd arranged matters over the telephone to be prepared if anything like that happened.

'Harry Brooke, alias Stephen Curtis, was kept at the police station in Camden High Street until Rigaud and I arrived back from Hampshire. Then he was brought round to Bolsover Place for formal identification by Rigaud. I told you, my dear Hammond, that Hadley's task wouldn't be pleasant for one of you three; and I meant you. But it leads me to the one word I want to say at the end.'

Dr Fell sat back in his chair. He picked up his meerschaum pipe, dead with white ash, and put it down again. A vast discomfort or something like it made him puff out his cheeks.

'Sir,' he begun in a thunderous voice, which he managed to tone down, 'I do not think you need worry unduly about your sister Marion. Unchivalrous as it may sound, I say to you that this young lady is as tough as nails. She will suffer very little harm from the loss of Stephen Curtis. But Fay Seton is another matter.'

The little dining-room was silent. They could hear the rain outside.

'I have told you all her story now,' pursued Dr Fell, 'or nearly all of it. I should say no more, since the matter is none of my business. And yet these past six years cannot have been a very easy time for her.

'She was hounded from Chartres. She was hounded, with a threat of arrest for murder, even in Paris. I am inclined to suspect, since she wouldn't show her French identity papers to Hadley, that she made her living on the streets.

'Yet there was some quality in that girl's nature – call it generosity, call it a sense of fatality, call it anything you like – that would *not* let her speak out, even at the end, and denounce a person who had once been her friend. She feels that an evil destiny has got her and will never let her go. She has at best only a few months more to live. She lies now in a hospital, sick and dispirited and without hope. What do you think of it all?'

Miles rose to his feet.

'I'm going to her,' he said.

There was a sharp scraping noise on the carpet as Barbara Morell pushed her chair back. Barbara's eyes were opened wide.

'*Miles, don't be a fool!*'

'I'm going to her.'

Then it all poured out.

'Listen,' said Barbara, resting her hands on the table and speaking quietly but very fast. 'You're not in love with her. I knew that when you told me about Pamela Hoyt and the dream you had. She's just the same as Pamela Hoyt: unreal, a dust-image out of old books, a dream you've created in your own mind.

'Listen, Miles! That's what threw the spell over you. You're an idealist and you've never been anything else. Whatever — whatever mad plan you've got in your head, it could only end in disaster even before she died. Miles, for heaven's sake!'

He went over to the chair where he had left his hat.

Barbara Morell — sincere, sympathetic, advising him for his own good as Marion did — let her voice rise to a small scream.

'Miles, it's silly! Think what she *is!*'

'I don't give a curse what she is,' he said. 'I'm going to her.'

And once more Miles Hammond went out of the little dining-room at Beltring's, and hurried down the private stairs into the rain.

Printed in Great Britain
by Amazon.co.uk, Ltd.,
Marston Gate.